T0206462

Readers love CALEB JAMES

Exile

"Caleb James has arrived—and his work is more polished, fascinating and truly top notch."
—Joyfully Jay

Hound

"It's so intricate, so well crafted and full of all those small details that you don't realise are important until it all begins to make sense. I'm going to miss this series, but I'm eager to read more of this author, who has managed to capture the world of the Fey in such a unique way."
—Divine Magazine

Dark Blood

"*Dark Blood* is gruesome, fast paced, and has a lot of tension-filled moments, with some very intriguing twists and turns."
—The Novel Approach

By CALEB JAMES

911 Vampire
Dark Blood

THE HAFFLING
Haffling
Exile
Hound

Published by DSP PUBLICATIONS
www.dsppublications.com

911

VAMPIRE

CALEB JAMES

DSP PUBLICATIONS

Published by
DSP PUBLICATIONS

5032 Capital Circle SW, Suite 2, PMB# 279,
Tallahassee, FL 32305-7886 USA
www.dsppublications.com

This is a work of fiction. Names, characters, places, and incidents either are the product of author imagination or are used fictitiously, and any resemblance to actual persons, living or dead, business establishments, events, or locales is entirely coincidental.

911 Vampire
© 2022 Caleb James

Cover Art
© 2022 L.C. Chase
http://www.lcchase.com
Cover content is for illustrative purposes only and any person depicted on the cover is a model.

All rights reserved. This book is licensed to the original purchaser only. Duplication or distribution via any means is illegal and a violation of international copyright law, subject to criminal prosecution and upon conviction, fines, and/or imprisonment. Any eBook format cannot be legally loaned or given to others. No part of this book may be reproduced or transmitted in any form or by any means, electronic or mechanical, including photocopying, recording, or by any information storage and retrieval system, without the written permission of the Publisher, except where permitted by law. To request permission and all other inquiries, contact DSP Publications, 5032 Capital Circle SW, Suite 2, PMB# 279, Tallahassee, FL 32305-7886, USA, or www.dsppublications.com.

Mass Market Paperback ISBN: 978-1-64108-262-4
Trade Paperback ISBN: 978-1-64405-938-8
Digital ISBN: 978-1-64405-937-1
Mass Market Paperback published June 2022
v. 1.0

Printed in the United States of America
∞
This paper meets the requirements of
ANSI/NISO Z39.48-1992 (Permanence of Paper).

For: G. S. Jayson

Chapter One
My name is Godfrey.
What's yours?

I CAME with no owner's manual. It was London, and the year was 1356. My father, Gaius, died in childbirth. His words seared in my brain—"You are smart, you learn, and you are funny." That last bit loses in translation and is open to interpretation. His last utterance, "Ti amo"—"I love you." With that, he slit his throat, and I was born in a cataclysm of blood and pain. But that's birth, isn't it? A fresh canvas. Who—or what—will survive? All new sensations as you barrel through the birth canal, or in my case, slosh drunk in an abandoned Roman bloodbath in what is now a London suburb, soaked from head to toe as he gushed out a rare distillation of unknown vintage and tremendous potency. Sorry about that. If graphic and gory offend, I'll keep it down, but you might want to download something else.

My vampiric birth, if that's what I am, at the age of twenty-four, was more akin to my first birth than different. Both cost me a parent. I never met my human mother; my stepmother was nice enough, but it's not the same. I was the last of nine and the only one to survive into adulthood. My decade with Gaius was brief, wonderful, and short. A black-plague love story that ended as expected. He died, when by rights it should have been me. But I don't die. I could—he did—and perhaps *one* day I will. Perhaps that's where this one ends.

Gaius knew what he was about when he picked me, though I'm not certain he meant to die. I mean, yes, a slashed throat doesn't often end well, but did he know? Or was he more like me—trying to figure things out, hunt for clues, find that fucking owner's manual?

Which brings us to today's tale. I don't know if I'll send this to a publisher, and if I do, which name I'll put on the cover. This is a conversation. If it's just between me, myself, and I, the return is limited. But when I finish a book and send it into the world, it feeds me. Which right there, if the thought of nourishing a vampire, possibly a succubus, with a wee bit of your life does not appeal, stop now. I won't be offended. I won't stroll up your drive in the dark of night… but if I do, you will not hear the scribble-scrabble as callused fingers scramble up your wall or the clink of broken glass as I enter and gaze with hunger upon your luscious and vulnerable body. You will dream, unaware of how beautiful you are—your tender breaths or drunken snores, the splay of your limbs, covered or bare. You are delicious. Don't let anyone tell you otherwise. And when you wake, you will mourn the loss of that dream—it's a juicy one—and wonder at the broken glass. You will see the fallen branch and think, *It must have been the wind*. You'll languish in bed, try to go back to sleep to find what you've lost, but you will not resent what I took. I promise. And sometimes, if you are especially tasty or comely or… convenient, I might return. Though here's a funny bit and something to store in the manual I hope to write one day. You will replace the glass in the window, but dialing for dollars, and dollars to donuts, you will never again lock it.

My, how I dribble. It's now five thirty on a Friday morning. Time to shower, shave, and go to work.

Chapter Two
Godfrey's Day Begins

"WHAT IN God's name were they thinking?" Frustrated, Kate muttered as she gripped a company tablet and wrinkled her nose.

"Something new?" I unzipped my hoodie and pulled a freshly laundered sky-blue work shirt from my locker.

"A whole new system for tracking overdoses. Like what the fuck? Like this is what we need right now? Who thinks up this crap? So not only do we have to revive the poor bastards who won't go to the hospital and run right back to the dealer who nearly killed them, we now have three new screens of boxes to click and a number to call and report the event. But wait—." She read off an email from the executive suite of Boston's Cavalry Ambulance Company. "—we have a whole twenty-four hours to get this done, to be… in compliance with the state mandate. Fuck this!"

I took a deep breath of the station house—a mix of sweat, detergent, a whiff of alcohol-based hand sanitizer, and someone's chicken parm from the night before that had been nuked too long. I thought of the Mr. Rogers show for children as I worked my fingers up the buttons one by one. "Where's Trevor?" I asked as I tucked my shirttails and got a funhouse view of poly-blended paramedic me in a warped Dollar General mirror fixed to the back of the men's locker room door.

"Hosing down your truck."

"Guess that means I do check out. What number are we in?" It was nearly eight and the start of a twenty-four-hour shift on the ambulance. I'd been there a year and would stay a second—a bit short, even for me, but time should never be wasted, even when you have lots of it. End of the day, it's all anyone gets.

"Seriously? You know he grabbed Eight. He always wants Eight."

"That's because it's new and shiny." I snatched a fistful of turquoise nitrile disposable gloves from the box and shoved them into my back pocket. There'd be plenty on the truck, but between the mask mandates, the constant spritz of hand sanitizer, and always wanting a fresh pair of gloves, it was good to be redundant. None of this was for my sake, but when you're a taker, it's essential to give. Nature demands balance.

"Yes, and it goes fast and has more siren options than any of the others."

"He sulks when he can't have it," I offered.

"Wouldn't want that." She followed me from the locker room to the clubhouse area with its mismatched tables and chairs and ripped vinyl couches.

It felt good, like clock gears. Kate would be on dispatch for the first eight of my twenty-four with Trevor. She'd gripe and moan and get things done with blistering efficiency. No checkbox would be left blank, no ED triage nurse would want for a patient's insurance information, and by shift's end, she would have memorized the overdose memo, devised a strategy to ensure the company would be 100 percent compliant, and forwarded an all-staff email with bulleted instructions to ensure said compliance.

"You've got something in your hair," she said, and without pause, without mask, without gloves, and without permission, she plucked a bit of white down from my shower-damp curls.

Kate's smell, a mélange of Garnier Fructis, well-crisped bacon, coffee with 2 percent milk and turbinado sugar—lots of it—and arousal sent a pleasant tingle from the top of my head to the tips of my toes. Her interested touch played in my hair. She knew it was wrong, but she couldn't stop.

"It's so unfair that you get hair like that."

I inhaled a gentle sip of her through the pores of my skin. It was clear she'd had home fries—diner ones with bits of red pepper and chunks of sweated onion. She, and they, were tangy and delicious.

Emboldened by my silence, she played with my silken corkscrews. She stretched one out. "It's so long and soft, and there's another… why do you have feathers in your hair?"

"Leaky pillow," I replied. I gathered my locks into a ponytail, tied it back with a blue satin ribbon, and tucked it beneath my shirt collar.

"Maybe you should get a new one."

I lingered for another gentle draw of tasty Kate and then pulled back. "Maybe it wasn't mine."

"Tease."

"Never."

"Details?" she asked.

"You wouldn't like them."

"You don't know that."

Sadly, I did. And this would not be the first or last time my morning shower neglected to remove traces of the night before. "Something to ponder between calls." My company cell vibrated inside the patch pocket on my thigh. "My steed awaits."

"I'll tell him you called him that."

"Don't be crude."

"Have fun," she said. Her gaze narrowed, "But you do, don't you?"

I smiled and strapped on a cloth mask with the company logo stretched over my mouth and nostrils. "Later." And I pulled out my cell.

As I pushed through the outer door of the substation, I was greeted by a toot of the siren. Number Eight, a spanking new half-million-dollar red-and-white panel truck, sparkled amid drips of sudsy water. Trevor, unmasked and eyes shaded, strong Celtic jaw, his thick auburn James Dean forelock tamed into a semblance of order, sat poised at the wheel. The flashers were on. With my cell on speaker, I put a finger to where my lips were hidden by the mask to get him to cool it with the horns. "What have we got?" I asked the city dispatcher.

"Twenty-seven-year-old male. Probable cardiac arrest. Unresponsive and pulseless."

As he fed me the details, I popped into the truck, and we were in motion with lights, sirens, and speed. The LED GPS gave us an eight-minute ETA, which did not bode well for unresponsive and pulseless.

Trevor's blue-mirrored gaze was fixed on the road. "I got you a coffee," he said in a half-tamed "South Boston by way of Brighton" twang. As he accelerated, he added the air horn to the siren to move a Mercedes S series out of the left lane. "Moron," he muttered.

"Thanks." I cracked the lid and took a sip of black and bitter goodness.

"I got donuts," he added as he threaded the needle of a tight curve with maximum speed and the tiniest sense that we might roll over.

"I'm good." I held back the rest of the sentence, *I just had some Kate*. Not that I don't like donuts. Though their flavor took a nosedive when they ditched lard for shortening, and it really went south when they eliminated trans fats. "How was your weekend?" I asked as the red line of our route shortened and the eight minutes got halved by Trevor's lead foot.

"Meh," he replied and tailgated sluggish cars who had not caught the siren's wail. "Eye on the prize, and it's not fair how you sailed through pre-med so easily. I'd kill for your GPA. But nothing I can do now. Just that stupid test."

"Just don't get behind." I braced as he took a fast sharp left. We were less than a minute away.

"I don't think that's it. You got secrets, Godfrey. Don't think I don't know that."

"True. I slept with all my teachers."

He cracked a smile over toothpaste-commercial-perfect teeth, minus one chipped incisor damaged in a high school brawl. "Probably." He braked and drove up onto the sidewalk in front of a three-family home in Dorchester that had gotten a San Francisco painted-lady makeover. I didn't need to check the address or the GPS. The scene in front said it all. Neighbors in bathrobes, some half-dressed for work, kids—none wearing masks—their gazes shifted toward us, and an empty police cruiser parked on the postage-stamp front lawn.

"He's on the top floor," a woman offered as we donned nitrile gloves and pulled the gurney from the back. Excitement surged as we rolled with our valentine-red kit box and a fresh green oxygen tank strapped across white sheets with the Cavalry logo that was meant to be a crested knight's helmet but looked more like an adult toy favored by segments of the gay community.

"Of course he's on the top floor," Trevor murmured as we hoisted and headed up at a cadenced jog with me in the front. We were like a pair of well-matched dancers. I was an honest six feet, and he had me by an inch, which back in the day was wicked tall. Now not so much. At least I don't shrink.

The stairwell echoed with our unison footfalls. I remembered when these affordable and spacious homes were the thing. A couple thousand dollars, depending on the bric-a-bracs, shutters, porches, and turrets you wanted. Sears Catalog castles for the Irish, the Italians, the Jews, the Poles. Plenty of room for the new arrivals, and after that you could rent out a floor or two. Everyone in everyone else's business. But no longer. This close to Boston, walking distance to the trolley, these two-bedroom flats were far beyond the reach of any new arrival.

A tangle of people milled on the top landing, where a uniformed officer tried to take a statement from an unmasked skunk-root blond in baggy sweats.

"When did you find him?" the cop asked.

"When I got up for work. He was…." Her voice flat.

"Which was when?"

"Seven. He had no pulse. He was cold." She shivered.

I shifted my gaze to the black-and-white-checked linoleum floor. Another officer, his broad back to us, gave CPR to a heroin-thin man, naked save for a pair of paisley-print boxers. He was cold, gray, and too young for a heart attack, at least the normal kind. Behind him was an open bathroom door where I spotted a small stack of glassine drug packets and a syringe and spoon on the sink.

Trevor whispered, "Overdose."

We set to work. "Did you Narcan him?" I asked the officer giving CPR as I knelt and felt for a carotid. There was no pulse.

"Once," he replied as he continued compressions. He glanced at a small pile of familiar black, red, and white pharma packaging. "I was just about to give a second."

"Good man. How long you been here?" I asked as Trevor handed me a light and a number six endotracheal tube.

"Less than five. I should give it?"

"Do it." I'd done enough of these to know that cold and gray does not mean dead. And while this dude might be headed toward that bright light, he wasn't there. He was in that room, confused and hovering over the stove, a small tether of his life still attached to his belly like an umbilical cord in reverse.

With practiced efficiency I tilted his head back, felt with the gloved fingers of my left hand for the right angle, slid the tube down his throat, tapped his larynx like a melon for the hollow ring that let me know it was in, reached back to where Trevor had the oxygen tube, hooked it up, and taped it down.

"Six liters?" Trevor asked as he cranked the tank.

"Wide open," I said.

"Should I keep going?" the officer asked, the muscles of his upper arms corded from his exertions and three days a week on upper body.

"One more set and then let's get him on the stretcher." My gaze fixed on that thin thread of energy between spirit and body. It hadn't weakened, and between the Narcan, the oxygen, and the blood being forced to pump by officer gym bod—or Gymbo as I'd dubbed him—we had a chance for a save.

We rolled the naked man onto our backboard, and the three of us hoisted him onto the stretcher. As he landed, I pressed two fingers into the notch of his neck. I waited and made eye contact with the disembodied specter. He spoke. *"Am I dead? Is this it?"*

I shook my head as I felt the sluggish surge of blood beneath the tips of my cello-callused fingers. *Not yet. Find your way back. Will yourself back into your body, back into this life.* And so began a fun and private conversation.

I fucked up, the almost-dead guy said.

Yes, you did. Everyone does.

I told Annie I'd quit for good.

I glanced up at the Annie in question and was struck by the depth of her anguish. It was moments like this that dropped the floor out of my world. It was clear that this naked man, with his Jesus hair, perched between worlds, was the love of her life. On him, she had pinned dreams of children, marriage—the whole enchilada. He was her one. *She'll forgive you.*

She shouldn't. This was the worst time. You don't understand.

Dude, people fuck up. We can't help it. But here's the deal—do you want to die or do you want to live and maybe do better? Annie clearly loves you.

I don't want to die. She shouldn't love me. I want to do better. This was the worst. What's wrong with me?

I'd missed something. He did not want to die, but…. *Why was this time the worst?*

She's pregnant. We're going to have a kid… she just told me. And this is what I do.

Do you want to be a father?

Fuck yeah. I've got to stop doing this. I don't want to die. I don't want to be a junkie. Leave my kid with nothing but a trust fund for a father.

Then grab on to that line and get your ass back into your body.

He nodded, and as the oxygen tank hissed, Gymbo pumped, and Trevor started an IV, the cold gray body came back to life. The lips turned from bruised-grape to pink, his nail beds flushed, and the board-hard stiffness in his chest eased. His bright blue eyes cracked open.

Annie whimpered, "Oh my God. Oh my God, he's not dead." She grabbed for his hand. "James, don't leave me. Not now. Not fucking now, you bastard! You promised me."

He tried to move his lips, but they were taped around the hard-plastic tube.

I put a restraining hand on his shoulder. "Don't," I said.

She put a hand on his chest. "He's not dead. He's not dead."

"He's not," I said. "We're going to take him to an emergency room. You can ride with us."

"He'll only walk out," she said, and the expression on her unmasked face shifted from relief back to despair. "He promised that he'd stopped."

At least their stories match, I mused. "People mess up, Annie. We can't help it."

She startled. "How do you know my name?"

"Call sheet," I lied.

"Lactated or Ringers?" Trevor asked, the IV in, flushed and open.

"Ringers." I looked at our patient, knew that he could hear me and would not remember our astral confab. "James, you had an overdose. You've had a lot of Narcan, and in a little bit you're going to feel dope sick. You know the drill. We'll bring you and Annie to an emergency room, and you'll want to leave. You're going to want to use, because you're sick. But we'll take you to one where they can start some medication so you don't get sick. Nod if you understand."

"He's supposed to be on that medication," Annie said. "He was… is. I can't believe he did this again. Oh God." Her hand flew to her mouth. "Oh God."

And here comes anger. I watched as James tried to make eye contact with Annie. She bit her lip and shook her head.

"I can't keep doing this."

"We good?" I asked Trevor.

"Yup."

"Let's roll."

We wheeled toward the door, and Annie hung back. "You should come," I urged and tried not to

stare at her belly. She didn't show, but her loose
sweatpants and top hid a lot. Her hair spoke vol-
umes. I'd assumed her dark roots were a COVID
casualty, but I reassessed and figured she'd ditched
the harsh chemicals at least three months ago, maybe
four, when she found out she was pregnant. Add a
month to that... and she was well into her second,
possibly third, trimester.

"I can't... I just can't."

James tried to rise up against the orange straps
across his chest and legs. I laid one hand on his
shoulder as I held her gaze. "Please come." And
just as there had been a tether between almost-dead
James and his body, there was a bond with his wife,
Annie. I knew it for what it was—love, two-way,
unconditional, deaf, dumb, and blind. Rare as hen's
teeth and not something you throw away. "Get your
purse and come with us. He needs you."

"Yeah. He does." She shifted her gaze back to
the now shivering man. "James. I fucking hate you."
She batted back tears, stuffed things into a brief-
case-sized bag, and trailed behind as Trevor and I did
the paramedic two-step down a nineteenth-century
stairwell with a twenty-first-century tragedy.

Outside, the crowd of neighbors milled with
little attention to social distance and only half with
masks—a solid COVID C-. I heard snippets of
on-the-money conversations. Everyone had a story. "This happened to my brother." "My friend at
work said she's had to Narcan her boyfriend six
times." "Kid I went to school with just died from

an overdose. He was twenty-two. What the fuck is wrong with people?"

With a "one, two, three," Trevor and I hoisted James up and in. "You want to hop in back?" I offered Annie.

"Sure." Her tone let me know this was not her first such ride.

"Trevor, let's take him to University."

"B.I. is closer, Godfrey. Don't you start…."

"What he needs is at University, and it's only three minutes more." I watched him struggle. He had the physiologic tell that so many with Irish blood get—the blush—and the more perturbed, the more it spread. On a ten-point scale, this tiny infraction of one of his beloved rules rated a two, as a tinge of pink rose above his mask and spread beneath his blue-mirrored shades.

"Fine." And he walked off.

I turned to Annie. "How many times you done this with him?" She took my arm to steady herself up and in.

"Five in an ambulance, and he's had a couple close calls at home where he wouldn't let me call 911." She found her seat on the bench and strapped in without being told.

I ambled over her and sat by James's head. I pulled out a fresh paper mask from a box. "You should put this on."

"Right, I forgot."

"No worries."

"We good to go?" Trevor called from up front.

"All set."

James struggled and gagged with the plastic tube down his throat. He no longer needed it, but paramedics are not doctors and are held to a dizzying number of silly protocols. While we can do certain stuff in the field, we are discouraged from taking out breathing tubes once they're in. But he was miserable. He tried to talk, and if he persisted, he would damage his vocal cords.

"James, chill," I said, and to both Annie and him, "If anyone asks, it fell out. James, relax your throat, take a big breath in through your belly," and without further instruction or warning, I ripped off the tape and eased out the tube. "Don't speak," I said, not so much because it would hurt him physically, but this was not the time or place for him and Annie to have couples therapy. I grabbed a plastic face mask, strapped it around his head, and set the oxygen to six liters. "Your job is to breathe and look pretty. Trevor, what's the ETA?"

"Seven. I can do it in four."

"Excellent. Annie, how you holding up?"

"I'm not. And I'm supposed to be at work in, like, fifteen minutes. I'm a receptionist at a clinic, which makes me an essential employee." She glared at James.

"Call out," I said.

"Easier said than done… but yeah." She pulled out her cell and told the requisite lies. "Must have caught that thing that's going around. No… not *that* thing. Yeah, sure, happy to take calls from home. I should be back by tomorrow, day after at the latest." She glared at James.

And for his part, he tried. But with each minute, every cell in his body hungered for drugs. It would worsen and become unbearable. Theirs was an exquisite and painful love triangle—Annie, James, and heroin… although I was sure this was fentanyl. He loved Annie but needed his opioids. And the tipping point between need and true love was the stuff of great art. "As long as he's alive, there's hope," I offered.

"So they say. I'm not sure."

"I am," I said.

"How can you be?" she asked.

"'Cause I've seen it, a lot."

"Really, you don't look that old." Her dark red-rimmed eyes sought out mine.

"Thanks, but with all the overdoses and the bad drugs, people do get better. And you can't predict who or when. But folks who've had far more near-misses than your blue-eyed true love have gotten to the other side of this thing."

"He is my true love."

Despite her paper mask, I heard the hard set in her jaw. Tears popped in the corners of her eyes. "That's clear."

"This is my fault… I shouldn't have told him."

"Told him what?" I asked, though I knew.

"That I'm pregnant. We're going to have a baby."

And despite my order for silence, James rasped through his bruised vocal cords and mask, "I love you, Annie. I'm so sorry. I'm sorry."

His eyes teared, and trails of mucus tracked from his nostrils. I grabbed a tissue and tidied him up. Gooseflesh popped on the skin of his shoulders not covered by the sheet. He felt hot… and tasty.

"Two minutes," Trevor shouted.

"Okay, Annie, James… we're taking you to University Hospital. They can get you back on your buprenorphine. But it's an emergency room and things take time. So what we have to do is let them know exactly what you need without being obnoxious and pushy. Are we in agreement with that plan?"

She nodded.

He did as well, but with the large doses of Narcan he'd had, he'd descended into full-blown opioid withdrawal. It was not pretty, and to be blunt, I wanted him out of the back of our freshly washed ambulance before he puked, shat, or erupted in a magically unpleasant combination of the two.

Chapter Three
Trevor's Turn at Bat

LET'S KEEP track, I thought, and I wondered how and when I'd started my surveillance of Godfrey. It was the kind of thing Dad would do with an arson suspect. I darted and wove through traffic, played the siren and air horn with a minute left till we'd roll into the ambulance bay at University. I monitored the action in the back through the dash camera. *What is he up to?* I'd stopped saying anything as he broke one state and federal regulation, one company policy after another. It was pointless. Removal of our patient's endotracheal tube was one in a litany of… I'd lost count. *And why count?* Thing was, it was the right move, the kind move, but not in the book. And… we're obliged to take people to the nearest emergency room, and University was not. Strike one. Strike two. *What's your problem, Trevor?*

The man was suffering with that tube down his throat, so Godfrey took it out—no hesitation, no "I'll get in trouble… or get my partner in trouble." *I can't do shit like that. But I let him talk me into it. I'm just as guilty, a sin of omission.*

I couldn't hear the whole conversation, but between the video cam and the rearview mirror, I got the gist. What's supposed to happen in the back of an ambulance is crisis stabilization and paperwork. He hadn't filled out a damn thing. His company tablet hung turned off on its hook, not a single box checked. He hadn't even gotten their insurance info.

"Godfrey." I felt guilty for stepping into what was probably more important than my ask. "Get their insurance. Triage hates it when we don't have that." *And now I sound like Mom. Why does he have to be so fucking weird?*

He gave me a thumbs-up but made no movement toward the computer. At least I tried, and I took the right up the ramp into the emergency department, spotted an open bay, hooked a J-turn, and slid on back.

We got James, our revived OD, out of the back with wife Annie at his side. I sensed the three of them had hatched a scheme and got an unpleasant déjà vu. The man on the outside—the patsy, the fool. *Fine, let him talk. And when the questions start? I'll be well and truly fucked.*

I held my tongue as we rolled up to triage. The nurse behind her COVID plexi window rattled questions, but her expression soured when she realized James was not a cardiac arrest as advertised, but an overdose. I hated that, and I felt all my own buried shit about trips to the emergency room with my sister

Grace, dead and buried—the loss of control, the need to rely on strangers.

For her part, Annie knew what she was about and clearly had seen this show before. And yes, it was familiar and sad and scary. I'd thought this shift was about to start with a dead twenty-seven-year-old. I still felt his cold flesh beneath my gloves. I'd thought he was gone, but not Godfrey. Did he know? How could he? He seemed so confident—no doubt, no hesitation. He knew James wasn't dead. I thought back to the scene and his eyes glued not to our patient but to a spot over the stove. I'd watched him do that before, like he saw something no one else could.

Annie produced the insurance cards while Godfrey did his thing.

"He was on buprenorphine." Godfrey locked gazes with the nurse. "Went off, or maybe had it stolen and got some bad bags of dope. You guys do the rapid bup induction here?"

"We do," the nurse replied, her interest no longer on the keyboard but on I'm-sexy-and-I-know-it Godfrey. And while guys aren't my thing, you look at him and think magazine cover or pirate on a supermarket romance novel, with his long black hair, olive skin, dark stubble, and amber-ringed eyes.

He leaned into her window, and I strained to hear. "What are the chances of getting him straight back and getting his meds restarted?"

"He needs to be medically cleared first. Especially since he was intubated." She shook her head. "He's supposed to be intubated. What happened?"

Godfrey shrugged, and a tendril of blue-black hair tumbled down his tanned cheek. "It came out, and he was awake and alert by then. Would have been cruel to put it back."

"I see." She swallowed, her fingers poised over the keyboard, her eyes on Godfrey. It was like the National Geographic Channel—the raptor with its prey. I had zero doubt of what would happen.

"You'll get him out of here so much quicker," Godfrey added.

"I shouldn't," she said.

"No one will care, and more importantly, it's the right thing for the patient."

"True."

That clicked with her. It was a card I'd seen him play before. He pulled it all the time on me. Ends justify the means.

She reached for her phone, had a brief conversation, and said, "You can bring him straight back to the pod."

"You're a saint," he said.

"No." She tried to break from his gaze. "I'm a sucker for a sad story."

"And for doing the right thing," he added.

"That too."

WE WHEELED through the ED that, like everything else since March 2020, had been retrofitted for COVID. The cloth curtains replaced by hard plastic barriers in steel frames, patients and their families no longer allowed to accumulate in hallways, and additional hospital real estate subsumed by the ED to keep people apart.

We stopped outside the door to the pod, a euphemism for the psychiatric part of the emergency room. It also handled overdoses, which were a daily, often multiple-times-a-day occurrence—an epidemic of fentanyl and heroin wrapped inside a viral pandemic.

The door buzzed, Godfrey bumped it open with his back, and we were met by a short psychiatric resident and two medical students, all garbed in full face shields, gloves, and green plastic gowns that made them look a bit like Alaskan fishermen. "Welcome," the resident said as she made a rapid assessment of her new charge.

"Excellent," Godfrey replied, "where would you like James?"

"You can put him in two." She held a white tablet. "He was intubated…." Her voice faltered. "He hasn't been medically cleared."

Crap! Here it comes. Let no good deed go unpunished.

"He wasn't intubated," Godfrey said without pause as we shifted cold and clammy James from our stretcher onto the waiting hospital bed.

He turned to her and her two younger charges. "And look at him, he's fine… other than being horribly dope sick from all the Narcan he got. What he needs, you have. You can do a lot right now."

James looked awful. He had curled up under the sheet. Annie was at his side, rubbing gentle circles on his back.

"Besides," Godfrey added, "you weren't the one who sent him back here without medical clearance. Not your fault. And done is done."

"True." She smiled through her plexi shield. "It's good to see you, Godfrey."

"You too, Raj."

"Will I get in trouble for this?"

"No. But you will save his life."

I fixated on him, her, and the two students who gaped like fish through their shields. I knew that my fascination with Godfrey was that I wanted to be like him… but not exactly. It ran to my core, to a promise made to my little sister Grace. *You'll be fine. I won't let anything bad happen.* It was a promise I did not keep. I tried. I failed.

"Okay, then," Resident Raj said. With regret she broke from Godfrey and headed to her new patient. "So, James, you've been on buprenorphine before. We'll do a quick verification through the state's database, but do you remember what dose worked best for you?"

I pulled our stretcher from the cubicle and wadded the sheets into a sealed red laundry bag.

Godfrey hung back in the now-crowded and decidedly not socially distant cubicle with James, Annie, the resident, and the students. "Annie, you're in good hands here. He'll get what he needs."

I watched and listened as I sprayed down the stretcher with antiseptic. She looked drained, and James was a sick mess, nodding and rocking and probably doing everything in his power to not say "Fuck it, get me out of here." Which is exactly what would have happened if… Godfrey hadn't just broken half a dozen rules and lied, lied, lied. Half the time we'd revive an overdose and they'd run off, unable to deal with the anguish of hours in withdrawal in some emergency department where people called them names and treated them like scum.

"Thank you," she said through her mask as she struggled with something more. "Before you go…."

"What?" Godfrey did one of his signature moves. He stopped, turned, and gave her his full attention.

My breath caught.

"You know about this stuff," Annie said. Her words came fast and puffed her mask in and out. "Tell me what I'm supposed to do with him. I can't keep doing this. He's going to die, and I don't want to be there when that happens."

Godfrey cocked his head at an angle as he listened. It reminded me of a wine connoisseur, his senses tuned to her, her words, the emergency room, the several sets of eyes glued to him. "He might not. They'll give him medicine and schedule follow-up. That will help, but not enough. Here's the truth, Annie. It's his soul that needs saving. The best thing for that is love—lots of it—forgiveness, a friend or two who doesn't use drugs and who he can call in the middle of the night when it gets bad, and work. Work is good. And exercise. Prayer too. Trevor likes that one." He caught me staring and winked.

Bastard.

Then he turned back to Annie. "But it's not for everyone. And the last bit you know—it's a long road. Don't think about the destination. Just think about today and this minute. He could have died and he didn't. He wants to change, he loves you, you love him, and those are wonderful things, and they matter. Now can I ask you a question? Or rather, James, I need to know a couple things."

And we all stood and did nothing as Godfrey pulled back his mask, leaned down, and whispered into James's ear. His long dark hair tied in a bright blue ribbon slipped from under his uniform collar and curtained his face. *Yup, pirate king.* A whole upstairs bedroom of my parents' house was filled with those books. And it wasn't just Mom who read them.

The sick man nodded, cupped a hand to Godfrey's ear, and answered.

"Good to know." Godfrey straightened and tucked his hair away. He smiled. "I believe our work here is done."

And what the hell was that? I hated when he did shit like that.

Back in the ambulance, I ticked off boxes on the call sheet that he should have completed. It fell to me. It always fell to me. The grunt work. *Then work with someone else.* I stopped.

"You okay?" he asked as he plucked the frosting rose off a chocolate crème-filled donut and popped it into his mouth.

Tell him the truth—that you're sick of getting stuck with the paperwork. I felt the weight of his gaze, and I knew the moment I looked into those eyes I'd lose my nerve. I swallowed and thrust the tablet toward him. "You do this."

"Sure." He took it, licked his fingers, and without using hand sanitizer, punched answers onto the touch screen.

That went better than expected. Go for two. "What did you ask that guy?"

Without pause he said, "Where he bought his drugs."

"Why?"

"Ask me no questions, Trevor, I'll tell you no lies."

"Yes, you will. You lie all the time." *Do not look at him.*

"True, and you pay attention."

I hazarded a side glance as he came to a free text box on the form. The fingers of his left hand typed ridiculously fast while his right held the half-eaten donut.

I hadn't realized he was a leftie. But no… ambidextrous. "Why do you lie so much?"

He looked at me, and there were those eyes, deep and brown, but with odd outer rings of gold. *Do other people have those? Don't stare. Look away.*

He shrugged, broke gaze, typed a final line onto James's call sheet, and handed me the tablet. "Convenience, doing what works. *A*, all of the above, *B*, none of the above."

"It's *A*," I said. "But you left off an option. K questions have five choices." I looked at his completed call log. My name alongside his at the top. That was true. Much else wasn't, like no mention of an endotracheal tube being placed—and then removed. And no discussion of how and why he decided Mr. James Grant did not require medical clearance at the hospital. But if anyone dug, we would not be on the hook. It would be the nurse in triage and cute Raj, the resident at the hospital, who should have refused the patient. I stared at my name over what was essentially a work of fiction and wondered, *Is this what will keep me out of medical school? Not like they're jumping over themselves to let me in.*

"They do, and how goes you and Stanley Kaplan?"

"Like trying to stuff too much into my brain. Seems there's a limit to what it will hold, and it's not enough." I added my electronic signature to Godfrey's account of our first run of the day and hit Send. And that's what Father Calvin would call bearing false witness.

"I wish you hadn't done that," he said.

"Why? You wanted to add something?"

The on-dash phone rang, and a jellybean lit on the screen of my tablet.

"That. I wanted to grab coffee before our next run."

"Sorry, next one." I hit the audio on the dash and touched the jellybean on the computer. It brought me to a fresh call sheet with a familiar name—Florence O. Cantrell, a ninety-two-year-old chain-smoking widow with renal failure, a killer apartment in the Back Bay, and emphysema.

Kate's voice came through the speaker. "Morning, angels."

"Morning, Charlie," Godfrey replied. "Terrorists in the south of France?"

"Close, we're down a truck of basics. We need help with the renal roundup."

"On it," he said as I backed out of the ambulance bay and glanced at the GPS, which offered three routes to Flo's.

"So, your heart attack was an OD?" Kate said, having just received his… *our* massaged account.

"Yes," Godfrey said.

"That's happening more and more," she said, "where they call it in as a heart attack."

"Word is out," he replied.

"What word is that?" she asked.

"You get better service for heart attacks than overdoses. Cops were there before we were. They'd already given him a Narcan."

"Good point," she said. "You have to fill out that new report for these."

"Do tell."

I glanced at him, unmasked and grinning. Months back we'd decided that masks were kind of ridiculous when you work a twenty-four-hour shift with someone three feet away. He slouched back un-belted into his seat, his boots on the dash, which I hated. "Get your feet off," I hissed.

"Make me, Mother."

"It's short... ish," Kate said. "I'll walk you through it."

"Wonderful." And holding the tablet like a gaming module, he booted up her new form, entered God only knew what, and hit Send.

Chapter Four
Flo's Three Husbands and How to Quit Smoking

As TREVOR sped and enumerated my sins like beads on the worn rosary in his pocket, I stared out the window. I never tire of the views, and Boston is a favorite—a true city, old for this country, young when compared to others, but vibrant, like a plucked string held taut around a center pitch. No virus would upend things, not without a fight. As COVID spring gave way to summer and now fall, the traffic had picked up. The Newbury Street crowd donned designer masks, and people queued for pizza and beer in neatly spaced lines that allowed infected particles to float and fall to the ground. It felt familiar, a plague of manageable proportions, not like others where a rash or single pustule in the morning would bring death by dusk. In my endless game of compare, contrast, and try to fit together, I rolled James and Annie into the hierarchy of disease and death. His addiction to opioids was much closer to the lethality of the black death, the great pestilence. Though his disease, unlike that plague, required no carrier fleas and rats. It was 100 percent man-made.

"She won't go on the stretcher," Trevor said as he pulled up in front of a hydrant.

"She prefers the chair." And I felt the stirrings of a minuet, something in three-four time. The Trevor and Godfrey Waltz.

"We're supposed to use the stretcher."

"We'll say we did," I replied as we opened our doors, *two, three,* walked to the back of the truck, *one, two,* opened it up, *three, one,* and he jumped in, *two, three.* He looked at the stretcher, *one, two.* Realized it will be a waste of time and make everyone feel like shit, *three, one,* and with a shake of his head, grabbed the folded wheelchair off the wall and rolled it back to me, *two, three.*

I stopped myself from offering him my arm to get down, as it would only end with me attempting to twirl him into the street, *one, two, three, one, two, three.* He wouldn't like that. Although... *maybe he would.*

"What's the joke?" he asked.

"You," I said.

"Asshole."

"I don't remember you swearing this much." I unfolded the chair and wheeled it up the ramp to Flo's building.

"I didn't, and I blame you," he said.

"That's pointless. Own your actions."

"Like you do?" He held the door for me.

"I do."

"But you tell lies."

"The two are separate. Words and actions… different animals."

He pressed the button for the service elevator. "I know you won't tell me the truth, but I've got to ask…."

Oh, Trevor, what are you up to? "Yes?"

"When we were in that apartment with the OD."

"Yes, James. He has a name." *Stop being a pedant.*

"Right, James… and Annie. When you called her by her name, you said you'd read it on the call sheet. It *wasn't* there. All we had was an address and a twenty-seven-year-old male with a probable heart attack."

We got into the elevator, and Trevor pressed 2. I let his question-cum-accusation linger. So many ways to respond, and it added a discordant note to my minuet that begged for resolution. "I must have heard it."

"I didn't."

"You don't have my ears." And that was true… ish. Because I did hear her name, from her almost-dead husband as he hovered between life and death.

"I hate you," he said as he rang Flo's doorbell.

"Now who's lying?" I resisted the impulse to touch him, which had become increasingly difficult over that year. Nothing pervy, just a pat on the shoulder… or the ass.

"Bastard."

We heard the scuff and clump of a walker on parquet floors. It shifted us from minuet to something slower and contemplative—a largo or lento. Each footfall a decision, nothing unintended, nothing wasted, maybe a sarabande, slow and courtly. My thoughts drifted back a couple centuries to scenes of stiff satin and lace, a season in London, a string quartet. *Might I have the pleasure of the next dance?* The jingle of a security chain, the twist and thud of a deadbolt, heavy breaths brought on by the exertion of twenty steps down a corridor. "Hold on," her voice a deep but anxious rasp. "Hold on."

"Take your time," I said. "We're in no rush."

"Godfrey?" Her anxiety was replaced by excitement as the knob twisted and the door yanked inward.

"You are a vision," I said, and Trevor be hanged, that was no lie. For there, perched over her four-point walker with two bright green tennis balls affixed to the back legs, Flo was a head-to-toe package in shades of puce and purple. Rows of chunky Bakelite beads hung from her neck and ears, and her acid-green tasseled loafers matched the trim on her dusky grape pantsuit. She wore full makeup that had taken her the better part of an hour, and a storied and color-coordinated leather handbag in the shape of a panther completed her ensemble.

"What a wonderful surprise," she said. "Come in. Come in. And take off that stupid mask. I want to see your beautiful face."

Before Trevor could kill her buzz and say something like *we're not supposed to,* "Of course, but we can't stay long."

"I know." She inched backward, gripped her walker, and pivoted around the jam-packed floor-to-ceiling bookshelves as she managed a careful fourteen-point turn.

I loved her rhythm—like a metronome turned all the way down—everything deliberate, nothing rushed.

"Godfrey," Trevor hissed at my back.

"Yes, Trevor."

"We're not supposed to do this."

I stopped, which let Flo get a couple steps ahead of us. I looked back at him, his irritation about a four out of ten, as his nimble arterioles flushed up his neck. "Think, Trevor. This *is* what we're supposed to do." I watched his lovely hazel eyes and waited.

He nodded. "I still hate you."

"Something's burning," I whispered.

"What?"

"Your pants."

"Dick."

"Language. Is this how young doctors are supposed to talk?"

"Dickwad."

"Terrible." I turned back to Flo, who'd made it another three feet in the direction of her cluttered but spacious living room with its tile-framed fireplace, plaster rosettes, and sun-faded Persian carpets.

"Could I offer you tea?" she asked.

"Absolutely not," I said. "Trevor, would you put on a kettle?"

"I will kill you for this," he whispered as he abandoned all hope for a timely turnaround on this call. He disappeared toward her kitchen.

"You are a sight," she said as she settled back into her electric riser chair. Beside it was a coffee table buried under mail-order circulars, coupons, and dozens of dog-eared romance paperbacks.

"It's been a while," I remarked, pleased at how the clutter had been tidied… somewhat.

"Too long. They won't let me reserve you."

I chuckled. "Like a library book."

"It's not fair." Her crimson lips puckered into a sulk.

"I know. Don't you hate it when you can't get your way?"

"I do, and at my age, exceptions should be made. I've complained all the way to the head of your stupid company. Cavalry my ass."

"Agreed, age should come with privilege. And I see you've been putting up with the nursing agency," I commented. "Your house looks better than I've ever seen it." *But something else… she's playing coy… what is it? Something is different.*

"They're not horrible, and once they stopped changing my aide every two weeks… you get one to finally understand how things are supposed to be and then they're gone. They all want to rush me. Do this, do that. Where do they think I'm going that I need to get there so fast?"

"And your nurse?" I scanned her world of layered memories. Three dead husbands in matching frames on her paisley-draped Steinway, photos of the grand- and great-grandnieces and nephews where children and grandchildren might have taken pride of place had she ever conceived.

"He's cute… but not like you. More of a lapdog to your… not quite certain what you are." Her water-blue eyes squinted. "Not like anyone I've ever met, which is saying something. I've known a lot of men, Godfrey, and you're different."

"I'll bite." Still trying to figure the morning puzzle—"What's different about me?"

She waggled a hand in the air. "When I was young, men just wanted to get me in the sack. As that faded, they came for my money. You don't want either."

"Not true," I said. "We could have a quick roll before Trevor comes back. Perhaps a threesome? But no, I don't need your money. It would be just sex."

She giggled, and without needing the visual aid of her Rubenesque portrait that hung above the mantle, I glimpsed the beauty she had possessed. Though to me, the lines and crinkles of her face and neck were lovely.

"It would kill me, but what a way to go," she said. "You have such beautiful eyes, like Sophia Loren. You probably don't even know who she was. And your skin… Greek?"

"Italian. My people were from Firenze," I offered as the kettle whistled from the other room. "And what have your doctors been saying?"

"Nothing new."

And then it hit. The overwhelming smell of cigarettes was almost gone. Yes, there was a golden nicotine patina on the glass of her framed botanical prints, and the nude oil she'd posed for in her early twenties was in desperate need of a spit clean, but the ashtray that usually perched on her side table was gone. "You quit smoking."

"Two months," she stated with pride.

"That's wonderful. But why?"

"Funny thing, that," she said. "After so many years of everyone insisting and nagging and bullying me to quit, I woke up one morning, thought of something you'd said, and just stopped."

"What did he say?" Trevor asked as he reappeared with mismatched mugs—one with a photo of her departed dachshund, Ziggy, and the other with a cartoon of the same name.

"Confidence and a tipping point," she said.

"I don't get it," Trevor replied as he searched for a bare spot on her coffee table to set her tea.

"On the armrest," she instructed. "But here." And she pulled up a loose sleeve to show her dialysis shunt. It was a ropy stretch of arm where the vein had been replaced with a hard-grafted artery where she could be hooked to a machine three times a week for four hours a pop for the rest of her life. "Doctor Doom-and-Gloom told me it was failing and that either I'd need to have one placed on the other arm or they'd have to switch me to dialysis in my belly, which I know too much about this stuff and the belly type doesn't work as well, you have a tube in your stomach, and it kind of means they've given up. Which I haven't. Not yet. So I asked him what I could do to save it. And he said the one thing in my power was to stop smoking, that whatever was wrong with this one would have a better chance to heal. He also said that no surgeon he knew would take the risk of planting a new one on a ninety-two-year-old chain smoker."

"Your tipping point?" Trevor asked.

"Correct."

I felt proud at how he attended to Flo. He listened and would make an excellent doctor. *And this is where you learn, Trevor, at the bedside.* Just as Gaius taught me. And not for the first time, I wondered why he hadn't been accepted to medical school.

She sipped her tea and sighed. "But I've had dire warnings before, and threats and ultimatums. But this time it was all on me. My shunt was failing. I fought to get this one placed, and… I thought of the second half of your equation, Godfrey. Confidence. It seemed silly, but the more I thought about it, that was what it's always been with me and the big changes in my life. Like them." And she gestured toward her three framed exes on the piano. "The love of my life who broke my heart, the mean one, and the cheater. Crises and tipping points come and go, like them, but it's whether or not I believe I can do the thing that determines the outcome. Peter, whom I married too young, died in the war. Alex was a possessive bastard, but again, I was too young to know. But it was a tipping point. Confidence and an excellent attorney got me away from him." She chuckled.

"Why is that funny?" Trevor asked.

"Because number three, Stanley, may he rot in hell, was the attorney. Who mostly wanted the settlement he got me from Alex. But lesson learned, the tipping point with Stanley came when I realized he was a cheater. I got a different lawyer, a female one. She had me hire a detective, who got the most adorable set of pictures with Stanley in the altogether save for a diaper, pacifier, and bonnet. We took him to the cleaners."

"Flo, bring the ship back into harbor," I said. "Tell Trevor how this helped you stop smoking."

"Those were big changes. Huge, and in those days, divorce was not like today. But I knew in both cases that I needed to get out. Once a man hits me, we're done, and Stanley, I think that was worse... being made to feel a fool. The confidence was there. I had no doubt of what needed to happen. No hesitation. Which is the dead opposite of my affair with tobacco. I started to smoke when I was twelve. I looked up to women like Garbo and Dietrich. They smoked and were strong, and... I was twelve. It wasn't for a couple decades before people started to think there might be something wrong with pumping smoke into your lungs. And in all those years, I might have hit that tipping point, or come close, but I lacked confidence and conviction. And when husbands and doctors would scold me, it made me want to smoke more. And I'd think, 'You're all wrong.

I'm ninety-two and they haven't killed me yet.' But the truth has a wicked way of seeping in."

Trevor shot me a look, which I imagined had everything to do with his previous critique of my honesty. "And the confidence," I prompted.

"Was borrowed," she said. "I thought of Stanley and I thought of Alex and how, once I'd made the decision, it was like an on-off switch had flipped. I would not go back. I focused on that, and I flipped the switch two months and four days ago with my cigarettes. I just quit. I had the aide take out all the ashtrays. I hired cleaners to steam everything they could. And when I get the urge to smoke…." She stopped and smiled.

"Yes," I urged. "Out with it, Flo. Mustn't tease."

"I shouldn't," she said. Her excitement was delicious, like a child who desperately wanted to show something secret and special.

"Of course you should."

"You can't tell anyone." She lowered her voice. "It was stipulated in Stanley's settlement."

"Who would we tell?" I asked. "And Stanley has been dead and gone for over twenty years."

"Still," she commented as her fingers plowed into the layers of ephemera on her table. Her grin was delightful as she hunted. "Here it is."

"At the ready, I see."

"Funny thing," she said as she retrieved a bulging and faded manila envelope, its closure flap half-torn. "I really shouldn't."

"Yes, but you've hit a tipping point, and your confidence couldn't be higher."

"Scamp."

And with the tease of a burlesque fan dancer, she drew out one black-and-white eight-by-ten glossy after the next and faced them across her lap in our direction.

"Well done, you," I offered as I took in crisp images of a paunchy man with a pencil mustache and thinning hair beneath the brim of a baby's bonnet, with his dark lips wrapped lovingly around a young woman's nipple. In another he was upside down across her lap, buttocks exposed, her hand upraised, about to deliver a well-deserved spank.

"Spare the rod," I observed as the next few documented his punishment.

"And ditch the bastard," she said.

For Trevor's part, Flo's home porn had rendered him speechless and beet red.

"It gets worse, and I really shouldn't," she said.

"Your call." Not about to let her stop, because *A*, she didn't want to and *B*, there is not a lot in this life, or any of my many, that surprises me. This photo montage deserved a showing.

"Okay, but this crosses a line." She clutched the edge of a picture.

And before I could say something snarky to Trevor about once seen a thing cannot be unseen, there it was in all its full-diaper glory. "Coprophilia," I said, the Latin making it a bit palatable.

"Hell no." Trevor pushed back. "That is not… no, no, no."

"Mustn't judge," I said as I took the photo from Flo. It was art. Beautifully framed, in perfect focus, and the expression on Stanley's face… rapture. "I wonder if these came before or after the spanking."

"Before," she said. "They're all numbered. Now give those back." And she retrieved the potent images, slid them into their envelope, and buried them deep inside the mound of papers.

"You know you owe him," I said.

"Excuse me?"

"That was over fifty years ago. They gave you confidence then… to leave him, and they still worked two months ago when you needed that confidence again."

"And this, Godfrey, is why I can't understand why they won't let you come for all my dialysis trips. It's not fair."

I looked at her empty mug. "Which, speaking of, it's time to get a wiggle on."

"They don't like it when I'm late," she conceded. "Can I blame it on you?"

Trevor stiffened.

"He'd rather you didn't," I said.

"I suppose that's fair. Fine. I'll play the dotty old lady who got her days mixed up."

"It'll work," I commented as Trevor retrieved the wheelchair.

"It will," she agreed, and away we went.

Chapter Five
Trevor Explains Mnemonics

"WHAT THE fuck, Godfrey. Are you kidding? What is your problem?" As we left Flo at the renal center for her thrice-weekly blood cleanse, I could not believe what Godfrey just said. Like it was no big deal. "You deferred Harvard?" My dad's Southie accent clanged in my ears. *This is a joke. A typical and fucked-up Godfrey joke.*

"I did," he said.

I had no words, but I wanted to hit him. It's not like I was the one who'd just given up the Willy Wonka golden ticket to medical school, which apparently COVID had made even hotter with 15 percent more applicants. It was him. Why should I care? Or was that just another lie? Maybe he'd never been accepted in the first place, or even applied, and this was just to cover his tracks—a lie on top of another lie. Maybe that was it. I checked my mirrors and the video cam and pulled out. Our next call was an organ harvest, already up on the GPS with a forty-five-minute ETA. The dispatcher had said there was no need to rush. I floored it and flipped on the lights and sirens. "Why?"

"Because *you're* not ready," Godfrey said.

I looked at him—so damn smug—and nearly clipped a Prius as it pulled onto the curve. "What are you talking about?"

"You've got another year, right? Retake your MCATs this winter. I figured I'd wait."

"Bullshit!"

"Seriously, Trevor, you never used to swear. You've got to do something about your vocabulary. And not to judge, but when you get upset that—*pahk tha cah in Hahvahd Yahd*—not good."

I turned onto Comm Ave and the fastest of three possible routes to the hospital near the Rhode Island border, where a transplant team now harvested organs from a twenty-three-year-old woman about to be taken off life support. "Are you even able to tell the truth?"

"You wound me. What don't you believe?"

"Where to start? Did you even get into Harvard?"

"Want to see my acceptance letter?"

"Yes, I would." Mostly just to see the thing, and maybe someday get one of my own. Though it wouldn't be to Harvard but to some offshore school in the Caribbean that I should have accepted before. It would cost a fortune and come with no guarantees, but this time I'd take it. "I'd love to see it." I expected him to say he'd bring it next shift, and then, "Oops, I forgot"… because it didn't exist.

"No problem." He pulled out his cell, flicked through emails, tapped on the screen. "Here you go." And he read, "Dear Mr. Hesse: It is our great pleasure to inform you that the Admissions Committee for Harvard University School of Medicine has accepted your application for the incoming class."

He could be making it up. "Give me that."

He passed me his iPhone, *a 12 Pro Max—and how the hell does he already have one?* And there it was on university letterhead—the Latin logo, hyperlinks to forms he'd have to complete, and a drop-dead date to accept or decline, which had passed. *Okay, so maybe it's not a lie. Dude is super smart. Of course he got in.* I imagined him in the interviews— funny, articulate, handsome—who wouldn't want him? My head throbbed as I processed the I-don't-give-a-fuck way he treated this thing I wanted so badly, had wanted since I was a kid. *When I grow up, I'm going to be a doctor who helps children. Like the ones who tried to save my sister.* And he gets it without trying, and....

Fine, Godfrey gets into Harvard, and then... I blasted the sirens as I hit the on-ramp to I-95 south. Traffic was light, and I was pissed. "Why would you defer? Are you insane? Do you know how many people they reject? Over ninety-five percent." *Like me. Twice. And my supervisor told me, "Don't even attempt the Ivies. You don't have the grades, Trevor."* I still had his pricey cell, my thumb on the screen. I read and reread that awesome first sentence. And then I noticed something else—his address. I knew he lived in

Brookline, but here was the actual address. I memorized it. And like how I remembered all the steps in the Kreb's cycle for glucose metabolism, I repeated it over and over, attached little bits of other things to the words…. Evert Road, like the Mount Everest of lies he told and rules he broke. The 446 was harder. Unattached numbers are. But the first two repeated themselves and four is a square number, and Godfrey is the opposite of square. Times two at least, so that's the 44, and then add two, for the two of us hanging out together for twenty-four hours at a pop. Or if you add two and four that's six. That will work, 446 Evert Road, Brookline. *And why did you just memorize his address?* "Why?" I repeated.

"I told you. For you. I want us to go together."

I wanted to hit him. "What are you talking about?" I passed back his cell, or more accurately, shoved it at him.

"You're a year behind. You have to retake your MCATs, get at least elevens instead of nines and tens, do your applications, buy a navy suit, possibly gray. Though with your coloring, navy is better. Then go on interviews… get accepted to Harvard or Tufts. I'm good with either. I'd even do UMass. It's a lot cheaper, and you won't have nearly the amount of debt when you finish."

I didn't know where to start. "That's if I get in… anywhere, which is a big if."

"You've been accepted once."

"It was offshore. It doesn't count." I glanced at the speedometer. It hovered between ninety-five and one hundred mph. While I normally care about the rules, and unnecessary speeding was both taboo and dangerous, it helped me focus.

"It does count, would have gotten you closer to your goal. But you felt it was… what?"

"Second best," I admitted, having struggled with the decision to turn down the medical school in Dominica. "And there was no guarantee that I'd be able to transfer over to a US school for my third and fourth years."

"I never took you for a snob, Trevor."

"Said Mr. 'I got into Harvard and turned them down.' Tell me you're joking." And the needle hit 110, and that forty-five-minute ETA was down to twenty-five.

"I didn't turn them down. I deferred. It's different."

"And they accepted your 'I love you, but not yet'?"

"Why wouldn't they?"

I fumed and sped. Of course they would, because he was Godfrey Hesse, and the rules that applied to everyone else didn't matter. If I listened to his madness, I could almost believe what he said—that I'd retake that stupid test and magically spit back the answers I'd need to get my scores up, and that my essays, which I had proofed and edited and compared to prizewinners from others, would now sway the head of an admissions committee—that I was who they wanted. He probably scribbled something on the back of a paper towel, wadded it up, and….

The GPS spoke and pulled my focus. "In two miles, your exit is on the right."

"You're not a snob," Godfrey said after I'd turned off the interstate and our destination loomed before us.

"Thank you."

"You're a coward."

I flicked on my blinker and turned into the hospital parking lot. "Fuck you, asshole."

"It's true." He retracted his legs from the dash. "You just said you turned down that school in Dominica, which by the way is one of the most beautiful islands in the world, because you were scared you wouldn't get into an onshore school. That's fear, Trevor. It's cowardice that stopped you. You need to work on that."

I shut off the engine and looked at him. I hated what he'd just said, because it was true. There was no smugness in his accusation. It had been an honest observation. "You're right. I wouldn't take the risk."

He didn't move, just stared at me.

"What?" I said. The silence stretched. I forced myself not to blink or look away. *Jesus, he has beautiful eyes.*

"You will get into Harvard, Trevor, if it's what you want. And you will make an amazing physician. I have no doubt. But here's the thing, boyo, if you can't get your fear under control, it's going to lock you in a little box that gets smaller and smaller until one day you can't move at all. And the saddest part is you won't even notice, and then you'll be dead." He shifted his gaze out the windshield. "It's like you'll have lived your entire life without having lived."

I waited as he got out, and I felt like I'd been punched. It was fear that had made me turn down that school in Dominica—fear of debt I'd never be able to repay, of more rejection when it came time to transfer to an American school to complete the training I'd need to get my medical license. But it ran deeper, like maybe this whole dream to become a pediatrician was just that, a stupid fantasy, and the universe was telling me to ditch it. I didn't need a shrink to tell me how, when, and why it started. I knew. Years of watching my sister Grace die in stages, the rounds of chemo and radiation. The surges of hope as her numbers rebounded, the crashes when they fell. Her sweet smile and her stupid jokes about losing her hair, the wigs she loved—the more outrageous pink, purple, and polyester the better.

I startled as Godfrey rapped on my window. "Earth to Trevor."

"Right." I opened the door and strapped on a company mask. I felt light-headed, confused, and played.

"Eye on the prize, Trevor. You *will* get in."

I wanted to argue, but instead held my tongue and reran the mnemonic for his address, just to see if it took. *Mount Everest, he's not square... times two and then add two and we've got 446 Evert Road, Brookline.*

Chapter Six
Godfrey Snacks

ORGAN-TRANSPLANT RUNS are a mixed blessing. They require zero skill and could be handled by an Uber or Grubhub driver. The catch is the cargo—a heart, a lung or two, kidneys, eyes, a life-sustaining buffet of bits and bobs.

"She's so young," Trevor whispered as we stood in the dimly lit observation room and watched through the glass.

Before us a gloved, gowned, and masked team of three surgeons—cardiothoracic, renal, and ophthalmologic, not in that order—did the harvest. The heart and lungs would be the last to go, and then the poor young thing who had hovered confused and scared for months over her artificially animated corpse would be free.

"She fell asleep behind the wheel," Trevor said. "She was higher than a kite. What a waste."

I barely heard as she stared at me as they tend to. Her thoughts were scattered. *"What happened? Am I dead? Am I in hell?"*

I met her gaze and supplied what answers I could. *"Drugs. You passed out behind the wheel. This is not hell."* Though who am I to say?

She floated from her body up to the observation window. The thinnest of tethers held her rooted to this plane. Her mouth gaped. *"No,"* she wailed. *"Did I hurt anyone? Did I kill anyone?"*

"Just yourself." I'd read through her electronic medical record, which included links to stories in the local paper. There were pictures. I showed her one in my thoughts. The twisted remains of a white Mazda. Hard to tell where her mangled car ended and the steel barrier began, the edges blurred by a seventy-mile-an-hour marriage.

She gasped. *"My car."*

"Was it deliberate?" I asked as I tucked the image away. *"Did you mean to die?"*

"No...." She stared back at her body, which was now minus two eyes, as the renal team tapped in. *"Not this time. What have I done?"*

It was a rich question.

And while Trevor was oblivious to my astral sidebar, he echoed the wraith's lament. "What is going on with these overdoses?"

Before I could respond to either question, the observation room door clicked and a masked middle-aged couple entered. Both had red-rimmed eyes. The man's spine was straight as a marine's but softened by the hand that clasped his wife's. She glanced at Trevor and me, noted our uniforms, and then forced her gaze to the scene before us.

She put a hand to her covered mouth, her eyes squeezed shut. "No, no, no."

Her husband's grip tightened.

The wraith whimpered. *"Mommy, Dad, I'm sorry. I'm so sorry."* She looked from them back to me. *"They can't hear me. No one does. Just you."*

I nodded.

"Tell them I'm sorry."

"They know," I said.

"I've put them through hell."

"True."

"Is that where I'm going?"

"Don't know," I admitted. *"But there is a light. When they finish the harvest and turn off the machine, you should go into it. Doesn't work out well when people linger."*

"I never meant for this."

I was distracted as the woman spoke to Trevor. "Are you here for her? For Rachel?"

"Yes. You're her parents?"

"I'm DeeDee. This is my husband, Ray."

"I'm so sorry," he offered.

"Thank you." She stopped in front of the observation window, but her husband stayed back, his eyes unreadable.

I sensed her struggle. "At least this is something," she said.

"Yes," I agreed, not taking my eyes from her daughter's tethered soul.

"We tried. We never gave up on her."

Her words lay heavy in the air. They swirled in my head and caught on other such conversations. I knew these parents—always alone, when in fact they were two of a massive army. "This is not your fault."

"So people say… at least some of them. But what if we enabled her? What if we'd been stricter?"

The wraith gasped. *"Tell her she's wrong. They did everything—never kicked me out, never gave up. What have I done?"*

Her husband moved closer, like a magnet pulled to his wife and dying child.

"DeeDee, in my experience," I said, "it doesn't help. You gave her more chances to beat this thing. That's not enabling. That's love, and this is not your fault."

"She'd just left rehab," her father said. "We'd just brought her home."

"I should have known," DeeDee added. "She said she was going to get a pack of cigarettes. I should have known."

The wraith flew anguished circles over her body as her right kidney was removed and placed into what looked like a small blue picnic cooler.

"I didn't want to die," Rachel wailed. *"I didn't mean to hurt them. I was going to get cigarettes. I was not going to use. I was going to have a life."*

"What happened?" I asked as the fresh blood on the surgical drapes made my mouth water. I glanced at the clock. Time flies on this job. It was midafternoon, and other than a little bit of Kate and some empty donut calories, I was peckish.

"I got a text from my dealer. Said he'd gotten some unlaced heroin. No fentanyl. Said he'd saved me some and I could have a couple bags for free."

"Got to love a bargain."

"I told him no… and then yes. I couldn't stop myself."

A second pair of medics entered the observation room. One whispered to Trevor, but loudly enough for everyone to hear. "Have they done the eyes yet?"

"Yeah, about thirty minutes ago."

"Thanks." She turned back to her partner. "Let's get our package and roll."

"Good," DeeDee said. Her shoulders slumped. "She has beautiful eyes."

"She does," I offered as I stared into them, or rather their astral remains.

Ray stood behind her and spoke. "And now someone else will be able to see because of them and because of her."

Trevor joined us. "And there's a young boy in Boston who has a chance for a normal life who will get her heart and years of life."

"Is that what you're here for?" Ray asked.

"Yes," Trevor said.

"They do that last, don't they? Ray asked.

"Yes."

He nodded. "And then that's it."

"Yes," Trevor said, and his voice wavered.

"I'm going to go find some coffee," I offered. "Can I get you anything?"

"No," DeeDee said.

"We're good," Ray echoed.

"See if you can find me a sandwich," Trevor said.

And he'd done so well too, asked the right questions, his empathy spot-on. But chowing down on a hospital ham and swiss while someone watched their child get dissected was crass. Then again, he hadn't eaten either. "I'll see what I can find."

As I left the amphitheater of blood, my hunger was tripped by the wonderful sights and sounds that have made hospitals, accidents, and crime scenes reliable hunting grounds. Though with their random slaughter and waste, the best by far are war zones. But here the Cavalry uniform was like Harry Potter's cloak of invisibility. In a year I'd trade it for a medical student's, then an intern's, and then a resident's lab coat. I might be a surgeon this time or some other flavor of practitioner; things have gotten so chopped up and specialized. Not certain if that's good or not. But time raced on, even with Rachel's harvest by teams of specialists, each one focused on their bit of flesh, the entire picture of who she had been or could have been locked inside the hearts of her parents.

I wandered the corridors, steered by the overhead signs and arrows. This was an older hospital— at least a century—that had been rebuilt and renovated. Like myself, it had gone through incarnations and was now one in a chain of related institutions, though that last bit was not so true for me. Placards announced its recent triumphs with the Joint Commission and how it was one of the twenty-five best Massachusetts healthcare employers in 2015 and again in 2018, at least according to one local paper.

But this was past lunchtime, and like Trevor in a hospital cafeteria, I needed nourishment that would not put me to sleep and that tasted decent. I headed to the gift shop, which before COVID had been a favorite place to grab a bite.

With my ponytail tucked inside my shirt, I perused limited options. There was a thirtysomething woman with a heparin lock in her arm, browsing through magazines, her right leg swollen and cellulitic. The clerk, an older volunteer masked behind a plexiglass window, let me know that only two people were allowed in at a time.

I spotted a bag of black licorice, one of my favorites, though Trevor hated the stuff, and snagged it. I made eye contact with the young woman with the enflamed leg. *You'll do.* I smiled, and though the mask diluted that charm, my gaze did what was needed. Like a fisherman with a lure, I waited for that first tug of her interest. *And there it is. Hello, my darling. You've been here a long time.*

She stared into my eyes. Her pulse quickened.

I paid for and pocketed my licorice as the women hobbled after me.

"Do I know you?" she said.

"You're a nurse," I commented.

"How could you tell?" Her eyes fixed on mine.

"Is there someplace we can talk?" I asked.

"I shouldn't," she said, aware that talk was not the proposed agenda.

But with a lick and a lash of my will, I stirred urges even stronger than the invitation to heroin from dying Rachel's dealer. It was a shame she couldn't see the rakish twist of my smile. "You shouldn't. Then again…."

"There's a family room on my floor that no one ever uses. We can lock the door."

I followed at her side as she headed toward the elevator. "What am I doing?" she asked as we entered and headed toward the sixth floor.

But it was too late. She had let me in.

She stumbled as we exited the elevator. "It's down here." She looked up at me, and I smelled her fear—not of what I might do, but that I might leave.

"I'm right here," I reassured as I started on the appetizer of her lust.

She opened a door with two signs taped across it—Please Observe Social Distancing and Masks Are Required.

Inside it was carpeted, color-coordinated, and cozy. She locked the door behind us and threw her arms around my neck. "I need to see your face."

"Of course." I pulled off my mask as she did the same. Her mouth clamped on to mine, and I drank.

Our bodies pressed tight, she tore at the fabric of my shirt and a hand found its way inside.

I drank. Spittle and blood, as tiny capillaries burst under the rasp of small retractable barbs on my tongue—sort of like a cat's, only pointy and stabby.

"Please," she muttered. "I want you."

"You have me," I said as I stroked the soft flesh of her uninjured thigh and warm blood seeped from her mouth into mine. With it came images—her house, her jogger husband, the garden she loved almost more than her two children, her coworkers, birthday cakes, barbecues, Costco circulars, and nutritious meals for four that could be assembled in under fifteen minutes.

She shuddered as my callused touch inched higher.

Her fingers scrabbled over my fly, and she tried to pull it down, but things had gone too far and too fast. With a shiver and gasp, she orgasmed and collapsed in my arms. Her pulse, like a moth at a flame, battered out of control. But unlike Rachel and James with their heroin, I stopped. This lovely nurse, with her wedding band, her blond hair that had gone months without a touch-up, and her cellulitis from a gardening mishap with a nest of ground wasps, would not die at my hands. I took a last swig—it carried aftertastes of antibiotics and peppermint lifesavers—and covered my tracks with a bit of saliva to stop the bleed. *Just a dream*, I whispered as luscious aftershocks rolled through her. *Just a beautiful, sexy dream.* I eased her down onto a leatherette armchair and, mindful of her injured leg, propped it on an ottoman.

Her lips hung open, and she snored. I grabbed a tissue and mopped a bit of blood-tinged spittle from the corner of her mouth. It would be sore and she'd struggle to remember how it happened, but the cells of the mouth heal wicked fast. In two days she'd be right as rain, and when her leg healed and she went home to her husband and kids, she'd have a little secret—a dark and dangerous fantasy she could replay anytime she liked.

I listened at the door, heard nothing, unlocked it, and left it ajar. And now, off to find a ham and swiss for Trevor and maybe a yogurt as well. He'd been eating too much crap.

Chapter Seven
Trevor Lets Godfrey Drive

RACHEL DENNIS'S grief-stricken parents made me stop and filter my mouth. If my grandfather Karel were still alive, he'd have cuffed me upside the head for as much as a *damn* or a *darn*. Can't imagine what a fuck, shit, or cocksucking son of a bitch would get me. Father Calvin had it down to a confessional equation. "The effort matters, Trevor. Let's bundle the swears into ten per Our Father or Hail Mary." No time like the present. *Hail, Mary, full of grace....* When I was little, I thought that was a reference to my sister.

I ran the prayer like a mantra, my gaze focused on the choreographed surgical drama in front of me. In a few years, that could be me, and was Godfrey right? Why did I turn down the school in Dominica? I'd told myself it was the money, the uncertainty of knowing whether I'd find a US school to accept me for the clinical years. But his words festered. It *was* fear. Did I blow my one chance? At twenty-four, it's not like I didn't have choices. I didn't have to become a pediatrician. Maybe that was the fantasy of a young kid who saw the sister he adored suffer, who watched his parents—so like the Dennises—have their hopes raised and dropped with each round of treatment.

I glanced at my phone as Rachel's second kidney, along with a different set of medics, came and went with their blue-for-renal picnic cooler. The cardiothoracic team had just gloved and gowned. Soon, like the last leg of the relays I'd run in high school and college, we'd speed back to Boston and pass Rachel's heart to another surgical team, where it would be placed into the chest of a fourteen-year-old boy with a congenital defect.

And what is taking Godfrey so fucking long? It had been more than an hour since he'd vanished, and I was starving, and…. But one of us needed to stay here.

"She was such a beautiful child," DeeDee Dennis said. "Our little star. So full of life."

DeeDee and I sat reflected in the glass, her husband barely visible deep in the shadows—three masked ghosts in front of her daughter's final moments of life.

There was nothing I could say, and Godfrey— per usual—had told me what was needed in situations like these. "Listen," he'd say, "but not with your ears. If words are needed, they'll come."

A silence fell, and then DeeDee spoke. "The part that kills me is we never knew."

"About what?" I asked.

"The drugs. Any of this. She was a straight A student, beautiful, had friends, did sports, played the clarinet, was going to be a social worker or school psychologist. She loves children... wanted children. And then it all went to this. We'll never see her children, and now I'm going to bury mine. Parents shouldn't. We're supposed to go first.... At least there's this," she stared forward. "Her life won't have been for nothing. Others will have a second chance because of her."

"Yes. They will."

Her husband moved closer; streams of his tears glistened in the glass. He shook his head as DeeDee reached back for his hand.

They stood frozen and trapped. An arc of light spilled in as Godfrey returned with a cardboard drinks holder with four embedded hot/cold cups and a white cafeteria bag. "I didn't know what people took in their tea," he offered, "so I brought an assortment."

"Thank you," DeeDee said as she accepted a cup and Ray did the same.

I envied Godfrey's ease. How natural for him to pass out refreshments in a surgical theater. Even his choice of cookies—both chocolate chip and oatmeal—were easy to handle, no mess, no fuss, and no wrong choice.

Without a word he slipped me a wrapped sandwich—turkey, swiss, whole wheat bread, mustard and mayo.

"You've got something wet on the corner of your mask," I said and grabbed a napkin.

As he moved back from me, I swabbed at the dark goo, the way I might do with my little sister,

Emma, my parents' unspoken replacement for Grace. "Stay still," I said.

He moved back into the shadows, pulled off his mask, tossed it into a wastebasket, and pulled a fresh one from his pocket. "Ketchup," he said.

I looked at the napkin. Yeah, it was red. "Did you hurt yourself?" I asked.

"I'm fine." But he wouldn't meet my gaze.

I wanted to ask him why he had blood on his mask, because that's what it was, but this wasn't the time. And after a year of being partners, I recognized typical Godfrey-in-the-afternoon kinds of things, none of which made sense. But if I asked him about them, he'd tell me lies that might work on a developmentally slow child but that pissed me off. Like why, in this very dark room, were the colored parts of his eyes wide, and why did those freaky amber rings practically glow in the dim light that spilled from the surgical suite. It should be the other way—pupils widen in the dark and obscure the uvea, the colored part. The most obvious cause for this reversal was why we were in that room—opioids. Was that where the blood was from? Was that his secret? He was an addict? And the hour he'd been gone had been spent in some hospital bathroom shooting up and nodding off? I glanced at the sleeves of his uniform, rolled up past the elbow, which we are not supposed to do, but they displayed the bulge of his biceps... and no track marks. My two years as a paramedic and two before that as an EMT had taught me people can shoot drugs into all sorts of places. He was alert, not what you'd expect from someone who'd just shot heroin or fentanyl, but what about cocaine or meth? *Is that what this is?* His strange shifts in mood, his otherworldly behaviors, at times laid back and now... animated, jittery. *He's stoned.* And just as quickly as I landed on my solution to the riddle of Godfrey, I found a hole.

They make us pee into a cup every other week, and they check for everything. *But people fake drug tests,* and because of that the company insisted that all tests were observed, which was hateful but, from their cover-your-ass perspective, necessary.

I cornered him and lowered my voice to where I hoped the Dennises could not hear either my tone or content. "What is up with you?"

"Not a thing," he said.

And there they were, two golden eyes fixed on mine. I fell dumb, like some fan kid who's come face-to-face with their rock-star idol. I batted against the fog. "What are you taking?" I hissed, and maybe that was it. Maybe it was some asthma inhaler or legit prescription med that caused the weird shifts in his behavior and physiology.

Before he could respond, DeeDee gasped, "Ray, I'm not ready."

Godfrey cocked his head and slipped from my gaze, his movements feline fast as he returned to the center of the room. "We have to go," he said to the couple. "And so does she. Tell her what you need to," he offered.

I gaped and stared, as did they. *What the fuck did he just say?*

"You did everything you could. And she did try. None of this is your fault. Plagues are not judgments. They just happen, like a tornado or earthquake. And people die. Tell her how much you love her and let her go."

"I can't," DeeDee said.

"You can," he said. "And Trevor and I will take her heart and bring it to a boy in Boston, and he's going to have years and decades of life because of Rachel. And because of you. You did everything you could, and I think the two of you will do much more. Her life mattered, but right now you have to let go."

Ray wrapped his arms around his wife. They stared into the operating suite as a nurse shut off the heart-lung machine, another covered the open wounds with blue drapes, and a surgeon secured Rachel's heart into a red-for-cardiac picnic container.

Which was our cue to move. His words puzzled me. "Why," I asked once we were out of earshot, "is it so important to let her go?"

"Because if they don't," he said as we headed toward the waiting nurse with the cooler, "she won't move on. She'll get stuck here."

"What? And now you're the fucking ghost whisperer?"

"Statement of fact." He pulled on a fresh pair of gloves.

I tapped on my tablet and logged in the time we accepted the harvested heart.

"And why don't I drive," he said.

"That's a change. You hate to drive." And he did, always wanting to be the one in the back with the patient. *And what if he is stoned?* But he sounded and acted fine, at least for Godfrey. I didn't argue. And like the handoff in a relay, we grabbed the cooler and jogged back to the ambulance, aware that every second a harvested organ is outside a body—hearts especially—increased the risk for rejection. The decision to have it driven versus taken by med flight was based on a careful calculation by the transplant team that included time of day, distance, and traffic. I stopped myself from heading into the driver's seat, took the cooler from Godfrey, and buckled in.

Initially I was glad to have a bit of time to finish our call sheets, but that faded fast. "Why didn't you put in the GPS?" I asked as he pulled out of the bay.

"Don't need it." He cleared the ambulance zone and with split-second precision clicked on the sirens. "Heigh ho, heigh ho."

"Need it or not," I said, and I retrieved the receiving hospital's address with current ETAs for all possible routes. "There it is."

"Thanks," he said and then, with a lead foot, shot onto the interstate, made a surgically timed bop-and-weave across three lanes, and floored it.

I looked from his left hand on the outer wheel, to his right fingers poised over the embedded siren and flasher controls, to our green dot on the GPS, to the late-afternoon rush-hour mess before us. At least we were headed in and not out of the city. At the start of COVID, traffic had been nonexistent. Now it was just about back to pre-COVID patterns.

As I thought about it, this was the first shift in a long time where we hadn't already had to transport someone who'd tried and failed to ride the virus out at home.

Godfrey pulled off his mask, as did I.

"So how's Shannon?" he asked.

"Good," I said, in no mood to discuss my girlfriend with my possibly heroin-addicted partner. Though the more I looked at him—his laser-beam focus, his eyes a bit too bright and glittery—it might be stimulants. *Maybe he has ADHD. Maybe it's Ritalin.*

"Have you thought about what she asked?"

I did not want to have that discussion. Wasn't that the point of twenty-four-hour shifts? You got to turn off everything else? Like why I wouldn't get into an American medical school, or how my girlfriend since junior year of high school was giving me very strong signals to propose. Or that I was twenty-four and lived in my parents' basement.

"She's right, you know," he said.

"About what?"

"It's shit or get off the pot time, Trevor. What's it been? Twenty years?"

"Six, and the two in high school don't count."

"Yes, they do. I think it's more like seven. You're twenty-four. So is she. Tick tock, tick tock."

"Shut up. I'm in no place to make that kind of commitment." I glanced at the speedometer—not up to my speed heading down. Then again, I didn't have this traffic.

"She is." He tapped the siren to scoot a Nissan out of the passing lane.

"I don't want to talk about this."

"That's apparent." He glanced at the screen and a yellow bar that indicated a construction zone two miles ahead on our current route. With his right forefinger, he clicked on the siren and made a series of lightning maneuvers that took us off the highway and wailing down the main drags of Mansfield and Canton. Even with the detour, we'd beat the computer's ETA.

I glanced at his profile, his dark ponytail with the ridiculous ribbon half out of his collar, his fingers long and nimble as he played the wheel and the buttons of the siren options like the keys of a piano... maybe a guitar. Godfrey was odd, and now I suspected high on something, and making better time with Rachel Dennis's heart than I would have. *That's why he wanted to drive.* It rankled.

"Spit it out, Trevor." He tapped a cadenced rhythm on the horn and eased through a four-way light and back onto I-93 for two quick exits.

"ETA?" Kate asked over the intercom.

"Four and counting," he said. And then to me, "Well? What stops you from sealing the deal with Shannon. She's beautiful. She loves you. She wants your babies. A hundred years ago you'd already have four or five. And it wouldn't matter that you live in the basement of your parents' and that your mommy still does your laundry and slices banana into your cereal, which she does because she loves you."

And with a staccato burst on the horn, he flicked off the siren and took a left into Longwood Avenue and the Emergency parking lot at Children's. "I imagine Shannon would slice your banana… if you wanted her to."

I was out the door with the cooler. *God damn him.* Even with ditching the highway, we'd made spectacular time. The handoff to the transplant team went without a hitch. Only here, a different pair of frantic parents, these filled with hope as their son was about to receive a miracle—a gift from Rachel Dennis and her grieving parents.

Our leg of this race was over. I felt a weird mix of emotions as we walked out of Children's into a warm fall afternoon—a kind of letdown as the adrenaline washed away and I envisioned Rachel Dennis, now dead, but her eyes, kidneys, and heart gifted to others. Hope and despair, a yin-yang wheel, and one that I knew. But for my little Gracie, dead was dead, though not a day passed when I wouldn't think of her, even talk to her. I wondered what she'd have to say about Godfrey. I climbed back behind the wheel as the radio bleeped.

Kate, about to go off shift, told us to get something to eat and booked us for a simple early-evening transport from dialysis. "I hope you have a quiet night," she offered. "See you next week."

"What you in the mood for?" Godfrey asked as he eased his legs onto the dash.

"Thai?" Glad that he'd ditched his previous interrogation about my intentions toward Shannon.

"Sure." And he snapped his fingers and in a ridiculously good tenor sang, "Hey, Mr. Tallyman, tally me banana."

Chapter Eight
Godfrey and the Great Pestilence

I COULDN'T stop myself. By the time Trevor and I landed back at the Cavalry station, after a packed second shift, it was near midnight and he was furious… with me.

"Why do you care?" he spat at me, with no need to lower his voice. From now until the morning shift wandered in around 8:00 a.m., we were alone. The overnight dispatch would come from either Cavalry's central office in Braintree or from the city's 911 hub.

He didn't wait for my response but stormed back to the dorm with its narrow bunks. I thought to follow, but I'd continue to needle him, and it would be better for us both if he got a couple hours sleep.

I meandered through the kitchen and tidied. There was a half-eaten box of donut holes, all the jelly, glazed, and chocolate gone. I tossed the remains, gathered a half-dozen mugs into the sink, and cleared the counters of crumpled fast-food containers. I grabbed a bottle of Clorox and a roll of paper towels and spritzed everything, the toxic antiseptic a potent reminder of just how far science had come. Millions of microbes torn apart by this heady elixir in its pump-action bottle. I started at one end and continued till every millimeter of the faded eighties linoleum counter and battered cabinets had been sanitized. I replayed the day that had been and strategized for tomorrow.

I am no stranger to plagues, pandemics, epidemics, outbreaks, and contagions. What I am not is a passive observer. The virus was beyond my skill set, but the tainted drugs that killed Rachel Dennis and nearly took James were another matter. In ways it reminded me of the great pestilence. It had the same virulence, alive and seemingly well in the morning and dead by night. Admittedly the numbers weren't the same, the streets were not piled with corpses, and Rachel's parents, grief-stricken and bone-tired, never abandoned their daughter. But others did. Plagues are like that—raw fear and uncertainty, unsure what course to take. Should you stay and fight? Or is the contagion too great and it is better to flee to the country, to hole up and try to wait it out? Because things do pass. Like much in nature, plagues have a beginning, a middle, and an end.

I heard a creak from the dormitory door. "Don't you ever sleep?" Trevor asked.

I turned. He had stripped down to a pristine white T-shirt and boxers. I stopped myself from commenting on his mother's laundry skills, or worse, telling him how hot he looked, from his well-toned arms and his runner's calves and thighs to his sleep-tousled hair. "Not tired," I admitted, "and I do sleep."

"Good to know." He headed toward the fridge and retrieved a brown paper bag, the kind that millions of mothers send their millions of children to school with each day. "You want an apple?"

"Sure, Eve."

He tossed it to me. "Don't be such a dick, Adam."

"I'll try."

"Why are you still up?" he asked.

"Thinking."

"About?" he prodded.

"Rachel, James, a good thirty percent of the calls we get."

"It's fucked-up," Trevor said.

"You're going to have to clean up your language when we go to Harvard."

"Enough," he said. "I'm tired."

"Then get some sleep."

"I will. It's just…."

"What?"

"You really pissed me off, Godfrey."

"Sorry about that. You're kind of easy."

"I know. But you were right, and that's what gets me so angry. I don't know what the fuck I'm doing with Shannon. I love her, and that should be all that matters."

Don't do it, Godfrey, I thought, even as the words poured through my lips. "It's not, and the truth, Trevor?" *Don't, don't, don't. Stop, stop, stop.* "You're not

in love with her, but she's the only romantic relationship you've ever had."

He stiffened. "You don't know that."

"Yeah, I do." I knew he wanted to argue the
point, would bring up girls he'd kissed and use his
Catholic School vernacular of what bases he'd made
it to with said willing damsels.

He didn't. Instead he sank into a battered
chrome-and-vinyl chair. "What am I supposed to
do?" His hands on his temples.

"Stop stringing her along. Either commit or let
go. It's not the worst thing in the world to marry
for reasons other than being in love, which usually fades. But commitment, shared goals, friendship,
children, retirement accounts… those matter. People
make them work, make them good enough."

"My parents are in love."

"Not everyone gets that," I said. "And they've
worked at it."

"Yeah. That's what my dad says. When my sister
died, I wondered if they would make it through or if
I'd lose them as well. It made them stronger. Like if
they could survive letting go of Grace, they could
survive anything."

It took all I had to not go to him. To hold him. He
looked so sad… so lost.

"I don't want to hurt her."

"Jesus, Trevor, you have to know that ship has
sailed."

He stared at his hands. "It's going to break her
heart."

"It will."

He looked up. "I've had my heart broken," he said. "It's the most awful thing. Pain like you can't imagine, only nothing's bleeding. Have you... had your heart broken?"

I nodded, as those I've loved and lost through the centuries passed before my eyes like the beads on his wretched rosary—*Amelia, Camille, Beatrice, Bernard, Lawrence, Cedric, Wan-Li*. And I realized something I should have seen sooner. I was in love with Trevor. *And how and when did that happen?*

"So you know?"

"Like dying," I said, "or some catastrophic injury, only no bones are broken. But the pain, unlike anything else. Like a piece of you has been ripped out," I gasped.

He twirled the stem of an apple he'd left on the wobbly side table. "Are you going to tell me the real reason you deferred Harvard?"

"I did." But I now knew that I'd lied to myself—a thing I avoid.

"Because you want us to go together."

"Correct."

"You realize how motherfucking insane that sounds?"

"Right there. That one has to be a sin."

"It's not. Swears don't count. Not in the ten commandments."

"Wrong, church boy. What about honor your mother and father? Seems like you just veered from grace."

"I'll ask Father Calvin. You might have a point. I'm going to try and get some sleep. You should too."

"I will, and I'm glad you're done being mad at me."

"Me too, but you know I won't get into Harvard. If that's really the reason you put it off, you need to reconsider and go."

"We'll see." And I watched as he headed back and let my earlier realization sink in. Strange how the most obvious things are the easiest to overlook or ignore. From the cowlicked tips of his bedhead to a pair of rubber flip-flops he'd slipped on over his bleached banded gym socks, I had fallen in love… again. *And it won't end well. It never does.*

I grabbed the apple and took a bite as my cell and Trevor's rang in unison from the on-call room.

I picked up. "What you got?" I asked.

"Probable OD," the dispatcher said as Trevor stumbled out bleary eyed and stuffed his uniform shirttails into his crumpled pants. I pulled up the call information and stared at the screen. The Southie address that popped up was familiar and too fresh. *No.*

"Let's go," I said. "I'll drive."

And with his shoes in hand, Trevor ambled in and we rolled out.

The moon was full. A haunting tune from Sting about a vampire adrift in New Orleans ran through my thoughts as I sped. *What did I miss?* I laid on the horn to wake a driver about to fall asleep at the wheel. She startled and pulled off to the curb. We didn't need any more business.

I found a cruel symmetry to the day as I parked up on the curb, likely in the same tire grooves Trevor had left earlier. A cruiser pulled in behind, and there were no neighbors milling about, though I imagined glances from behind curtains as we gathered our kit and raced in and up, to the same kitchen, the same linoleum squares, the same James, this time slouched against the toilet with a spike in his arm, breathless, lifeless, and gone. Just gone. Perched on the sink were a well-used spoon, its outer bowl black, a wad of cotton, three crumpled drug baggies with visible residue, and a book of matches. By the faucets stood a bundle of still-full waxed-paper bags. They were stamped in black with an image of a skeleton on its knees and the logo "Pray for Death."

I searched for any trace of him, as Annie, in different sweats from this morning—red, not navy—stood back and stared.

Trevor dragged James out of the bathroom and laid him flat on the kitchen floor. As he did, I pocketed half the unused drug packets. We then did what was expected and futile. Gone is gone. Alive and well… enough, in the morning and gone by midnight. *Pray for death, indeed.*

Trevor started compressions as I drew up, administered Narcan, and eased another plastic tube down dead James's stiff throat. A rib cracked as Trevor counted, "One, two, three, four, five. One, two, three, four, five." If James was still in the room, if there was a chance to bring him back, I'd know. Gone is gone. Dead is dead. At least I'd managed to give him a heads-up about the light, though that scrap of 211 had made the rounds.

A pair of masked and uniformed officers entered the apartment. One looked me square in the eye, the question on his face clear—*He going to make it?*

I shook my head in the negative and tried to put the pieces together. Three bags of fentanyl in the insulin syringe I'd removed from his arm, several more at the ready. Either he'd gone out after he got home from the hospital… or what? Had a stash? Waited till his pregnant wife had gone to sleep?

"He's gone, isn't he?" Trevor whispered as he searched for a pulse.

"Yes."

"Goddammit!"

I said nothing. I looked back at Annie and knew that she knew. This morning she'd caught him in time, but now… *dead is dead.* "You want to ride with us?" My ask an echo from earlier when hope still existed. But it, like James, had gone.

"Yeah, let me get a few things." Her tone flat. All sense of urgency gone from the room.

What happened next was going through the motions. We gathered our dead patient, though he wouldn't be declared until we got to the emergency room. But rites of passage matter. Not to the dead, but to the living—to Annie and her unborn child, to his parents, to everyone he had touched.

Like pallbearers at the ends of a stretcher, we carried him down and out. Oxygen hissed as it pushed air into his lifeless lungs. We hoisted him up, and I offered Annie my arm for her second ride of the day. I got in and closed the doors behind. Protocol would have me start an IV, but right then, James was not the patient who mattered.

"I knew this day would come." Annie stared at his eyes—glassy, blue, and fixed. "He loved heroin more than me."

There was some truth in that. Then again…. "He was addicted," I said. It's a concept that's evolved, but the core feature, the immutable bit, is this moth-to-the-flame compulsion that seldom ends well.

"Whatever that is." She clutched her satchel tightly. It was smaller than it had been this morning.

"Yes." And I waited.

"James," she whispered, "I hope you're at peace." She looked at me. "He did try."

"He certainly did."

"It must have been in the house," she said. "I didn't leave his side since this morning. Called out sick, would have taken FMLA… again. I don't know where he could have gotten it. I never left him. He should have been okay. It must have been in the house." She glared at her dead husband. "Bastard. Everything was a lie. He must have waited till I was asleep. Probably thought about it for hours, yessing me all the way till…."

"Probably," I agreed. "Addiction is like that, like a parasite that must be fed."

"Why couldn't he stop? If he loved me, he would have found a way." She reached into her bag for a packet of tissues. As she did, I glimpsed a familiar red box of Narcan that tumbled amid the contents.

"Not how it works… sadly. And he did love you. Anyone could see that. My guess, this would have happened five years sooner if not for that." I thought about the Narcan in her bag and wondered why she hadn't used it. There weren't any discarded packages at their apartment. They'd been prominent in the morning, but not this time. *Curious.*

She nodded. "That's when it got bad. Though with all his lies, it's hard to know. But yeah, five years back I knew he was using needles, and then he got hepatitis… and gave it to me. I nearly left him, probably should have."

"But didn't."

"I couldn't."

"And neither could he." I wondered if she'd pick it up.

"Love and heroin," she muttered. "Yeah." She gave a hard laugh through her tears. "The ultimate bad relationship. Bastard. What am I supposed to tell his parents? As much as he lied to me, he was worse with them. They'd take us out to dinner and he'd shoot up in the bathroom. And you know what the worst part was?"

"Tell me."

"I covered for him. Over and over. I have been such an idiot. Should have left years ago. And now…."

"The thing is done," I said, though I knew what she needed would be time. Lots of it. I glanced out the back windows and felt the van shift as Trevor looped into the emergency bays at the same hospital we'd taken them to that morning. I struggle in these situations. Death is a part of existence. Everyone wants more life, and I seem to be the only one who gets extra.

"Yeah, it is. And then again…." She placed a hand on her belly.

"When are you due?"

"January." Her gaze met mine. "He said he'd pull it together for our daughter. All lies."

I saw emptiness in her eyes. Despair.

The truck stopped. "Take your time, Annie," I offered. "Is there anyone we can call for you?"

"It's too late," she said in reference to both James and the time of night. "What happens now?"

"Paperwork." Though I wondered if her question was more metaphysical than procedural.

"Yeah. I saw you take those packets off the sink. Why?"

"Evidence."

"You're not a cop."

"True."

"Then why? Why not just flush them? I wish you would. Just make this be over." And like a mantra, "Just make this be over."

Before I could formulate a plausible reason, Trevor opened the back doors.

"It's time to go." I scooted out and offered Annie my arm. We were the only ambulance in the lot, and as we wheeled James through triage, there was no line.

I spoke with the nurse and let her know what was needed—"Pulseless and breathless on arrival"—and went down the list of futile activities we had gone through, because those were the rules.

She nodded and paged the attending doctor.

"This is his wife, Annie," I said.

"I'll just need a bit of information," the nurse instructed from behind her plexi barrier. "I'm so sorry for your loss. Why don't you take a seat."

"Of course."

In silence we transferred dead James to a hospital stretcher. I passed Trevor the tablet so he could fill out the forms. And by 2:00 a.m. we were back on the road.

Chapter Nine
Trevor Discovers the Fourth Law of Physics—Godfrey's

"WELL THAT just sucks," I said as I wiped down the stretcher. Before Godfrey could respond, the dispatcher came through the onboard radio. "Cavalry Eight, you guys free of University?"

Godfrey pressed the microphone. "Affirmative."

"We've got a multiple-vehicle MVA—three cars and a semi on I-90. Multiple casualties. Sending the coordinates now."

"On it," Godfrey said.

I flicked on the lights, but with no traffic, we didn't need the horns, and away we went. "No sleep for the weary," I said.

"Not tonight."

"I felt awful about that last call. That poor woman," I said. "I'm sick of all these ODs."

"Everyone dies," Godfrey said, and he flicked on the police scanner.

"Aren't you Mr. Sunshine." But my focus was pulled to the incoming reports of our next call as I counted four, five, then six sirens headed in the same direction, with our ETA still three minutes and three miles away. "This is bad." I gunned it. It would be an all-available-responder situation.

A mist formed on the windshield and turned to a drizzle.

"Good man," Godfrey said. "First in is first out."

I barreled up the on-ramp to the Pike and flew past another ambulance and a fire truck, all headed toward the left lane. Traffic had backed up. As we neared the accident, I spotted a pump truck, and a broad plume of water shot across a jackknifed refrigerator semi. Its side was gashed open, and a thick fluid oozed from its side. A Corolla, half buried under the dark goo, smoked from a crumpled hood, and behind it, two other cars had collided, their interiors obscured by deployed airbags.

"What the fuck is coming out of that?" I pulled onto the grassy median, as that was always the better choice when it came time to skedaddle.

"Treacle." He unbuckled.

"Treacle?"

"Molasses."

"Is that even combustible?"

"Only if it gets wicked hot," he said. "They're being careful." An orange-striped panel truck of city medics was first on the scene, which meant they were triage.

We headed toward them as the mist turned to a soft, cool rain.

"What have we got?" I asked, having spotted five, six, seven casualties, but all vertical and on their phones. Their expressions were a mixture of shock, anger, and relief as they pulled family and friends from their beds to let them know they'd been in an accident but were going to be okay.

The EMS medic, in his tan-and-brown uniform, looked us over and saw that we were with one of the privates. "Take your pick of the walking wounded. If you could take two, that would be great."

"Not a problem," I said and turned to Godfrey. *Where the hell is he?* The rain hissed off the half-buried Corolla. *Where did he go?* I squinted through the downpour as a spotlight illuminated the collision site, and what had at first appeared to be a series of significant but not life-threatening bumper-car crashes took a dark turn. There, under the arc of a streetlight, I spotted Godfrey's uniformed body as he disappeared through the opening of a mangled steel guard rail.

I should have said something to the triage medic, but he was in discussion with a pair of city EMS, and... I ran back to Eight and grabbed the go kit. Not slowing, I pulled out my mag light and shone it down the steep embankment. I caught movement as Godfrey waved back from the butt end of a BMW sedan, its rear tires still spinning.

He shouted, "We've got three—two adults and one in an infant seat."

I shone the light around the scene and checked for downed power lines and imminent dangers. Lesson one, day one for all first responders—assess and secure the scene. Because a dead hero is no hero. Rule number two—scoop and screw. So down I went. It started well, but the ground was slick with rain. My toe caught on a loose stone. "Shit!"

I tripped, scrabbled for purchase, and fell headfirst. I had the sick realization that I was about to get hurt bad, or even worse. My life didn't pass before my eyes; there was just a pit in my gut that I'd been stupid and would pay for it.

Something hard thumped against my chest. At first I thought it was a tree, but it held me and pushed me back to where I could feel the ground beneath my feet. *Trees don't do that.*

"Klutz," Godfrey said. His gloved hand splayed across my chest like he was holding a melon. Only it was me and my full 185.

He smiled and was weirdly calm. It was hard to breathe as I squinted past him and tried to get my balance. His fingers felt strong. I'd never realized how big his hands were or had to be to hold me like that. *One-handed, and I'm 185. Is that possible? And he's doing it.* "I'm good," I said, knowing I'd almost made a bad situation much worse.

"You sure?" His hand firm against my chest, his eyes fixed on mine.

"Yeah." But I wasn't. My pulse rang in my ears, and I gasped for air. "Thank you," I managed and steadied myself on knees that did not want to function, my thoughts too scrambled for purchase. *It wasn't really 185 pounds. My feet were on the ground, sort of.* But, but, but, and goddam my year of physics, one of the few premed courses I aced. I had substantial momentum and forward velocity. Even if my feet had been rooted, which they weren't, still aren't, the impact would have been far more than 185. I skittered over formulas memorized for tests gone by and that I'd need for the medical school entrance examinations I'd have to take again.

"No problem," Godfrey said.

A voice shouted from behind us, "What you got down there?"

Godfrey's hand stayed put as I sank my heels into mud and tried to pull my gaze from his. The freaky amber rings around his irises reflected brightly as an arc light flooded the crash scene with the upended BMW, hood smashed, sumac branches wedged against the doors… and the two of us.

"You're okay," he whispered and then yelled up, "Two adults, one kid. We need a basket."

"What's their status?"

"Kid seems okay. One adult is conscious. Can't tell about the other."

"You got it," the responder shouted, and the light vanished as he went in pursuit of reinforcements and the required equipment and truck.

Godfrey's hand eased off my chest.

"I dropped the box." It was hard to catch my breath.

"Doesn't matter," he said. "We need to get them out."

A crack of lightning overhead, the wind picked up, and branches swayed and groaned.

"Come on," he said as he shone his light around the interior.

The child, not more than three, was still strapped in but too quiet. I saw movement from one of the adults in the front, but it was hard to see, as the front and side airbags obscured much of the windows.

I reached for the handle of the back passenger-side door, but it was either locked or jammed shut by the collision, a bent sumac, or some combination.

"Hateful things." He grabbed the trunk of the sumac and bent it back and down to where he could stand on it. He smashed his foot onto it, and I heard it crack. "Better."

His fingers slid next to mine. "Together," he said. "One, two, three," and surprise, surprise, surprise, the door opened.

The kid stared at us. He seemed frozen and confused. "Mommy, Daddy."

The woman in the driver's seat moaned. The other… nothing. I reached a hand into the front and sought purchase in the man's carotid notch. There was a pulse—*good*—and something warm and wet oozed down my fingers—*not good*.

"What's your name?" I asked the little boy. A towhead like I'd been at that age.

"Jeffie."

"Good man, Jeffie. I'm Trevor and this is Godfrey, and we're here to get you and your mommy and daddy out of here. You're first. You need to be a good boy and do everything we tell you. Yes?"

"Okay."

"Does anything hurt?" I asked as Godfrey shone his light, which got a boost from the return of the arc light that now flooded through the back window.

"My tummy."

"Big hurt or little one?"

"Just a little."

"Okay," I instructed, "if it gets any bigger, you tell me." I reached in and unbuckled him. "Put your arms around my neck."

He was light as a feather, or maybe it was all that miracle adrenaline strength people are supposed to get in these situations. And maybe that was the 100 percent reasonable solution to Godfrey's one-handed catch.

"Good man, Jeffie." I squinted against the lights and the driving rain and spotted a firefighter easing down the cliff, his hand clutched to the side of a teth-ered rescue basket. His progress was awkward but a hell of a lot better than mine.

"You're going to get my mommy and daddy?" Jeffie asked as we strapped him into the basket.

"You bet," I said, and from behind us, I heard a stomp and crack, which I now equated to God-frey breaking tree limbs with his booted foot. *Don't think about it. Dude is strong. How the fuck did he catch me?*

Jeffie seemed unhurt, but the risk of internal in-juries from his seat belt straps and the force of the collision made the extent of his wounds unknowable.

We hoisted him up and out. The fireman who'd come down with the basket now pulled without success at the driver's side door. Godfrey had managed to open the passenger's. "Scalp wounds," he said. "Lots of blood. He's got a decent pulse and breathing."

"All good things." And I tried to help the firefighter. The door had bent inward and was jammed shut by another one of those stupid sumacs that grow like weeds. Its bark and a bit of the wood had been ripped by the car. "Let's try to bend it back." *If Godfrey can do it, why can't we?*

We grabbed the supple tree. It wasn't massive, the trunk no more than five inches in diameter, and we bent it back but not enough. Its rain-slicked bark slipped through our hands and banged hard against the door. "It ain't moving," he said. "We need the jaws."

While we all love those can-opener tools that make short work of fine German engineering, they take time, and scoop-and-screw is about speed—get your victim and get them out.

The firefighter rapped on the window. "Ma'am, can you hear us?"

I trained my light inside and saw Godfrey's progress with the male passenger. He'd gotten the seat belt off, and with his hands, those wicked strong things, ran a quick survey over his body for potential bleeds and obvious fractures or dislocations. There was blood, a lot of it. It matted the man's hair and soaked his shirt. But what disconcerted me was how much had gotten onto Godfrey—all over his face, especially around his mouth, like a kid with his first popsicle.

The firefighter shouted across to Godfrey, "Can we get her out that way?"

"Possible...." He sounded doubtful.

"You need a hand?" I asked.

"I will," he said.

"Go," the firefighter said. "Get him out first."

Behind us the basket descended, along with a city medic.

I inched around the back of the car while the mud grabbed at my shoes and I gripped with my toes to keep them on. Godfrey had the man under the arms and had mostly dragged him from the car. "Help me with the basket," he said.

And half falling against the vehicle, we got him strapped in and launched up the hill.

"Two down, one to go," the firefighter said, his words broken by a crack of lightning and the now-familiar sound of Godfrey's foot shattering the trunk of a sumac—the one that both the firefighter and I had tried to bend and snap.

As we inched our way around like old ladies at a funeral, steadying ourselves with the wrecked BMW and trying not to faceplant in the mud, we found Godfrey with the driver's door open and the sumac trunk splintered six inches from the ground.

"Jesus, you're strong," the firefighter muttered.

"Physics," Godfrey replied, his head buried inside. "Shattered sternum," he said.

The woman moaned, "Jeffie." She started to wake.

"Jeffie's fine, and so is your husband," Godfrey said, his tone calm and filled with reassurance.

"Everyone is going to be fine. You had an accident. We're going to get you out of here. Jeffie is fine. Your husband is hurt but fine."

"What...?" she managed.

"An accident. You're going to be fine. Everyone is going to be fine."

As I kept my beam focused on him and his patient, it was hard not to believe what he said. Although the blood smeared all over his unmasked face added a horror-show dimension. *But yeah, Godfrey was here, and just saved me from getting impaled on a tree or at least getting multiple fractures, and he could snap trees with his foot that two grown men couldn't... or physics. That's all. Physics.*

Chapter Ten
Godfrey, What Big Eyes You Have

"YOU'RE HURT," the triage medic said to me.

"Not my blood." And we transferred the soaked and injured woman from the extrication basket onto a backboard and then up to our stretcher.

"We'll transport her," I said, not about to let those yahoos steal our patient. More importantly, it would keep Trevor occupied. He was exhausted, working on fumes, and itching to ask me questions I would not answer.

"You might want to wipe it off," he shouted after us as we wheeled her to our truck.

"Please do," Trevor said. "You look like Dracula."

"I'll clean up on the ride," I said. "But people in glass houses, Trevor. You look like a drowned puppy."

"People like puppies," he shot back. "Vampires, not so much."

With a silent one, two, three, we collapsed the wheels, loaded up, and locked her to the side rail. I climbed in behind, and Trevor took the wheel. I knew it was a joke, but he was quick, and we'd just slipped into dangerous but familiar territory. I call it the Little Red Riding Hood zone.

I caught my reflection in the cabinets over the patient, and yeah, not a good look—hair soaked and curling like mad, face and neck smeared with blood, eyes a bit too bright and too feral. *Why, Granny, what big teeth you have.* But first things first. I transferred the woman's oxygen from the portable to the on-board tank, even though the ride would be short.

I gave report to the accepting hospital, where her husband, the source of the blood on my face—and I only snacked on what was already outside his body, seriously, waste not—and the child would already have arrived. "Pulse is eighty-four and stable, respirations twenty-four on six liters of O2, BP 110 over 80. No visible lacerations, but possible crush injury and likely fractured sternum where she impacted the steering wheel. Visible bruising across the chest from her seat belt."

"Do you have a line in?" the ED doc asked.

"Not yet. You want one?"

"Yes, please. What's your ETA?"

"Five tops."

"We'll be waiting."

I cut away the sleeve of her jacket and silky blouse. They had been coming back from a small gathering at her in-laws' home. I'd seen a bit of it in her husband's alcohol-enriched blood, and it was best he hadn't driven.

I wiped her arm with alcohol and started an IV. Then I gave my face a quick scrub with alcohol and gauze. At least the end of our shift was in sight. Maybe some time apart would let things quiet in Trevor's mind... *or more likely fester and grow*. And why did you have to snack on that dude? *Because you were hungry, and he was bleeding... and delicious.* I still smelled him, a man in his prime ticking the boxes as he progressed like a corporate samurai. He tasted of ambition, sex, want, and lots of single-malt scotch. I licked a tenacious bit of dried crust from the corner of my lips, and it released afternotes of affection for his wife, his child, and his parents. *That was reckless. You must be more careful.*

I grabbed a handrail as Trevor took a fast turn off the highway. I glanced at him, his gaze fixed on the road, the angles of his face up lit by dim cabin lights, like a Caravaggio saint. *Shit. How did this happen?* I've been here before, and one of the first signs that I have grown attached is I get careless. But that's not it. I become like a rooster, peacock, or toad in heat. I wanted him to see me, or at least the better parts of me. *And now he did.*

Which, after we'd deposited our human cargo— one Brittany Corrigan, mother of Jeffie and wife of tasty Brad, all of whom would survive the night— the interrogation began.

"How the hell," Trevor started, "did you snap that tree?"

"I work out."

He timed the early morning lights on Mass Ave, though I would have just used the flashers. "Liar."

"Fine. What's your explanation?" *I should not have said that.*

"No clue, Godfrey. No fucking clue. And yeah, thanks for saving my life, but… you stopped me with one hand."

And here it comes.

"I weigh 185 and I was in free fall. How the hell did you do that?"

"What do you want me to say, Trevor?"

"I don't know. The truth."

I hated this part. "I'm strong."

"No shit, you're strong. Something does not add up. It never does with you."

"You're tired, Trevor. It happened. We got lucky. I managed to stop your fall and got a good grip with my legs that let me brace you."

He shot his head around and glared. "What are you doing with me?"

It caught me unawares. "Riding in an ambulance. Finishing our shift. Starting to wish I had let you fall on your pointed head."

He glanced to the road and then back at me, was about to say something and then stopped. Reconsidered and then spewed, "I'm not gay."

Not what I'd expected. "Okay. Never said you were."

"Just wanted to be clear." His eyes fixed on the road, his pulse fast and visible in the notch of his neck.

"You think I'm trying to get into your pants?"

"Aren't you?"

In truth it went beyond that, but he wasn't wrong. "No, Trevor. I'm not trying to get into your pants."

"But you sleep with guys, don't you?"

"How did we warp from saving your life to my sex life?"

"Because I can't figure you out."

"Why do you have to?"

His jaw twitched. "I just do. Everything about you is wrong."

"That hurt."

"That's not what I meant. But is anything you tell me true?"

"Not a lot," I admitted.

"Goddammit, Godfrey."

"That one counts," I said.

"It does." He cracked a smile.

"Can I ask you something, Trevor?"

"What?"

"Why does it matter? Why do you care how strong I am or who I sleep with? And yes, I have slept with men. I have slept with women. I have slept with men and women together. I like sex. And I would never force myself on anyone, in case you're worried that some night I'll crawl into your bunk and do nasty and unspeakable things." *Though I have considered it.*

He swallowed and focused on the road. "I don't know. Because we've been doing this for a year, and I think of you as a friend, and I don't know if anything you say is real. Which, if it's all lies, that sucks."

It was obvious there was more he did not say. Seven hundred years of human observation let me know that had I reached out to him—a tap on his shoulder... or thigh, and.... But no. He was tormented, which, combined with no sleep, too much caffeine, and waves of adrenaline, gave him a battlefield fervor. It looked good on him—primal and raw. "We're off in two hours," I said. "Go home, get some sleep, and maybe you should work with someone else?"

"You don't want to be partners?"

"Not what I said. But clearly there's something about me that disturbs you."

"I don't want another partner."

"Neither do I." And with that, the interrogation came to an end. Like a Band-Aid on a cut. He'd go home, sleep, study for his examinations, and try to organize all the things about me and how he felt about me that were wrong. I wondered how much he'd share with his confessor, Father Calvin. But now was not the time to pester and prickle. The rain had ended, and rays of dawn pushed up through the night sky.

We rode in silence back to the station.

"You want to stop for coffee?" he asked.

"Sure." And a line from something I wrote several hundred years ago flashed to mind. *A sin kept hidden is a sin only half forgiven.*

Chapter Eleven
Trevor Reflects

"HOW WAS work, dear?" Mom shot out from the kitchen as I vanished down the basement stairs.

"Long. Fine. I'm going to get some sleep." I did not want to talk. And in this COVID fall, my quasi in-home quarantine provided an easy excuse. As a first responder, I interacted with dozens, maybe a hundred or more people over the course of a twenty-four-hour stint. My parents and ten-year-old sister, Emma, did not. And I was not going to be the one to infect any of them.

"Shannon called," she offered. "Wanted to know if she'd see you later."

I'd made it to the bottom door. *So close.* I just wanted to get through it, play a couple mindless rounds of something where I shot things dead, and God willing fall asleep. "I don't know."

"Call her." I heard footsteps, and there was Mom at the top of the stairs. "Just call her, hon. I know you're exhausted, but do that. Relationships take work."

"Yeah." From the shadows to the entrance of what had been dubbed Trevor's Cave, I felt every inch the fourteen-year-old who'd first laid claim to this unpermitted two-room basement suite that Dad and I had drawn up and framed, had Uncle Bob the electrician wire, had Uncle Al the plumber hook up the minimal bathroom, and voila, the teenage son goes down to the basement and his little sister Emma can have the upstairs bathroom to herself. "I'll call her."

"You okay?" she asked as she turned on the stairwell light.

I squinted. "Fine. Tired. Long shift." Not wanting to say more, my head a jumble of thoughts, images— *how did he catch me?*—and emotions. "I'll call her later." I opened the door and felt the cool, dry basement air against my face. *I just need sleep.* "You good?"

"We're all fine. Though I don't know how much of this back-and-forth of virtual versus in-person schooling I can stand. I wish they'd make up their minds."

"I'm glad you've been able to stay home," I said. "It's safer."

"It's a pain in the you-know-what," she said. "But what is it you kids say… it is what it is?"

"Yeah." And maybe those were words to ponder. "Emma's good?"

"Yes, Trevor, we're all fine. Get some sleep. But call Shannon."

"I will." Hand on the doorknob, interrogation near its end.

"You want something to eat first?"

"No, we grabbed breakfast after our last call."

"Did you get any sleep?"

"Not really."

"Okay, hon. We'll talk when you feel more human." And she switched off the light.

On the one hand, it probably didn't say great things about me that I was twenty-four and happiest in this windowless and illegal apartment. But with my bedroom to the right and a combo living room and study with a fireplace that had gone unused for the first twenty years my parents had owned this Cape in a suburb of Boston to the left, I felt safe, relaxed, home.

But my usual adrenaline letdown at shift's end was not to be had. I reflected on the weird day that had been, but mostly on that last call—my fall, Godfrey's catch, the rain, the blood on his face, my weird outburst and accusations. I stood in the dark. Something was wrong… with me. He'd just saved my life, or at the very least stopped me from landing in the hospital with multiple fractures and a concussion, and I responded like the ingenue in one of the romance novels my parents devoured.

I flicked a switch, and the room flooded with a muted amber light. The bedroom furniture had been my grandparents'—a 1920s suite gifted by their parents on their marriage. The wood gleamed from a century of waxing and polishing, its mahogany and satinwood veneers and patterned grains cut into geometric patterns that repeated on the bedframe, the tall dresser, the short dresser with its balloon-shaped mirror, and the cedar-lined hope chest that stood against the wall with a big flat-screen and two piles of neatly folded laundry on top of it.

I should call Shannon. I should go to sleep. I should study. I should... I caught a whiff of myself. *Shower.* I grabbed a clean pair of boxers off the stack and stripped. The air purifier roared to life, sensing something wicked this way had come. It was just twenty-four hours' worth of sweat, but I was rank. I glimpsed myself in the dimly lit mirror, face smeared with grime, my uniform muddied, my sweat socks caked and beyond what even bleach and Mom could salvage, good only for rags.

"Why did you say that to him?" I felt like shit.

It's just... I gathered my clothes and dropped them into the hamper outside the bathroom door. Mom would gather them and do her magic, probably tomorrow when I was at work, and they'd be ironed and good as new. *And why the fuck does a twenty-four-year-old man let his mother do his laundry?*

Because he can.

I turned on the shower, waited for it to get hot, and stepped into those first wonderful rushes of warm water through my hair, down my back, my legs, my cock. I soaped up and scrubbed away crusted mud from my ankles and matted hair. Filthy bubbles tinged with blood swirled down the drain as unwanted thoughts raced in.

I sank to the bathtub floor. Water pounded over me as a hateful pit grew in my gut. Twenty-four years old, living in the basement, two attempts at getting into medical school, working on the third... three strikes and you're out. Shannon. Godfrey's bullseye comment. *Shit or get off the pot. Why haven't you put a ring on it?*

Why indeed? I pictured Shannon, from the awkward girl who played tuba in the marching band—"What was I thinking?" she'd say—and who still played it in a salsa band. She was on track with everything, had just graduated from an intense five-year program and started her first job as an occupational therapist. She was funny and smart and wicked hot.

I breathed in steam and the smell of soap. My pulse pounded in my ears. I'd come close to asking her to marry me many times but had always stopped. I swallowed hard as I thought through all the reasons that held me back. I'm not ready. I haven't gotten into medical school. And when and if I do, it's years of my life where I'm going to be chained to books or on call or… no kind of life for someone newly married. And what about kids? She wants two. Do you?

My cell rang from the bedroom. I turned off the water and listened from the tub.

"Trevor, you up? You up?"

I ambled out and grabbed it. "Hey, Shann."

"Hey back. Wanted to say hi before you went unconscious. How was your night?"

"Long, hard… weird."

"Good weird?"

"Weird-weird. What's on your agenda for the day?"

"Work."

"Right." It was Saturday, and for her, a nine-to-five shift at the rehab facility.

"You want to come over tonight?" she asked.

"I would," I said. Something about that felt so right, so comfortable, so….

"Great. If you're coming from Kaplan, just let yourself in. I've got a chicken marinating, so if you popped it into the oven with a couple potatoes at around four thirty…."

"Will do. Or… we could go to Carlito's."

"Good answer. You'll call for a reservation?"

"Will do," I said.

"See you then, sweetie. Pleasant dreams."

"Back at you."

"I'm going to work," she reminded me.

"Then the work equivalent," I said. "Whatever that is."

"Don't kill anyone?" she offered.

"Works for me."

"Love you," she said.

"Love you too," I repeated. We hung up. Naked in my bedroom, cell in hand, I felt frozen. This lump in my throat would not let up. "I love Shannon," I said to the man in the mirror. But the truth, and not sure that it mattered… *but, yeah, it does*—"I'm not in love with her."

Chapter Twelve
Godfrey Meets a Drug Dealer

I TAPPED the red looping pedal with my foot and the tracks of the Romberg sonata I'd just laid down soared clear and loud through balanced speakers in my Gothic church. I breathed in, bow met string, and the dance began. Three-part harmonies exploded and bathed me in mournful, at times seductive, E-minor chords. I danced triplets up and down the fingerboard. Point and counterpoint. The echoes of baroque composition, the rule of thirds, the rise and fall, passion and loss, hunger, want, desire. The raw sex of music. I pictured the nurse I'd enjoyed earlier. I felt her arousal as my fingers played across the strings. A flick with the pad of my forefinger for the harmonic, the hard jam of my callused thumb as it served as a fret, and a manic trill ended in a courtly turn. The movement was an allegro hyped to a blinding Ramones speed—way too fast but so much fun as I careened toward the inevitable climax. Triplet on triplet on triplet, the crisp under tracks of quarters, eighths, and sixteenth notes, the pulse of desire, more than two hundred years old and fresh as the day Bernhard penned it. Hairs broke on my bow. I held back a bit, the downside of playing with your-self, your recorded self, that is—you can't change tempo once it's set. For that, you need live players, which presented a different set of issues. But now the conclusion. I dug in for the final chords, let them fly, and tapped the pedal to stop the tracks.

I threw back my head, let my mouth drop open, and listened. Bernhard would be pleased. He would have loved this—the electric band that wrapped around my three-hundred-year-old Italian cello that hooked into the looping pedal and from there to an amp, mixer, and studio speakers, all connected to a laptop on a carved oak pew with a USB microphone, where I could adjust, warp, and twist Bernhard's beautiful composition. I knew, not only would he not have minded, had he been there….

I bit back a tear as my gaze drifted from the dark crossbeams overhead to the sun-illuminated stained-glass Golgotha over the altar. I imagined my old friend with his floppy bangs and round red cheeks would appear, cello in one hand, bow in the other. More than anyone, he pushed my playing to a next level. In truth, he did that for all cellists. I remem-bered how upset he'd get with me, that I could play faster than he, and his accusations… not unlike Trev-or's. His German accusations. *I think you are some-thing not quite human, Godfrey Hesse. Why, Granny, what big teeth you have. And what fast fingers… and why is there blood on your mouth? And Trevor said I looked like a vampire.*

I looked up toward the altar, my attention away from the crucifix to the panel on the right—Christ risen, the Magdalene and the Virgin Mother in blue cowls, a band of ecstatic apostles. *He rose from the dead, and no one called him a vampire.*

I stared at the Resurrection, put bow to string, and played the Fauré elegy. I felt them, all of them, and tears flowed. Whatever moron said it's better to have loved and lost than to have never loved at all was mistaken. I missed Bernhard, and Emilie, and Paulo, and… and every time I went to ground and reinvented myself, I'd make a promise to never love again. You'd think that, with seven hundred years under my belt, I'd have achieved some restraint. I've become a damn good cellist, because let's face it, no one has practiced as long as I have. I've written lots of books—again, I've had some time to put pen to paper. I've even learned to not break the fourth wall, though loneliness fights against that, if you hear me. Do you hear me? Sorry.

But when it comes to love and having my heart break again and again, I don't learn. I make promises to myself as I start again or pick up threads of a previous life. "This time," I'll say to myself, and it's a joke, and not a funny one, "this time I will walk alone. There will be no lovely young man or woman, no wise or funny or insanely talented companion." And I do, for a time, and I build a life, and I feed, and I watch, and I learn, and I take a job on an ambulance, and I meet Trevor, and I make him blush, and he makes me laugh and shares all his fears and worries and desires. He brings me to life. And if I am not careful, I will destroy his. It's what I do.

I stopped my bow in mid passage. "Not good." I put the cello, a gift from a dear friend and wonderful harpsichordist, into its cradle. I thought to call the station. Kate would be on. I'd have her switch my shift. If not the next one, all the ones after. I'd offer a plausible excuse as to why I couldn't work with my partner of the last year, and that would be that. Maybe I'd see him at change of shift or maybe I wouldn't. *Let him go. You've done it before. You did it with Bernhard. You've done it with others. Let him go.*

But like the gears on a complex timepiece, the day shifted to a new hour. And like Scarlett O'Hara, who would think about things tomorrow, I had places to go and people to... well, we'd see. I had unfinished business from yesterday's shift.

I grabbed my phone and dialed the number I'd gotten from dead James. I unblocked it to decrease the suspicion of whoever picked up. And they did, but they said nothing, just air and expectation over an open line.

"Hi," I said with a friendly, breathy, hungry voice. "My name's Godfrey. I got your number from James Grant."

"Yeah?"

"He said you deliver."

"Yeah. It's five for twenty, minimum order is ten."

"You take plastic?" I searched for information in the man's clipped sentences. Bit of a Boston twang and layers of professional wariness that bordered on paranoia.

"Sure, but cash is king."

"I have cash." *Bit of humor, street sense.*

"How much you want?"

"You do bulk discounts?" I matched my tone to his.

"Hundred, cash only, gets you an extra five for free."

"Hundred cash it is." I would be his new favorite customer.

"Address?"

I gave it to him. "How long?"

"Twenty. You need supplies?"

"No, all set." Curious to see he was a full-service supplier.

"Okay." He hung up.

I shut down the speakers, the amp, and the laptop—careful to do it in the right order, having blown many a piece of equipment, and I liked my current arrangement, from the speakers to the pedals where I could play one track on top of the next. For fun, I could take an entire orchestral arrangement and play every part, one over the next, run it through a mixer—that took me forever to learn—and there you have it. Beethoven, Brahms, Mahler, Stipe, Lennon, Parton in all their glory. Though technology whizzed forward, and just when I thought I'd figured out a thing, I would find it obsolete… or considered so. Tremendous amount of baby-with-the-bathwater arrogance with each new generation. *Maybe that's not it. People don't know what they don't know.*

I headed out the side door with its carved arches and left it unlocked. The air smelled cool and sweet. COVID spring and summer had shifted, seemingly overnight, to COVID fall. The side yard of my property was a scenically derelict gravel drive, the surface pocked with weeds, bits of thyme, and grass that had wandered from tidy squares of lawn in the front of what had once been Saint Margaret's. An eight-foot wrought-iron fence, overgrown with roses and dark green Swedish ivy, created a dense barrier to my next-door neighbors—a sprawling complex of two-story redbrick post-war apartment buildings that housed mostly seniors who'd lived there for decades and would pass their spacious two-bedroom units to children eager for the chance to have an affordable rent on public transit and fifteen minutes from downtown Boston.

I deadheaded vivid red and magenta roses, and fragrant satin blooms fell apart between my fingers, the vines healthy. The more manure and decomposed the waste, the better. The cycle of life, death, decay, sex, and rebirth—it's all here. I ripped out clumps of ivy and grabbed an offensive root, wrapped it around my wrist, and tugged. Concealed as I was, a good hundred feet from the road, no worry that someone might find it strange how such deep roots would come out in my hands. And this was midmorning when my strength is at half-mast. I thought of Trevor's wide-eyed expression a few hours back when I

caught him in mid fall. So many emotions. And then
I had to snipe about his poor long-suffering and un-
betrothed Shannon. *You should not have done that.*
He and I had hit a turning point. Once things entered
the Red Riding Hood phase, decisions needed to
be made. Or to quote the Clash, "Should I stay or
should I go?"

I attacked the ivy, careful not to make holes in
the living screen that blocked me from the neighbors. But left unchecked, it would overrun the heir-
loom roses.

As I pruned and weeded, I kept attuned to the traffic sounds on the secondary road that led commuters
in and out of the city through Brookline without ever
having to get on a highway. I heard my visitor pull up
in a throaty but not new dark green Subaru.

I waved, motioned for him to come down the
drive, and tossed a thick wad of tangled ivy into a
black garbage barrel, one of several dotted around
the property.

I peered through the tinted windshield as he approached. The lone occupant was young, a teenager
with silky jet-black hair, dark glasses, and the broad
facial features of an Amerindian—a Mayan from the
Yucatán or possibly farther south.

His window lowered and affirmed my initial im-
pressions, but even younger. Maybe not old enough to
drive, at least legally—no more than sixteen or sev-
enteen, no facial hair other than wisps of down that
would one day turn into sideburns. I caught a whiff
of him—potent surges of testosterone, adrenaline, and

cheap cologne doused to cover his sweat. The combination was ripe, acrid, and filled with sex. I've always wondered why no one has bottled the stuff. Teen Spirit, indeed. *He's fourteen, tops.*

"There's a turnaround in back," I said. "I'll meet you there."

He smiled and had not understood a word.

I repeated it in Spanish.

"Sí, gracias." He drove back toward a long two-story five-bay garage, its doors painted brick red and its walls, mostly buried in ivy, carved from the same Vermont granite as my church.

I followed the Subaru and reached back for my wallet. The kid had turned the car around, its hood pointed straight at me and a quick getaway if needed.

He seemed nervous… jumpy as I headed toward his open window. I let the hundred-dollar bill flap over my hand.

He nodded and pulled a small white envelope from beneath his seat.

I gave him the money.

He gave me my drugs.

"Narcan?" he asked, his accent rural, Mexican, Yucatán.

"Sí, gracias," I answered. *Curiouser and curiouser.*

He reached over to the passenger side and pulled out a two-dose red box of the overdose reversal medication I'd used on James.

"¿Cuanto?" I asked.

"Nada, es gratis."

"Gracias," I reached for the box and fixed him in my gaze. I felt the connection, his initial confusion and inevitable surrender—no translation needed, the universal language of hunter and prey. *Please, come into my web, said the spider to the fly.* "¿Como te llamas?"

"Ricky?" He removed his glasses.

"Cuántos años tienes?" *How old are you?* I asked.

"Quince."

"¿Donde estan tu madre y tu padre?" I'd missed by a year. He was fifteen, which made all the sense in the world. If he got pulled over by the cops, they'd turn him over to ICE and send him back to whatever small village he came from, too young—at least I hoped—to be incarcerated with adults. He wouldn't survive that, so what was he doing so far from home, delivering what I assumed to be fentanyl-laced heroin like it was a large pepperoni?

I invited him into the church.

As he got out of the car, he asked if I was a priest.

I told him no, that the church was my home. I asked if he wanted something to eat or drink as he tagged at my heels. At the side door I'd left open, my attention was tripped by a discordant sound. Another vehicle had stopped out front, which is common; parking is always at a premium, and half the time people will risk the ticket and even take the spaces in front of the hydrant. I stood as he entered and listened. *Was he followed? Is he under surveillance? Have a partner?* I heard a car door open and footsteps. I stepped back into the drive and looked toward the road. Not a parking space to be had, but something played in my mind, a warning bell. There was something there, but just beyond my grasp.

Probably nothing, and even if it is the cops, wouldn't make a difference. And for those of you, dear readers, concerned as to my intentions with young Ricky, no blood, or any other bodily fluid of the innocent, will be shed today. However… and….

I kept him for the better part of an hour—fed, watered, and interrogated. Before he left I coached him through whatever answers he'd need to satisfy his bosses, who I quickly learned were not kind men, as to his long turnaround. It was time well spent, at least for me, and I gave him a thousand dollars in crisp one hundreds.

As he downed a delicious meal of leftover Chinese in my kitchen, I held him in thrall and learned a great deal—about his life in a small village in the Yucatán, about growing up on his family's farm, and how there was no money, except for those who went north and sold drugs. He told me of his plans to return home and build a better house for his mother and father. How he now lived with three other boys from his village in a single room in a bad neighborhood where they were scared to go out. How he'd made it across the border with the promise of this job in Boston. And how almost every cent he made he sealed in envelopes and posted home. As he ate and answered my questions, I was struck by his fear and by his courage. He just wanted to go home. He knew that the drugs he delivered were *muy malas*, but he saw no way out.

"There is no other way," he explained, "to make the money that was needed." His eyes brightened as he imagined his hero's welcome. His suitcases bulging with Levi's jeans and other gifts to be dispensed. The girl he intended to marry finally able to say yes, because he would be a man who could provide.

I asked him if he knew James. And yes, he had delivered drugs to him on many occasions. "And to his woman as well, though just once."

That last revelation surprised me, as Annie had said she did not use. "When? When did you bring her drugs?"

"Not long ago," he said.

Though I suppose it was no shock. Sometimes giving in to a partner's addiction is the safest thing. Beats having them drive intoxicated to a liquor store, but here… the drugs were delivered.

My glamour over him faltered when I told him that James was dead.

"No." He put down his fork and broke the connection. He crossed himself, and his gaze darted over several of the small single-panel stained-glass windows in the kitchen, each with an apostle's symbol.

He crossed himself and again asked if I was a priest.

I reminded him that I was not.

"Me voy al infierno." *I'm going to hell.*

"No." And I pulled him back into a light thrall. If hell exists, this kid had already sampled much of it. From his harrowing border crossing, to beatings and threats from his employers, to the constant threat of arrest, an American prison, or worse, a Mexican one—all of which and more caused him to wake in a cold sweat. "Tell me about your bosses," I instructed in Spanish.

He resisted, his fear of them, of what they might do to him and his family, almost stronger than my hold. A mother's love will do that. And Ricky loved his parents and his village and a girl called Cecee he hoped to impress with the house he would build. And they would marry and have children. I encouraged those wonderful dreams as I pressed for details about the duo who'd brought him and the others north. I got names and numbers. The one named Rod sent spasms of panic through the poor boy. I wanted to press further, but his fear was so intense, it would shut him down.

And before I sent him on his way, I told him, "Si quieres regresar a México, vuelve aquí. Si no estoy aquí, espérame, y te llevaré allí." *If you want to go home, come back here. If I'm not here, wait for me, and I will get you home.*

Chapter Thirteen
Trevor's Fears are Confirmed

I AM not a stalker, I reassured myself as my pulse leaped and I sank into the driver's seat of Mom's Prius. *But what the hell?* I left my car, because if he spotted it, he'd know it was me... and that wasn't stalkerish. Or that I'd told myself I was going to Stanley Kaplan's to cram three hours of bio and organic chem drills. I'd even brought the books, because maybe I'd do that. Or that I'd memorized Godfrey's Brookline address from his Harvard acceptance letter, popped it into the GPS, though three years on an ambulance—two as an EMT and one as a paramedic—had given me a back-of-my-hand knowledge of greater metro Boston. But it was reassuring to see it there as I drove past the church, not once, not twice, but three times before it sank into my brain that this might be where he lived. At first I figured it had to be wrong, and I meandered back through the apartment complex on one side and the retail and office space on the other. "He lives in a church," I muttered. "And

I live in my parents' basement. Maybe it's his parents' church."

And then I spotted him, mostly hidden in the shadows, dressed in a pair of baggy sweats and a tight black tee, his lush dark hair loose around his shoulders, his focus on a wall of roses that separated him from the drab brick apartments on the other side.

What the fuck am I doing? My focus riveted on him. *And that's not creepy.* I pulled out my iPhone, flicked to the camera app, and went from bad to worse. I framed him in the viewfinder and spread it apart with my fingers to enlarge the image.

I couldn't imagine how or if I'd bring this up with Father Calvin. Because I knew, knew, knew this was sin or sin adjacent. And that was one of several issues that I did not want to contemplate and how and why I'd rationalized this surveillance. Godfrey had wormed his way into my head. I wanted him out. Over and over I relived that moment—the trip, the fall, the catch, his eyes in the dark, his hand like… living steel against my chest, just holding me. In no hurry. His breath against my face.

I swallowed and scrutinized. He'd moved from deadheading roses to ripping out ivy. His hands blurred, like trying to capture a bee or hummingbird in motion. Now he'd looped a great hunk of vines around his wrist all the way to the elbow, and with his other hand, pulled at the roots.

"Shit!"

No stranger to Virginia creeper, wild grapes, and ivy that threatened to overtake Mom's back garden and that I dutifully attacked twice a year, what Godfrey did, that I recorded for later review, seemed impossible. Foot after dirt-caked foot of thick and twisted roots came out. He didn't even strain.

He stopped and turned.

I ducked. *I am not a creepy stalker. What if he comes over? What if he saw me? What am I going to say? Drive away.*

I peeked.

A dark green Subaru slowed and turned into the church drive. Godfrey waved toward the driver as he shucked the thick mass of vines off his arm and into a black barrel.

It was hard to get a clear view, and then the green car with its mirrored windows disappeared down the drive and around the back of the church. *And now is a good time for you to leave, get your ass to Kaplan.* With cell in hand, I clicked open the door.

I ducked again and froze as Godfrey turned and looked out at the road… right at me. Though no way he could see me as I was still in the car, behind the door, not a stalker. I held my breath and waited. Seconds stretched into a minute. I half expected him to yank open the door and say something snarky or worse. But nothing.

I turtled my head up and looked to where he'd been. There was no one, just a quaint gray Gothic church with two squares of manicured lawn in the front surrounded by hedges, the rose-covered wall and drive to the left, and a bit of side garden with an arbor and iron gate to the right. I couldn't see the green car, couldn't see him, should have driven off, but got out.

It felt like a tunnel, like a dream where everything seems normal when it's anything but. It's a Saturday in Brookline, I reminded myself. This was a road I'd driven hundreds of times. Right by this church, not bothering to notice it or that it had no marquee in front. And this was the address on his letter from Harvard. *He lives here.* Maybe he gets a break on his rent for taking care of the gardens. I peered over the hedge. The lawn was free from weeds, the edges clipped and mulched. *Probably has an apartment.* It was a great location, and if he went to Harvard, an easy… ish drive to Cambridge, or just hop on one of the buses that stopped in front of the apartment complex.

It kind of made sense. An old property owned by the church, assuming it belonged to the archdiocese. It looked Catholic, could be Episcopal, even Lutheran with the squat square turret. Whatever denomination, maybe they had to close it for safety reasons or more likely a drop in parishioners. But the property had to be maintained. I stopped at the edge of the gravel drive. It vanished around back, where I glimpsed a two-story garage, likely where his apartment was. He probably lived there rent-free. It made me feel better about my own rent-free basement cave.

There was a door on the side, but it felt too exposed. I doubled back toward the front of the church. The wrought-iron gate was locked, came up to my shoulders, and was connected to an even higher iron fence embedded in the evergreen hedge. But it wasn't that tall. I looked around at the busy street behind me and a group gathered at the bus station a couple hundred feet away, everyone in their own little bubble, eyes and ears glued to cell phones, watching for a bus, car and truck drivers oblivious to all but what was in front of them.

No harm in going in for a closer look.

I pressed back into the hedge at the corner of the property farthest from the apartments. Branches scratched at the exposed skin of my neck, arms, and head. They were thick and strong and tore my jeans. A conifer branch pierced my shirt under the right arm. *And from stalking, we go to....* I muscled back with my legs, twisted around bigger limbs, and felt the hard metal of the gate against my back. I turned to where I now faced the church, my body concealed in the hedge, or so I hoped. My nose tickled, and I sneezed. My arms were covered with a fine yellow pollen, and my eyes teared. *Why are you doing this? Go home. Go home.*

I dug a toe into the fence and grabbed for one of the cross-shaped iron spikes above. Up I went. In fairness, this was not the first church fence I'd climbed. As a product of the Catholic school system, I was no stranger to the risks and benefits of seeing what lay on the other side.

I got over with zero grace, minor cuts and abrasions, and a T-shirt that would join last night's socks in the rag bag. Before me, the building was more impressive than it had seemed from the street. Well below a basilica, but with a square Norman turret a good four stories high, walls of gray granite, and soaring stained-glass windows. A keystone on the right read 1865.

I looked at the gate and was relieved to see a latch mechanism, so at least my exit could go smoother. *And now what?*

I snuck around the side away from the drive. There was a rose-covered arbor and a striped lawn edged with mounds of Montauk daisies, purple asters, and remnants of spring and summer perennials that had been cut back for the fall. It looked like a wedding photograph.

The windows were well above my head. Unseen, or so I hoped, I jogged toward the back. The Subaru was parked, and my earlier assessment that his apartment was in the garage seemed wrong. The long building with its five bays appeared derelict. The brick-red paint on the upper level was peeling, and the granite below was covered with vines.

I looked around, kept to the periphery, and tried the side door of the garage. With a shock, it opened, and cool oil-scented air filled my nostrils. I held still as my eyes adjusted. Minimal light entered the cavernous space through dirt-smeared windows on the sides and the open door behind me. The glass panels on the bay doors had been painted, but what I did see made little sense. In the center stood Godfrey's vintage Jeep—a Korean War relic that I'd help him tinker with during slow shifts. It was a great vehicle that could be broken down into its component parts and rebuilt in a matter of hours.

The four other vehicles added to the puzzle. A black 5 Series BMW sedan, an Acura SUV, a vintage 1950s two-tone Jaguar coupe that had been exquisitely restored, and a racing-green Miata. I could almost rationalize the BMW and SUV as church vehicles, though a bit too pricey, and that would piss off parishioners. But the Jag and the Mazda?

I had this sick-gut sense. *These aren't church cars. These are his.* And what did I really know about him? Yes, we had been partners for almost a year, which meant twenty-four-hour chunks of time living on top of each other. But what did I know about him? *He has money. Maybe that's why stuff doesn't matter to him.*

Saltwater flooded my mouth as I felt for the door. I needed to get out, needed air.

I sidled on cracked asphalt and gravel toward the church. I looked at the Subaru, with its dented door and darkened glass, not certain what I'd say if he stepped out. *I should not be here.*

But he didn't, and as I walked up the side drive, thinking maybe I should just get out of there, go to Kaplan, and… I saw a half-open door up a flight of stairs.

I stopped, listened, and heard faint voices, one of them Godfrey's and both speaking Spanish. I knew he spoke Spanish—one of his many accomplishments and super useful on the ambulance.

I froze. Climbing a fence and going into someone's garage were bad, but now… *the door's open.*

*Yes, and? Not like he's going to have you arrested for
breaking and entering… or stalking… or….*

I looked toward the road, so far away, and the
door was open.

I smelled Chinese and went inside to an oak-pan-
eled hall. *Chinese?*

So, he had a guest and was making him/her lunch.
The voices grew louder and clearer as I passed a
coatroom, men's bathroom, women's bathroom, and
came to an open doorway where I glimpsed a wall
of white kitchen cabinets and dark butcher-block
counters. My three years of high school Spanish was
not up to the task as I pressed against the wall.

Certain words I caught—*drogas*, something
about a village near Mérida. The kid, which is what I
took him to be, spoke about his mother and father and
someone named Cecee, money and his *jefes*, which
caused his voice to crack. In a couple places he sounded like a boy in the throes of puberty, which couldn't
be if he'd driven the car, and again drogas—drugs—
his bosses, and a girl named Cecee.

Godfrey's voice was calm and had that weird
soothing tone that made everything plausible. *We'll
go to Harvard together.* His words spilled fast and
smooth as oil. He used an accent that mirrored the
kid's, something I'd noticed before. If our patient
was Dominican, he sounded Dominican. If Mexican,
you'd swear he was from the same city or village.
With this kid, it was like an older and younger brother chatting in their mother's kitchen about drugs and
scary bosses and girlfriends.

I was torn between wanting to look and fear of discovery. It's not like he would kill me or anything... drugs, scary bosses, unexplained high-end vehicles, unexplained high-end church living. I pulled out my phone, tapped the camera app, and played with the angle to where I caught the back of Godfrey's head and the teen, who devoured a plate of dumplings between swigs of cola. With my thumb I snapped pictures and then pulled the phone back to enlarge. There was something on the table—an envelope. As I spread the image wider, I realized what it was. And things fell in place.

It was a stack of drugs in the same envelopes as the ones that had killed James. While I couldn't see the full graphic or the wording, the cartoon skeleton on his knees was unmistakable. *This was a drug deal.* What I didn't know, because my Spanish sucked, was if Godfrey was the scary boss or a customer... who invites in the delivery boy for some tasty Chinese.

I eased the camera back up as the kid pushed away from the table. He was talking faster and gesturing with his hands. He mimed a gun to his head and pulled an imaginary trigger. The anguish on his face made it clear it was no joke.

Godfrey stayed calm. "*Claro,*" he said, followed by liquid sentences that had something to do with *dinero*, *pasaje aéreo*—airfare and something about his mother, his father, and Cecee.

The kid pulled up a sleeve, and I saw bruises—some fresh, some yellowed and fading. *Not good.*

And as a mandated reporter of any form of child abuse—as was Godfrey—another line was crossed.

The kid shook his head and spoke too fast for me to follow. He pushed back from the table and stood.

Godfrey's tone stayed calm but matched the speed. My camera caught a flash of green in his hand that he thrust toward the kid. At first the boy shook his head no.

Godfrey said something about a secret and again mentioned airfare.

The boy took the money but seemed more frightened and something else. Resigned? Maybe this wasn't just a drug transaction but something more lurid.

My heart pounded as I watched and waited.

The boy's gaze was fixed on Godfrey as he stood with cash in hand, the bruises on his arm a testament to whatever hell he'd landed in.

Godfrey laughed and reassured the boy. At least that's what I hoped. "*Vámonos*," and they headed toward me.

I bolted into the dark coatroom and hid behind the door. As I held my breath, I realized several things. At the top of the list, I knew nothing about Godfrey. The man who rode beside me, bunked over me two to three days a week, and who had just saved my life was not just a stranger but something worse. *At least he didn't put the moves on that kid… yet.*

The two stopped outside the cloakroom. The boy asked Godfrey, "*¿Puedo usar tu baño?*", which even my high school Spanish managed.

"Claro," he replied as I pictured him on the other side.

I tried to sort what I'd just seen and heard. I'd suspected Godfrey took drugs. I didn't know which ones and was kind of freaked to learn it was the garbage fentanyl that masqueraded as heroin and was responsible for dead James and Rachel Dennis, whose organs had been disbursed through the night and early morning. The proof was strong, though I'd never seen him shoot up… as if that's something people do in public. But he did have a habit of vanishing throughout a shift, like at the hospital yesterday. And when he returned, *all bright and bubbly. He snorts it*, I reasoned. And now he's humming. I strained to catch the tune, familiar and old, and then he started to sing. It was soft and sent a tingle down my spine. I caught the words, "Who's afraid of the big bad wolf? The big bad wolf, the big bad wolf…."

A toilet flushed, then water in a sink and the kid's voice, "¿Vives aquí?" *You live here?*

Good question, I thought.

"Sí," he replied.

The answer was too brief. The kid did not disappoint and hit the logical follow-up.

"¿Porque en una iglesia?"

"Acústicas buenas."

"¿Eres músico?" *Are you a musician?* I translated in my head.

"Sí."

"¿Eres famoso? Rock star?"

"Sólo en mi imaginación."

Typical Godfrey. Vague and tells little.

The boy did not let up, his voice tinged with awe and something else, like he didn't want whatever minutes or seconds he had left with Godfrey to end. The drug deal was done, and now this kid had to return to his horrible bosses, but there was something else, and I recognized it, as he pleaded for just a little more… of Godfrey.

"Cántame algo, una canción, algo. Por favor. Solo una."

Godfrey chuckled. And in a rich, gut-tingling baritone, belted, "Who's afraid of the big bad wolf…."

He sang as they headed out the door, and it closed behind him. I wondered at his choice of songs. I could still hear him, like some great Welsh baritone, like Tom Jones, who my mother adored and binge-watched on YouTube. Was he toying with that boy? But as I skulked in the church cloakroom, the only conclusion I could make—because the boy's English was nonexistent—that children's ditty was not directed at him… but at me.

Chapter Fourteen
Godfrey Plays Detective

I SANG, much to Ricky's confusion and amusement.
I could have done it in Spanish, given it a salsa beat,
but this teenage fentanyl delivery boy was not the
intended little piggy. I left the door unlocked, something I'm loathe to do. Nothing worse than returning
home to a burgled house, though the possessions I
treasured—my collection of instruments, mostly cellos and de gambas, a theorbo, two Turkish ouds—
were all valuable but tough to fence. The rest was
just stuff. It's not like Trevor was a thief.

He is a snoop, I mused as I clicked the remote
for the second bay. As it raised, I spotted the open
side door to the garage that someone—not I—had
left open. I waved goodbye to Ricky, hummed, and
watched his Subaru turn right, toward the city.

Not wanting him to get too far ahead, I got into
the Acura SUV and settled in for an afternoon of
follow-the-leader. I'd been sincere with my offer
to send him back home. He should have said yes.

Strong forces played with the teen. He had come north with a mission—make money, make his parents proud, and one day return to his village, if not a hero, a success.

His was a great story, though the laced heroin dampened its purity. He was no Galahad nor even Lancelot, off on his hero's quest, but an unwitting delivery boy of death. All of his good intentions, I mused as I synced my GPS to the tracker I'd slipped under his rear bumper, would end up… "Malo. Muy malo." Best scenario, he'd get arrested and deported. But just as easily, he'd piss off his bosses or an inner-city gang would catch wind of him and his crew's encroachment into Boston, and he'd be dead. His parents might never know what had become of their boy, and Cecee would move on to a more sure thing.

For the next couple hours, I trailed at a distance as he met customers in shopping malls and plaza parking lots. The transactions were quick, none more than a couple minutes. Two random cars, their COVID-masked occupants sharing a brief conversation, the exchange of cash for product, and then on to the next.

He was quick to drive off, and his customers varied. A couple wiped down their purchases with disinfectant wipes, and one, his forehead beaded with sweat and in obvious withdrawal, shot up in plain sight of any Walmart shopper who cared to look.

It was about four when Ricky turned onto Route 128 south toward the burbs. He stayed in the middle lane and never went above the speed limit. He signaled and took the exit for the commuter town of Dedham. I followed him down the main artery past well-maintained single-family homes. I thought this would be another delivery, but as the houses gave way to strip malls, car dealers, and nurseries, I reassessed. *Too far.* He put on his blinker and turned into an autobody shop and used car dealer wedged between a junkyard and small plaza with a Thai restaurant that had a cardboard sign in the window—Open for Takeout—a barber shop, two empty storefronts for rent, and a music shop. I turned into the plaza as Ricky's Subaru drove into an open garage bay. And the baby bird returns for....

There were two other cars in the plaza, and no customers in any of the shops. The music store window was filled with stacked amps and guitars and signs that advertised instrument rentals and "Lessons for All Levels." In this middle of nowhere it would have looked odd to stay parked in the car, and I do like a music store. I checked the GPS on my phone and clicked the alert button should Ricky be on the move.

I half expected the store to be closed, but the door opened with a tinkle of chimes. I was greeted by an unmasked middle-aged man and the competing smells of patchouli and cannabis. One meant to mask the other.

"Greetings," he said. "Can I help you find something?"

With mask in hand, I realized he had no intention of putting on his. Out of courtesy, I strapped on mine. "Just poking about. I see a music store and I pull in."

"I'm the same," he said. "You never know where you'll find a hidden gem or learn something new."

"Truer words." I took a quick inventory of the wall of guitars, overhead display of violins suspended by their necks, a jumble of black-cased instruments, dust-covered amps with hand-written price tags, keyboards, a couple vintage uprights, and racks of sheet music. There was a family of made-in-China cellos that started with a full-sized instrument and marched neatly down to a quarter-size, suitable for an ambitious six-year-old or more likely their Mensa-minded parents.

It was a large space, and off to one side was a corridor with soundproofed practice rooms. "You give lessons?" I asked.

"Used to. Can't now. Health department won't let me."

"Yeah, rooms are too small for social distance."

"Yup, the whole thing is a clusterfuck," he offered. "Don't know how long I'll be able to stay open."

"What do you teach?" I asked.

"Piano up to intermediate and anything with frets."

"Anything?" I asked.

"Try me."

"Theorbo."

"Not much call for those, but sure."

I looked around. "Do you have one?"

He looked through his window that hadn't been washed in a year or more. "Yeah, come with me."

I followed him back into the shop to a shadowy repair room that smelled of turpentine, varnish, and oil. A row of counter-height windows leaked in late-afternoon light and a panoramic view of wetlands. Beneath was an expanse of wooden workbench, its surface covered with instruments in various stages of deconstruction and repair. A fiddle with clamps spaced every two inches around its body, a guitar with a shattered neck, coffee cans filled with files and rasps, and cabinets of tiny drawers with labels in faded ink.

He clicked the overhead fluorescents. "I'm Ben, by the way."

"Godfrey."

We both fought, and acknowledged, the impulse to shake hands.

I opted for a courtly bow.

He laughed. "I'm sick of this COVID shit," he said.

"Part of being human… plagues."

"I guess."

"You're a luthier," I commented.

"A dying breed."

"But an important one." I scanned his workbench—more wrecked guitars, a couple violins, a student cello that had met with an unfortunate accident or child's tantrum.

"It's all that pays the rent, and even that's not steady. No one's buying squat." He headed toward a darkened corner of the room, where cases of varying sizes and bespoke shapes stood rows thick.

My focus lit on a battered wooden cello case, the kind that hasn't been made in over a hundred years. "Anything in that?"

"Yeah, but nothing great. German, so-so quality. You play?"

"I do."

"And the theorbo?"

"Less well."

He stopped and sized me up, as though deciding if I was worth the time and effort. "Professional?" he asked.

"I have been. Not now."

"You're not that old."

"Thanks."

"I might have something you'd like." And he waded through the cases, one hand on the wall to brace himself. From deep in the shadows, he retrieved a 1970s brown Swedish fiberglass cello case covered with airline labels from Rome, Paris, London, and New York.

"Looks like it's been here for a while," I said.

"Occupational hazard."

I helped him lift it out from over its many neighbors.

"No idea what shape it's in," he said. "I haven't looked inside for over… ten years. Jesus!"

I stood it on end, noted the faded paper repair label dated June 12, 2001, clicked open the latches, and beheld beauty. Unexpected and… "French?"

"Yup, Mirecourt, 1880s, belonged to a player with the BSO."

"He abandoned it?" I removed the golden-red instrument from its velvet-lined shell. It felt solid and, for lack of better descriptors, special.

"Died."

"And the heirs?"

"Didn't want to pay for the repairs. Told me to keep it. Morons."

I held it just below its delicate carved scroll. The rosewood, not ebony, fingerboard was well worn, and several sealed cracks on its spruce belly gave truth to its age. Without looking inside for the maker's label, I knew this was a masterpiece. From the gorgeous double rows of inlaid ebony purfling to the delicate f-holes and the voluptuous curves of the upper and lower bouts. The strings hung loose, and the bridge was about to fall off. "Do you mind?" I asked.

"Is the sound post still up?"

I held it in both hands and gave it a gentle roll from side to side. Nothing rattled. "We're good."

I glanced at my phone, mindful of my mission, but… Ricky's Subaru hadn't moved, and what I'd intended to do next was best kept for after dark. I grabbed a stool from under Ben's bench, laid the instrument across my lap, and pulled out the tailpin.

"You want an A?" he asked.

"It's in my head." I eased old but high-end steel strings up to pitch. "You got a bow?"

"Just carbon fiber ones."

"Don't knock 'em," I said. "They do the trick."

"True. And for the price, you can't beat them."

He vanished back into his shop as I centered the bridge in line with the f-hole notches, turned the pegs, and plucked.

Ben returned with a bow and a small electronic tuner. He tapped for the A, and I plucked the cello's top string.

"Perfect pitch," he said with admiration and rosined the bow.

I ran my forefinger across the open strings. Clear fourths rang out. I took the bow, looked out toward the marshes of the Charles River estuary, and dug in to Fauré's fiercely passionate *Après un Rêve*, *After a Dream*, with its askew intervals that skated near atonality and then pulled back. The piece is less about the fuzzy head one gets after a too-long nap and all about the end of love, or more aptly, being in love.

Oh my, I thought as this dormant beauty burst to life. The strings and pitch held, and as I reached for the final note, high up on the G string, my phone dinged.

I handed the bow back to Ben.

"You play beautifully," he managed. "I had no idea it sounded like that."

"Thanks. You do good work." I pulled out my cell and saw that Ricky was headed back to the city. I ran through possibilities. Perhaps he'd driven this far to deliver some drugs, but he'd stayed too long for that. This was more in the nature of the worker bee stopping at the hive. "The auto body place next door, any good?" I asked.

"Never used them," he admitted. "But they seem to do a decent business. And they work hard."

I smiled, my hand on the cello's neck, appreciating the transition of the varnishes from blond to golden red. I pushed it away from my body and turned it in the fading light. "How can you tell?"

"I'm here late a lot," he admitted. "Between gigging, customers who need things finished fast, and students who want after-work and after-school lessons, I'm here at least a couple nights a week. So are they. A couple of them live above the shop."

And we have a winner. But what to do? I examined the cello, every inch of it a testament to its maker's skill and artistry. The flamed maple back had been chosen with care. A master's hand and eye had claimed the best timber for this instrument. It had been made to order. "So you play anything with frets?" I commented.

"Yup," he handed back the bow and pushed up from the stool where he'd listened to my impromptu concert. "You got a few minutes?" He reached for a twelve-string guitar.

I placed the cello's slender neck back on my shoulder. "Always."

"You know this one?" he said, and his fingers danced the opening of a Bach two-part invention.

I nodded, caught his tempo, and joined in.

Afternoon faded into dusk, and between Bach, concerti by Corelli, Scarlatti, Vivaldi, and Marcello, night fell. We drank beers, smoked some weed, and lost any sense of time. At some point he turned the Open sign to Closed and called his wife.

"You know you should buy that cello from me," he said after we'd finished the second allegro of a Corelli mandolin concerto. "It's meant for you."

"I hope to. What do you want for it?"

"Just what they owed. It's on the ticket."

I reached back and turned it in my fingers. "It's worth a hell of a lot more than $1200. And this was almost twenty years ago."

"It's what I want for it."

"Not happening," I said.

His shoulders slumped. "I'd do it in installments," he offered, "if that would help."

I still hadn't checked for a maker's label or a brand. And in older instruments, half the time if they're still there, they're fakes. "Twenty years ago you were owed $1200. With interest… I'll give you twenty for it."

He seemed confused. "Twenty thousand dollars?"

"You know it's worth at least that. Probably a hell of a lot more if you took it to an auction house and had it properly valued."

"I just want the $1200."

"Ben, you're struggling to pay the rent. Gift horse, mouth, don't look inside."

He snickered. "You don't have twenty thousand dollars. You're a kid."

"Again, older than I look, and you can hang on to the cello until my check clears. Cool?"

"No. It's yours. If you stiff me and the check bounces, it's on you. And I'm still good with the $1200, Godfrey."

"You're a strange bird," I commented as I laid my new cello across my lap, collapsed the endpin, and settled it back into its case.

"And we have to flock together," he said. "You want another beer?"

"I need to hit the road."

I pulled out my wallet, counted out twelve one-hundred-dollar bills, and retrieved a folded check. I grabbed a pen off his workbench and filled it out for the remainder.

His expression saddened, and I wondered if he regretted his decision to let me have the beautiful French cello. "What's wrong?"

"It's stupid. I don't want you to go."

I stopped and looked at him. As transported as I became with music, the same was true for him. We had woven a spell, and now it was broken… and something more. At times I'd had the urge to feed on him and had resisted. No blood had been drunk, but there had been an exchange through the music. I had tasted him, and he had drunk off me.

"You play wonderfully," I offered.

He nodded and looked at the cash and the check. "You won't come back, will you."

"No." And I was not about to explain all the reasons why that would be a bad idea. I got up, grabbed my prize by a well-worn leather handle, gave a second courtly bow, and left.

Chapter Fifteen
Trevor Seeks Grace

I WAS screwed, and I knew it. I color within the lines, and my behavior defied rational explanation. I broke into Godfrey's home… a church, he lives in a church. *I had reason. He bought drugs…. And you're not a cop. That kid was a minor. You have to report that.*

I'd gotten almost zero sleep during our last twenty-four-hour shift and maybe three hours tops this morning, which had ended with a dream… about Godfrey. That's what started this, as studying got pushed aside and I drove toward Saint Mary's and the one thing that could make things right, make *me* right… a little Saturday confession, preferably with Father Calvin.

There was so much I did not want to think about, at least not on my own. I pulled into the parking lot between the diocesan high school I'd attended and the affiliated brownstone church. *He lives in a church… that you broke into.*

I got out, checked the time on my phone, and hoped he'd be there. I needed perspective and direction and penance and... *please be here*.

I pulled open the heavy oak door, entered, and took deep breaths. Rows of votives glowed in red glass jars. I touched two fingers of my right hand into the holy water font, turned toward the sanctuary, and crossed myself as I genuflected. I looked to the confessionals and was relieved to see no one in the adjacent pews. The door was closed on the priest's side, and the curtain was drawn. Grade school rhymes came to mind—*Don't come knocking if the confessional is rocking.*

I took a seat in the nearest pew and waited as I organized my thoughts. *Where to start?* What part of this freaked me out the most? Was it how he stopped my fall or the teen who'd sold him drugs... and yes, I'd done a good and thorough snoop after he left. A thick bundle of fentanyl was left out on his kitchen table in the same baggies as the drugs that had killed James.

The curtain pulled back and an older woman came out. She glanced at me, smiled, and gripped the side of my pew as she retrieved a walker from the row behind.

I held back. "Do you need a hand?" I asked.

"No, dear. You can go. It's a marvelous thing, isn't it?"

"What's that?"

"Grace."

"It is." My dead sister's name sent a shock, as did the memory of her smile. *"I am the state of Grace,"* she'd joke. And she was.

I swallowed and forced myself into the booth, pulled the purple curtain closed, and opted for the bench versus the kneeling rail. "Bless me, Father, for I have sinned. My last confession was over one month ago, and these are my sins." And out they spewed.

"I have lied on multiple occasions. I have let my partner at work do things that were against the rules, that I knew weren't right, but the way he does them, they tend to turn out... better than if we'd followed the rules. But I know that's wrong." I strained to hear or catch a glimpse of who was on the other side of the pierced wooden grill.

"You sound troubled, Trevor. Give me an example, and take your time."

I let out a breath at the sound of Father Calvin's deep voice. I told him about the way Godfrey had intubated James, removed the tube, lied about it to the triage nurse and the psych resident, and how I'd been complicit with all of it.

"Yes, you lied," he offered. "But not to have done so would have caused greater harm to your patient. Under those circumstances your lies are not a sin. You did not bear false witness."

"And he died anyway... later on." There were big-ticket items here that I needed to cover. "I've had impure thoughts." I stopped, unable to voice the jumble inside.

"Go on."

I did. *Don't do this, Trevor.* But I had to, and like a game of pool I went to the break shot that kicked this off-kilter day into action. "I had a dream this morning about my partner," I said, grateful for the grill between us.

"Godfrey."

"Yes. We kissed in it, and if I hadn't woken…."

"You were aroused in the dream."

"Yeah." And I held back bits of information, but God sees all and knows all. I just couldn't give the grotty details—that I'd been hard as a rock as I forced myself into an ice-cold shower and tried to conjure Shannon and have impure thoughts about her. And the erection did go down, but the feel of his hand against my chest persisted. And his eyes…. And this wasn't the first dream I'd had of him.

"Is there more here, Trevor?"

"I don't know," I admitted. "I've never had these kinds of feelings for a guy before. It's pretty gay, Father."

"It is, but other than the dream… or dreams, have you entertained these thoughts?"

"Yes, Father."

"Have you acted on them?"

"No."

"You hesitated."

"Which brings me to my next sin."

"Go on."

"I broke into his house."

"Why did you do that?" I heard concern in his voice.

"Last night there was a bad accident on the Pike, and we got the call. I tripped. It was stupid, and I fell headfirst down a ravine." It played like a flashback. "He caught me." The feel of his hand like a rock on my chest. "Literally stopped me from bashing my brains or getting impaled on a tree."

"And that led you to break into his home?" His tone incredulous.

"It's hard to explain, and maybe it was all adrenaline, but he shouldn't have been able to catch me like that."

"And you repay him for saving your life by breaking into his house?"

"Yeah. Did I mention he lives in a church?"

"No. Is it important?"

"Not so much… but…."

"Go on."

"Before I broke in… and to be fair, the door was open."

"Were you invited in?" Father asked.

"No."

"Then you're still on the hook for that. You stole, Trevor."

"I didn't take a thing," I said. "I wouldn't."

"You most certainly did. His privacy, his trust. And you know that."

"Damn."

"Language, Trevor. So, continue…."

"I watched him purchase drugs from a minor."

"You're sure of that?"

"I am. Because after he left, I looked at the drugs. They were from the same batch that killed a man we transported."

"The one who was intubated and then later died?"

"Yeah." And this was why Father Calvin was the best. He connected the dots.

"And your partner, for whom you have developed sexual thoughts, appears to have purchased drugs from this same dealer."

"Yes."

"Are you concerned that he too will overdose?"

"No." I hesitated. "I should be, but I'm not. Like, I don't think he would do that, but he obviously uses drugs."

"You've seen him take drugs?"

"No."

"But you saw him purchase drugs from the same dealer who sold them to a man you'd both tried to save the night before?"

"I did. At least that's what it seems like. Same bags… it's no coincidence."

"Agreed," Father Calvin said. "And you've never seen him take drugs?"

"True."

"So, at this point, you don't know if he takes drugs or not. In which case, saying he does is bearing false witness. Correct?"

"Yes, Father." I felt like a worm on a hook or one of those formaldehyde-soaked frogs or fetal pigs, everything laid bare.

"And you've entertained impure thoughts about this man."

"Yes, Father." It seemed like we were nearing a conclusion. And there would be penance, and likely

I'd need to make amends to Godfrey—so far, not awful. Bad, but workable.

"Which brings us to bearing false witness toward Shannon."

"Oh crap."

"Language!"

"Sorry, Father." I fell silent.

"You know how this works, Trevor," he reminded.

"Yeah." And I knew where this had to go. He was also Shannon's confessor, which added a layer of ick. I knew he'd never divulge anything I said to him, but… "Godfrey accused me of stringing her along."

"Are you?"

"I don't know, Father. It's possible. She seems so certain of us and our future—marriage, kids, all of it. Doesn't really care if I go to medical school or not."

"And you're not certain."

"No," I admitted. "I think I should just push the button and do it, ask her to marry me, all of it. Everyone would be happy. It's what they're expecting. But I can't."

"You haven't told her this."

"No."

"Is it because of Godfrey?"

"No," I said, faster than intended. "I'm not gay."

"Being gay is not a sin," he reminded me.

"Yeah, it is," I argued.

"It's not. The church position is that the act is a sin and impure thoughts are sinful."

"Kind of narrows things down," I said.

"It does."

Something in his voice sounded different… sad.

"So what's the damage?" I asked.

"It's significant, Trevor. You have serious soul-searching to do. You need to contemplate how your actions, or lack of action, affects those around you and those who care for you. You have borne false witness toward Shannon, for which amends must be made. You continue to let her believe that your intentions are to move forward with a life together. If that is not the case, you must tell her the truth. So too with your partner. You stole into his home and took his privacy and his trust. Finally, for the impure thoughts…."

We finished, and Father Calvin absolved me and released me with a "Go in peace."

I thanked him, crossed myself, and left the booth. Two others had taken up spots to go in, and I felt an additional pang of guilt for having taken more than my share of the Father's time. I drifted toward a pew under the window of Lazarus's resurrection, but I had no sense of God's grace. Father Calvin's words cut deep. Even before I'd begun to work with Godfrey, I'd felt a drift between Shannon and myself. Her path and vision were crisp, and I'd assumed it's how things would happen. In truth I knew that if I let it, we'd be married in this church, buy a starter home close to our families, and within a couple of years I'd be a dad. The problem was, the more I considered that, the less I wanted it. I worked my fingers over the beads in my pocket as familiar prayers of penance spilled through my lips. They brought neither solace nor calm.

I stared at Lazarus as he emerged from his stone tomb to greet Jesus. Whatever artist had made this window had decided that Lazarus was young, or maybe the resurrection made him look that way. His clothes were tattered, he was mostly naked, and he obviously worked out. Maybe it was his long hair, or the way his eyes glowed amber from the sun that streamed through, like Godfrey's. And that horrible sex dream that had kicked my shitshow Saturday into motion. And now, like some cherry on a turd Sunday, I had to make amends to him and to Shannon… who I did love and all through junior high had pursued like the hormone-riddled teen I'd been. It wasn't till sophomore year of high school that she agreed to a first date… a Friday night dance in the parish hall. Our moms there as chaperones. Shannon in a light blue dress, the feel of her silken hair against my cheek for that first wonderful slow dance. I would have married her then. I was convinced that it was one and done. She was my soul mate. I honestly believed that. *When did that stop?*

Father Calvin's directive to soul search was like a dentist's hard probe. Because while I may not be gay, and maybe it's not a sin—hate the sin and not the sinner—I could not stop thinking about Godfrey and his beautiful eyes and Lazarus hair, his humor and his intelligence, the way he looked at me. I prayed for guidance, and I prayed to be free from sin. I even prayed to be free from him. *Please, God, take these thoughts and feelings away from me. I don't want them. I don't want him.* But right there, that was a lie.

Chapter Sixteen
Godfrey Plays with Dolls

MY CURIOSITY drives me—one of the attributes Gaius identified—"You learn." But yeah, when things don't add up, there is a reason, always. But sometimes you must dig for it. Things don't just happen. Everything on this planet is caused. James's OD death would be determined an accident. It's what they write on all of the autopsies unless it's an obvious suicide with a note. But it was not an accident, or new, or even different. Opium and all its many new children have been around long before me and probably even before Gaius. And those in the know recognize its many useful properties—takes away the pain, stops the shits from cholera and dysentery, and in a stiff enough dose, removes an inconvenient wife, boss, or political rival. It's a favored go-to of assassins and suicides. And it's why I now parked the Acura, with my wonderful new cello in the back, in a convenient stretch of gravel half a mile from the body shop next to Ben's. Last night's crescent moon was a bit plumper, though clouds blurred its silver glow with a now-you-see-it, now-you-don't rhythm. I clicked the locks and knew if anyone bothered my vehicle or the treasure it held, the alarm would sound and I'd be back faster than the cops.

The last movement we played bounced in my head—a Vivaldi allegro agitato. I hummed and drank in the fall night. Wetlands to the left with cattail heads falling to seed, frogs croaking and bellowing in search of mates, cars zipping past on my right, the occupants oblivious and fixed to the sliver of road ahead of them and whatever music, radio pundit, or audiobook they'd chosen.

A marvelous night for a stroll, though aren't they all? It was nigh midnight, my favorite time, rife with darkness, possibility, and strength—my strength— that ebbs and flows with the moon and the tides. I chuckled. "Just me trying to figure stuff out." But I am strongest and fastest after dark, which likely has a lot to do with how vampire myths—if that's what I am—evolved. But it was other special skills I now needed, ones that didn't jibe with anything Bram Stoker, Polidori, Anne Rice, the Twilight twinks, or the True Blood fangers covered. It's core to what I am, and one of the few things Gaius told me before my bloodbath—*"I first found you in a dream."* At the time I thought it romantic; in hindsight there's a significant creep factor to what he did to me and what I was about to perpetrate.

Security lights illuminated the body shop—a two-story cinder block building with eight bays below and a retail space on the far right with a red neon Closed sign. Beyond it, a single spot lit the parking lot to Ben's music store and the attached restaurant and spaces for let. His parking lot was empty, and I wondered what he'd tell his wife about his day's windfall. Maybe he wouldn't say anything. *Naah. He'll show her the check and not say a thing about the cash.* It's what I would do.

But now. I hid among the grasses, bramble, and scrub sumac that bounded the back and one side of the body shop. I stood still and opened my senses. An owl screeched, frogs hopped, and something splashed and flopped behind me. My focus drifted to an agonal drama as a lusty bullfrog was yanked from a lily pad by the talons of a raptor. His ardor turned to terror as he was flown off to the bird's hungry, but fluffy and adorable, brood.

Like a stagehand with a spotlight, I shifted my focus to the upper story of the body shop. A dim light, probably a bathroom, and all else dark. I stepped forward, noted red lights on security cameras, and pressed my body against the cool painted cinder block. My fingers gripped and clung as I scribble-scrabbled up the side of the building. I salivated at the smells of the all-you-can-eat buffet that awaited—two of them, one to the right off the bathroom and the other to the left, both asleep.

I crooked my neck to survey the options. Both bedroom windows were open. *Eeny, meeny, miny, moe.* To the right I went.

Careful not to dislodge a pair of coital stone-white tree toads camouflaged beneath the sill, I lifted the window, caught the edge of the sleeping man's dream, and crept into his bed and into his head.

Once inside I took control of a rather humdrum work dream. The guy was doing an oil change, and the pan wouldn't stop filling. I felt his… *Jeff's*… anxiety ratchet as he raced to find an empty pan. But every time he found one, it was filled with oil.

I poked and stroked. *Calm down, Jeff. Day is done. Work is over. Time to enjoy a bit of play, a bit of pleasure. Isn't that nicer?* I spilled into his dream, caught an image of a buxom lingerie-clad strawberry blond, and dove on in.

"Hello, Jeff," I cooed through ridiculously plump red lips.

"Candy." He reached for me.

"Candy is sweet," I purred as I wrapped my legs around him. "Oh, Jeff, you feel so good. So strong. Such a man. A real man."

He buried his face in my silken mane, his mouth hot against my neck, his tongue in my ear, his hands like a beggar's at a banquet, not certain where to go, wanting it all. On my full breasts, working under the lace edges of my panties.

"No rush, Jeff. I love you so much. Need you."

"I love you, Candy."

"I know you do." And my mouth was on his, both within and without the dream.

His tongue sought Candy's as my barbed tongue pricked the first sparkle of his blood, like popping the cork on a bottle of Cristal.

He moaned and pressed into me, and I drank. Candy did not disappoint as she and I brought him to the edge of release and held him there. Surges of thick sweet energy pulsed as I fed. Candy thrashed, moaned, and delighted. She fulfilled his every fantasy. Her green eyes held his as she performed acts and assumed positions he'd never have a woman do. "You're real?" he asked, incredulous at his good fortune.

Unable to speak, her lips wrapped around his cock, she gazed deep into his eyes and gave a throaty grunt as her tongue slid up and down the underside of his sex.

The part of his brain that controls pleasure released its rich cocktail—delicious stuff that science has determined contains dopamine, a hormone called oxytocin that's associated with nursing mothers and love, and natural opioids. Candy and I pushed him toward the swoon. It's a place beyond orgasm, and for me, the portal into a person's entire library of experiences and memories. As I drank and Candy performed acts that included contortion, we gave Jeff his money's worth. His engorged penis throbbed and spasmed with ropes of cum as he whispered into Candy's ear, "I've always loved you."

"And I you," she said as I went to work and Jeff fell into the swoon.

Mindful to not take more blood than he could spare, I pulled for the information I wanted. I began with images of Ricky. It was a quick hit, and I saw a scene of him in a small office with the man asleep in the other bedroom. There was an open safe, stacks of money, and Ricky, who seemed nervous, handing over wads of cash. Jeff counted the bills as the other man—Rod—circled behind Ricky, who appeared increasingly scared. The man cuffed the teen behind the head as Jeff accused, "Where's the rest of it, you little shit!"

Rod pulled at Ricky's ear and translated for Jeff in less than perfect Spanish.

Ricky cried and told them that he'd given them everything.

Jeff smiled and looked at Rod, who now twisted the boy's ear to where it drew blood.

He nodded, and Rod released his pressure but didn't let go.

"Maybe you're telling the truth," Jeff said as he arranged the bills into stacks of a thousand dollars and threw them into the safe. From a drawer in the desk, he pulled out a brown-paper-wrapped package, removed a string, and counted slender opaque bags of the same drugs I'd found at James's.

It's a start, I thought, and I latched on to the image and the feel of that package. I reached into his swoon, and in Candy's rich alto, purred, "Mmm, Jeff. Where did this come from?"

"Oh, Candy… Claire."

And we were off. Like a nest of Russian dolls where Ricky was the tiny one in the middle, Jeff and his brutal partner Rod were next, I glimpsed doll number three. She was unexpected. I wondered if the Candy fantasy had somehow contaminated his actual memories. But now I saw him and his partner in a different light as a strawberry blond woman in a dark blue suit drove her white BMW into an open bay.

She appeared to be in her midthirties, and Jeff was afraid of her but also fantasized about her... frequently. Their transaction was quick; she never left her car, just popped the trunk. Boxes were exchanged, the trunk was shut, the bay opened, and away she drove. I stared through his eyes as the white sedan sped off. I felt his hunger, but that's not what I wanted. I focused on her plate, but all I saw were breasts.

I poked around some more, like going through the files on a computer, and found stacks of similar encounters with this woman and cash/drug transactions with Ricky and dozens of other mostly teenaged Mexican boys.

I noted Jeff's frequent masturbatory coffee breaks—two or three a day, either in his bedroom, at his computer, or in the grimy bathroom off of the shop—and this woman—Claire, not Candy, was a frequent star.

"Should I be jealous?" Candy whispered through his swoon.

"No, I love you. Only you."

I could not find a last name for Claire. No surprise, but I did find a cache of prison and court memories. The trick here was to put them in sequence. I drew up a memory with flashing lights. Not an ambulance but cops, an arrest, being pushed up against a patrol car, cuffed, arrested. Related emotions—this wasn't his first time—resignation, despair, even traces of guilt, but faint. Then some particularly awful scenes that nearly broke the swoon. Thrown into lockup when still hooked on dope, cold turkey behind bars, puking, sitting on a stainless toilet in an open cell, gooseflesh, and sweats. An angry judge, a useless public defender, behind-the-scenes plea deals, two years served, making the most of it by getting into an autobody repair program, then mandatory drug treatment. A halfway house in South Boston, everyone wearing ankle bracelets, and that's where he met Rod. "My uncle has a repair shop. I could get you a job." He knew it wouldn't be just oil changes. "Sure, why not."

I ferreted more. But there comes a point where the lemon has been squeezed. Candy/Claire and I eased out of Jeff, and I bathed his wounds with the barbs on my tongue. He'd wake with a sore mouth, a sweet sense of loss, and crusted boxers.

Jeff rolled onto his back and snored. I felt full but unsatisfied. There was more here, and a smell in the background grew. It was familiar. *Ricky.* I sniffed. It didn't emanate from here, but from the hall. I followed my nose and blood-heightened senses past a grotty bathroom to a closed bedroom door.

Ricky's scent and a rank medley of others wafted from inside. *Okay, Rod*, I thought as I twisted the knob. It was locked. I twisted and it snapped in my hand. *Let's see what you've got.*

It started with rich odors, some fresher than others, a patina—sweat, urine and feces, fear, stale beer, lust, mold, dead rodents, dust, jizz, and cheap brown liquor. I let them waft through me. If I were a perfumer, I'd name it... *Despair*. And then we had Rod, flat on his back, slack-jawed with days of stubble, strands of long gray hair splayed out around a bald dome that glowed silver in the moonlight. Dressed in a pair of yellowed tighty-whities, the waistband stretched and half obscured by the roll of his belly, he was *Despair*.

I've seen, smelled, touched, and tasted worse... much. What puzzled me as I slid around the space with its piles of soiled work clothes and empty beer cans, were the layers of fear that emanated from Rod's bed. Not from him, I noted as I sank onto the bare and stained mattress. I breathed in deep—*terror*.

Okay, then. I stretched out next to Rod, caught the end of a sonorous beer-fueled snore, grabbed it by its figural tail, and dove in. He was drunk. It washed over me, and I wanted a clear head. I'd also had my fill of his partner and had no appetite for this dish. There is truth in the adage, you are what you eat.

I felt around for the edges of his dreams. Fragments and images flew past. *Damn*, this would take a while. Alcohol does that, and in Rod's case, it wasn't just booze I had to contend with. As the night progressed and his blood alcohol levels fell, he slipped into withdrawal and a vivid and frantic dream state. *Here we go.* And suddenly I was beside him in a white Solara, top down, his bald spot red from the sun, an open bottle of tequila in the cup holder, eighties metal blaring from the radio as we sped through changeable dream landscapes—here a bit of Mexican scrubland and there a flash of Kenmore Square.

Rod drank tequila and passed me the bottle. His eyes were bright, and there were smudges of cocaine under his nose. But now I was no longer Jeff's Candy/ Claire. I was young, too young, with silken black hair and dark eyes, and I was scared. I shook my head. I did not want his tequila or anything to do with him. His smile broadened, and I felt his lust as he shoved the liquor back into the cup holder and grabbed my thigh. I pulled back, which is what he wanted.

"Mio Carlito," he said, and he clawed under the legs of my jean shorts.

And then we were no longer in the Solara, but in a room, at times this one, at times different motels, curtains drawn, booze, and despair.

"No quiero esto." *I don't want this*, I said.

"Pero yo sí." *But I do.*

I fought against him, and he forced me back and ripped my clothes as dozens of faces flew out of him. Their terror fueled his lust. And then I saw Ricky and smelled him. He'd been in this room earlier in the day.

What did you do to him? And I pushed Ricky's image forward to guide the flow of the dream.

"Mi pequeño Ricky."

I fell into a bank of related memories—a village with a central square outside of Mérida, a bar with beer and tequila so cheap Rod wondered how they could do it, and all the beautiful young boys. So eager, so willing to hear what the man from the north had to offer. Like fish in a barrel, and there was Ricky, fresh and sweet, just what the doctor ordered. He loved his mother.

"Of course you do." And he drank and told the boy all the wonderful things he could do for his mother and the girl he hoped to marry. "Build a big house. She'll never have to work the fields again. Yes, we all love our mothers. We would do anything for them."

And then we were back in the Solara. I was now Ricky, and the more frightened I became…. And then it was the motel room, and he was on top of me, making me do things, hurting me. I was scared out of my mind, which is what he wanted. My fear, my tears. It made him hard.

His words, his threats. "What would Cecee think if she knew her Ricky was my whore? Your mother will be shamed. Your father will disown you."

And then it was this room and different threats. "You hide money and I will kill them all. And Cecee, I will sell her to the highest bidder. You do whatever I tell you to do. Do you understand?" His fingers dug into my shoulders; his grime-caked nails broke the flesh.

I pulled out of his dreams and out of him.

I pushed back on the bed, wrapped my arms around my knees, and stared at Rod. His erection tented the front of his shorts, and his snores pulled at me. I'd seen enough, too much. Ricky's terror clung and touched something deep and old within me. It's not that Rod was a pedophile, a sadist, and rapist, but it dredged up my own near misses, centuries ago, as my family and the entire world was plunged into a death spiral. For some, the great pestilence brought out unparalleled valor and sacrifice, while others used it as an excuse to give full rein to their basest instincts. *"If we're all going to die, why not?"*

I trembled as I unfolded my legs, got off Rod's bed, and went down to the shop and the back room. The safe was locked, but it wasn't cash I wanted. In a closet, hidden behind a false back I'd glimpsed in Jeff's dreams, was a storage room filled with drugs, boxes of overdose reversal medication, sterile syringes, and even alcohol pads, cotton, and bandages.

Ricky's tear-streaked face would not let go. And I get it. For many the world is a terrible and frightening place. But this... I grabbed three, then four, and finally five bags of the fentanyl-laced dope that had killed James, found a disposable lighter in a desk drawer, cooked it, and drew it up into an unused syringe.

A refrain from *The Mikado*, like a balm on my troubled thoughts, broke through. "To make the punishment fit the crime," I sang to myself as I walked back up to Rod's room, "the punishment fit the crime."

I stopped myself as one of Gaius's truisms sprang to mind... or maybe it was from a La Fontaine fable—look before you leap, don't act in haste, a fool and his money.... I'd come there for information. *Right.* Awful as it had been, I forced myself to reenter Rod's dreams. I drew on Jeff's fantasies of Claire... nothing. But as I flashed the image of her BMW into his brain, it took hold. A different desire, as he got the car up on the hydraulics and pretended to change the oil, his fingers on the paint, the interior wood trim, the smell of leather. *Mine. I want this.*

"Good boy. This is nice," I coaxed. "Beautiful car."

Mine, and his vision twisted to this car on a Mexican road, radio blaring, AC on high.

"Keep going." I pushed him toward a gas station with a lovely young male attendant. "Just your type." The car now another tool to be used to seduce and to violate.

He got out, and I became the boy. "What a beautiful car. You must be very rich." *Look at it. Look at it.*

"I am," he said. "Muy rico."

He tried to grab me. I laughed and headed toward the back of the car. *For the love of God, look at it.* Uncertain if he'd even registered the information I wanted.

"¿Te gusta el dinero?" *Do you like money?* Rod asked.

"Yes, I like it." And I smiled and sank to the ground.

His grin, his filthy tartar-caked smile, widened, but as he advanced on me, I caught Claire's license plate and memorized it. *And that's enough of that*, and I fled from his dream.

I ran the combination of six letters and digits in my head. There was a strong chance they'd turn out to be confused dream garbage, but I'd done my best.

And now… mindful to not break his drunken slumber, I tied a filthy tee around his upper arm and rebooted *The Mikado*. A vein popped, I injected the entire syringe, released the tourniquet, and sat. *"To make the punishment fit the crime, the punishment fit the crime."*

His snores loudened, and then he gasped—a coarse snore, a gasp, a pause, hint of a snore, gasp, pause, gasp, pause, pause, pause.

Frogs croaked from outside the open window. Rod's spirit separated from his flesh. He looked bewildered as he stared down at his body and then at me.

I pointed toward the light that glowed behind him.

He seemed frightened. "It's fine," I said, no idea if that was true or not, but a spirit as vile as his did not need to remain on this plane.

He nodded, and I followed his bald head and baggy shorts till they vanished into that wondrous white light.

Chapter Seventeen
Trevor Goes for Supper
and Gets a Root Canal

"YOU WENT to confession today?" Shannon asked. Her unmasked face was lit by a space heater, string lights, and the single red candle on our socially distant table, one of eight inside a tent erected for the cool weather and COVID at our favorite neighborhood restaurant, Carlito's.

"I did."

"I'll go next week." She reached for the basket of warm rolls our masked and gloved waitress had just left.

"Strange, isn't it?" I looked across at the girl, now woman, I'd been with since we were high school sophomores at Saint Mary's. So pretty, her blond-streaked hair loose around her shoulders, her blue eyes a few shades lighter than the silk blouse that peeked from under her jacket. A small gold crucifix she's always worn around her neck, not much makeup.

"The Father Calvin thing?" she asked as she tore open two packs of butter.

"Yeah, you have to wonder what he makes of us."

"I do." And with buttered roll in hand, she looked me dead-on. "Trevor, something's up with you."

"You're sure of that." I tried for a relaxed smile.

"Spill it."

Where to begin? And not certain that this was the time and place. "It's a bunch of stuff."

"Did you go to Kaplan today?"

"No."

"I thought you always went before confession."

"I didn't."

"And? What did you do?"

I was not about to start with my episode of breaking and entering. I also did not want to lie, *bear false witness*. I grabbed my beer and took three long swigs.

"Oh shit," she said. "That's not good."

"It's a lot of things, Shann. Work, the realization that I'll probably never get into an American medical school, stuff with my partner, the fact that I'm twenty-four years old and living in my parents' basement, that my mother still does my laundry… and I kind of like it."

"So, what's up with Godfrey?" she asked with laser precision.

The waitress returned with our salads and a steaming platter of fried calamari with chunks of gorgonzola, hot peppers, and a ramekin of marinara. Before she left, I said, "I'd like another," and pointed to my beer. "You want more wine?" I asked Shannon.

"I'm good… on second thought, bring me a cosmo."

As she left, Shannon persisted, "Godfrey, what did he do this time?"

"Saved my life."

"What?" With a chunk of tentacle in her hand, she stared at me. A drop of marinara fell to the tablecloth.

I told her about my klutz dive down the ravine and his one-handed catch.

"How is that possible?" she asked.

"Exactly. He caught my full weight."

She popped the squid into her mouth. "It happened, so clearly it's possible," she offered. "With the angle he stopped your fall, if he's in good shape…. You're lucky. It's all about the mechanics. So, what else did he do? There's more."

"Just his usual weirdness." And why, I wondered, was she so fixated on Godfrey?

"Like?"

"Like he got accepted to Harvard Medical."

"Oh, Trevor…. Seriously?"

"Yeah, it gets worse."

"You do know you're supposed to be happy for your friends when they get things they want?"

"I know," I said, "but…." I drained my beer as the waitress returned with the fresh one. "So, what about you?" I said.

"I'm not the one who seems like… I don't know, like you've got this weight on your shoulders, Trevor. It's been there for a while, and whatever it is doesn't get lighter, just… I don't know."

And there it was, the total and absolute realization that this woman loved me and cared about me. I felt it in my chest and in every inch of my being. *Do you love her? Yes. Are you in love with her?* "So work is good?" I asked.

"Work is great," she said. "I love my patients, I could kill the computer system, I'm sick of having to wear a mask and a splatter screen, and I'm tired of the gloves and all of that shit… but it's good enough. So… Godfrey got into Harvard, and you're pea green with envy."

"I am, and he deferred."

"Deferred Harvard Medical School? Why would he do that?"

I couldn't meet her gaze, but I felt it. "That's the weird part." *Don't do this. Please don't.* And I had that same sick sensation as when I was in free fall down the ravine. And there was Father Calvin's voice and his conclusion that my lies and omissions weren't the sin, but the intent, bearing false witness and deceiving Shannon, was. "He said that he deferred because of me." I gripped the cold beer in both hands. The condensation, or maybe it was sweat, dribbled down my knuckles. The words sounded bizarre in my head and just as strange as I forced them through my mouth. "He said he wanted to wait so we could go together."

"Does he have a thing for you?"

"I don't know," I admitted and felt her scrutiny. I sensed what was coming.

"I guess the bigger question, Trevor… is do you have a thing for him?"

"No, I don't." And I drank.

"Because if you did," she said, and her voice quivered, "or thought you might, you have to let me know… like now."

I put the glass down and looked at her. "You're my bedrock, Shannon. I love you."

"I love you too, but something's off. I know it. You know it."

"Off how?" I asked, and I saw that, like my beer, her cosmo had vanished.

"Hard to put my finger on it." She swallowed and paused. "Like you're here and not here at the same time… but that's not it." She waved for the waitress and raised her empty glass.

I wanted to argue, but she was right. And maybe this had nothing to do with Godfrey.

"We're in a holding pattern," she continued, "and I don't know what to do about it."

"What are you saying?"

"Us. Vickie Sue and Bobbie Joe. High school sweethearts, the last two twenty-four-year-olds in the continental United States who go to fucking confession and share their sinful premarital sex lives."

"Is that what you discuss with Father Calvin?"

"Of course," she said. "If you can't imagine him blushing on the other side, where's the fun?"

I smiled, and our waitress reappeared with our entrees and a third round.

"We're all we know, Trevor… romantically. And yes, we both had a thing or two in college, and that was the deal."

"It was." I looked at my eggplant parm. Carlito's was our joint. We could get sloshed and either cab or take a long walk home. Maybe I'd land at her place; maybe she'd follow me down to my basement. The food was dependable, not great but good enough—lots of melted cheese and well-seasoned breading. The sauce on my parm identical to the one that came on the side of our calamari. All good enough, familiar, comfortable.

"Like this," she said and pointed to her plate. "Saturday night at Carlito's. Will we each have three drinks or two? You'll order something eggplant based, and I'll have chicken. We get one of the same three appetizers, and…."

"You're reading my thoughts." I played with my fork at the edge of a sea of melted mozzarella. I caught the tines in it and twirled.

"So, back to you and Godfrey," she said.

"There is no me and Godfrey," I corrected.

"Maybe not sexually. Though if you were going to turn gay on me, he is hot."

"Excuse me?"

"Godfrey is hot. Like, cover-of-a-magazine hot. And don't pretend you don't see it."

"Fine. He's a good-looking dude. And believe me, he is aware of that."

"He's pushing your buttons, Trevor."

"He is," I admitted and could not force myself to lift that fork to my mouth. All appetite gone.

"I don't think he'd be able to do that if there weren't a button to push."

"I'm not gay, Shannon. You should know that better than anyone."

"Yeah... but tell me the truth, and I mean it.... Have you had impure thoughts about Godfrey?"

I felt buzzed and naked. Glad for the COVID distance between us and the other diners. It wasn't just years of Catholic school, Mass, and confession. God sees all, and so could Shannon, at least about me. I didn't want to lie, and the truth, once it left my mouth, would leave us forever changed.

"I've had dreams... about him." I forced myself to make eye contact.

"Sex dreams?" she asked.

While she said it without emotion, I knew her. There was pain in her eyes, pain I caused. I did not see how any of this would help or absolve my sins, but the time for lies and omissions and false witness had passed. "Yeah."

"More than one?"

"Yes."

"For how long, Trevor?"

Our Saturday night now felt like a trip to the dentist. She'd found a bad tooth, taken out her steel probe, and gone straight to the exposed nerve. "A while."

"How long?" she persisted.

"Since we started," I admitted. "Since we started working together."

"So... a year."

I nodded and felt nauseated. The booze did not help.

"You've kept this from me for a year."

I swallowed and started to reach across the table.

"Don't." She recoiled and pushed her chair back. "A year."

The weight of those words brought it home. A year is no small omission. It was enormous, and I knew it. "I shouldn't have kept this from you."

"No, you shouldn't have." She took the napkin off her lap, put it over her uneaten chicken bolognese, and stood.

"Just dreams," I said. "Nothing more."

She glanced around at the other diners and back to me. She gritted her teeth and kept her voice low. "It is more, Trevor. It's a year of lies, a year of saying you love me. And I think you do, but I don't think you're in love with me… not anymore. And I think maybe…." Her mouth twisted, and I wanted to wrap her in my arms, to tell her that I was just kidding, to go back to what we had. "I think you're in love with Godfrey." And she grabbed her pocketbook from off the back of her chair. "I need to get out of here."

"Let me get the check and I'll walk you home." I started to stand.

"No!" she spat out. "Let me go. Do not come after me." And she left.

Numb, I sank back into my chair and watched her walk away… from me. She was hurt and furious. I looked at her shrouded plate. The truth, once in the open, was hard to ignore. This was no small cavity. It went deep as a root canal.

I caught the glances of diners, mostly couples, who must have caught bits of the conversation, or at the very least understood the universal dance of a breakup. *Did we just break up?* The enormity of what had just happened registered.

Patty the waitress returned with another round of drinks... our fourth. I couldn't remember ordering them. She looked at Shannon's plate. "Should I wrap that?" she asked.

"No."

"Can I get you anything?"

"No."

"Okay, let me know if you need anything."

My hand played over the side of the fresh-frosted beer. I had no desire to drink it, just wanted the cold—something, anything to break this dread that engulfed me. *What have I done?* Shannon's words, the pain in her voice, echoed. *Are you in love with Godfrey?*

I'm not gay. I picked up the beer and drank. *And that's not the question, Trevor.*

Are you in love with Godfrey?

Chapter Eighteen
Godfrey has a Nightcap

I'D HIT a wall.

It was still dark when I eased the Acura MDX into the church garage, retrieved my new cello from the back, and headed in through the unlocked side door. I tumbled pieces of what I'd learned as I turned the deadbolt behind me and headed to the kitchen, where the drugs I'd purchased lay stacked, though not as I left them. "Trevor, Trevor, Trevor."

I fanned the rubber-stamped envelopes with their kneeling skeletons. Just like the ones I'd drawn up into Rod's fatal dose. *And why did you do that?* I still tasted the taint of him and of what he'd done to so many boys like Ricky. He needed to go.

But the problem I now faced was, where did I go… next? I love puzzles and am fascinated with plagues and epidemics. It's my catnip and what Gaius knew when he poured his life into me. My hunger is less about the blood and sexual energy that keeps me alive and more about figuring stuff out. Because everything, once you find the pieces, fits together. If I had a religion or philosophy, that would be it—everything makes sense.

Rod was vile, but he made sense. And his miserable life connected bits of the puzzle that killed James, organ-donor Rachel, and a multitude of others. This was not the first opioid epidemic on the planet, not even the biggest, though the COVID virus had worsened it—one plague that fueled another. Again, not new. Indeed, what Gaius thought back in the mid-1300s, science has substantiated. The great pestilence, the bubonic plague, black death, whatever you call it, was not a single pathogen but at least two and possibly three or more—a great war of the microbial world against humankind. Sort of amazing we survived.

The packets of fentanyl were just another disease. As I've learned through centuries of medical study, diseases require several things. It's like a five- or six-spoked wheel. If you lose a single element, it can't turn, and the disease is stopped.

I looked at the kneeling skeleton and ran through the factors. You need a pathogen—in this case opioids, potent, cheap, and available. Then it must be given at a high enough dose to take effect. In the case of these drugs, it seemed to be around two weeks to two months of habitual use. By that time, the person was good and hooked, which also covered the third spoke—a susceptible host or victim. In this case the millions who had become enslaved to the drugs. But that's all cart-after-the-horse, isn't it?

"Vectors, you need vectors." These are the agents of transmission. I ran the ones I knew—Ricky, Rod and Jeff, the mysterious auburn-haired Claire, even that village in Mexico. Rod didn't visit there by accident, but with intent. I'd seen it in his dreams. He knew the bartender and others like him. The locals were frightened but drawn to him and his crap Spanish, like a flea that pushed the disease from one body into the next.

I saw big holes. Claire was a lead to be followed, but other than Jeff's dream and the snippet of a license plate in Rod's, I had nothing. I wondered if killing him might have been a mistake. Then again…. And from what I'd glimpsed with Jeff, Rod had been the dominant force in their partnership. Yet Jeff was the one who met with Claire. Though I couldn't rely on that. Dreams are truth, but more emotional than factual.

Leave the sequence of vectors for now. Though it rankled. *Tomorrow is another night. You could go back.*

"Mode of transmission," I said aloud as I emptied the glassine drug packets down the kitchen sink. I flushed the water and flicked the switch for the disposal. I held an empty packet.

How one becomes infected is nuanced. People take their drugs many ways. It usually starts with pills, and then someone learns to crush and snort them, maybe skin pop next. And as tolerance builds and the person gets less bang for their buck, the needles start.

But just like the pestilence, COVID, Spanish flu, malaria, cholera—pick your plague—there's more that makes the wheel spin. Despair, depression, poverty… pain. That's at the heart of this one. It's the poppy's greatest lure. It numbs pain and replaces it with joy… in the beginning.

But because this was not my first adventure with the poppy, and now its potent and deadly children, I examined the final spoke and what prevented this disease from fading into the background—money. Trillions of dollars. Ricky's fantasy of a home for his mother, Claire's BMW, the wads I'd seen in Rod and Jeff's dreams.

"Economics." I put the packet with its brethren on the table, and headed back through the chapel and up a narrow flight toward the organ-and-choir loft that served as my bedroom. I put my cell in the charger. It was after three, and in five hours my next shift began. *Plenty of time.* I stripped and sank into my nest. And whoever invented memory foam deserved a prize. Propped up on pillows against the rows of organ pipes that served as a headboard, I had an unobstructed view of the rose window over the church's eastern apse. In a few hours, it would burst into life, and if I were smart, I'd have grabbed every minute of sleep available. But these twenty-four-hour shifts screwed with my normal rhythm. And that's one piece of the vampire mythology that's true for me—I'm strongest at night.

Sleep would not come, nor did answers to the mystery of these killer drugs. I thought about a different case, months back—Pete, who we'd revived on three separate occasions. He had a heavy habit, no interest in stopping, but did not want to die. I asked him, "How many times have you OD'd?"

"More than a dozen," he said. "Occupational hazard… especially now."

We'd just given him Narcan, and he'd already signed our against-medical-advice paper. "I'm not going to the emergency room," he said without hesitation as he shivered and the sweats began.

Trevor pleaded with him to stay and get help.

"What's the point?" Pete said. "They treat you like crap 'cause you're an addict. You stay for hours. No one helps or even talks to you. You just get sicker. No… I'll take my chances out here."

"They're not good chances," Trevor argued.

"Yeah, but it is my life."

"Agreed," I said and wondered how many more times before we'd find Pete dead. "I got to ask, though." And I knew he dealt drugs, mostly to support his habit. "It seems like a crap business model."

"Which part?"

"Killing your customers."

"That's because you don't understand."

"Then educate me," I said.

"Economics. The profit has gotten so big, it outweighs everything."

"I'll bite. How big we talking?"

"Massive since fentanyl came along. So big you wonder why more don't do it. And that's the thing," he added.

"What is?" Trevor asked.

"When people find out just how much money can be made, they want in. And yeah, lots of people die." With that he thanked us for our services, took the free box of Narcan, and went in search of his next fix.

I wondered if Pete was still alive. How many times can someone be resurrected?

And while the night and unquiet thoughts buzzed inside of me, I napped.

I dreamed.

It was a good one... ish. Back to the beginning and the smells of fourteenth-century Venice. Raw sewage flowed in the canals, but not even that covered the stench of rotting human flesh. I was in a market square that had once been filled with vendors with treasure from around the world and wooden stalls heaped with the season's produce. Now it was a struggle to find a few onions and a turnip to bring home to my sole surviving sister and my father. The stalls with butchered pigs and country game were long gone. Anyone lucky enough to still own livestock kept them hidden. All the dogs, cats, and even horses had vanished. But rats were big, bold, and plentiful. Skinned and boiled with the onions and half-rotted turnip, they weren't awful.

Piles of corpses waited for the morning procession of a priest and their servants who hoisted the dead onto carts. A boy of maybe seven or eight brought up the rear, swinging a pierced and smoking thurible. I watched, kind of like Trevor and I at the head and foot of our stretcher. Only here the count of "*Uno, due, tre*" ended with a body sailing up to the top of their load. I spotted Rod, James, and Rachel among the dead. The priest examined his cargo, the cart almost too heavy to move. He said something to his servants, and despite two other bodies, a woman and her child that someone had bothered to arrange against the side of a shuttered shop, he instructed them to move along.

I watched and breathed in incense of sandalwood and the stench of plague and rot as they lurched and struggled toward the docks.

"You mustn't linger, Giovanni," a familiar voice urged.

I turned and beheld my first love, Gaius Aurelius Maximus. He was gowned and hooded in black, with an elaborate leather plague mask that ended in a long crow's beak.

"I bring gifts," he said, and from a pocket, I glimpsed a bunch of beets and carrots with their leafy greens still intact.

I could not see his face, but his voice pushed away the nightmare that had overtaken the world. "It is time to go," he urged. We crossed the Ponte della Paglia and headed toward the docks.

"But my father."

"Gone," he said.

I felt for the onions and turnip, but they'd vanished.

"I have to go home. They're waiting for me. They'll worry."

He stopped, and I felt a shiver as he laid thick talons on my shoulders.

"You're not Gaius," I said as the man turned into a blackbird.

"All dead," he cawed as a small boat pulled up to the quay. "Look." His robe sprouted feathers, and he waved an oily black wing across the water.

Packets of skeleton-stamped drugs bobbed to the surface.

"There is only death here." And he shoved me off the bridge.

I fell and kept falling. He faded into the distance, his beak gone, his flowing silver-streaked mane whipping around his face. "Ti amo, Giovanni," he shouted.

"E ti amo," *And I love you*, I whispered and fell. I felt something wet around my mouth as I looked back. A hard and familiar knot of loss filled my gut. E ti amo, Gaius. *Don't leave me. I don't want to be alone.*

Just a dream, I thought, and I tried to comfort myself, but the warm wet that now covered me and coated my vision in blood was a sick reminder of how I came to be. A scream welled inside of me. *Why? Why couldn't he have stayed with me?*

He was gone, in life and in this dream, so I fell. Beneath me a whirring sound, faint at first, but then like rotors on a turbine.

Great, I'm about to get sucked into a jet engine.

I rolled in midflight and spread my arms. Gusts of wind billowed the folds of my garment. I looked at the fabric—black, iridescent, and made of millions of tiny feathers. "Nice… wings." And I looked down at the source of the noise as I swooped and soared. Not a jet engine but a spoked wheel—*ruota del destino*, the wheel of fate.

I hovered above it as the colors shifted and it morphed from a medieval cartwheel to something like the sectioned game pieces in Trivial Pursuit.

Eeny, meeny, miny, moe, I muttered as the spaces became doors. I tried to remember what Trivial Pursuit topics went with the different colors. *No clue.* I gathered my wings in tight and dove toward the green door.

I landed in a dark bedroom. The air was cool, clear, almost subterranean. But no, a basement bedroom on the outskirts of Boston. I gazed on the figure asleep before me—beautiful, albeit snoring, and the smell of bourbon and beer oozed from his pores. His naked arms snaked around a pillow, his legs splayed—one under the sheet, the other over. Gaius's final words echoed through my lips. "Ti amo," I whispered.

A fat and fluffy tabby mewled at me from the foot of the bed.

"Ti amo."

Chapter Nineteen
Trevor Falls

I WANTED someone to blame. I'd stayed at the socially distant table for two at Carlito's, the food long gone and the beers replaced with bourbon. *Hi, my name's Trevor, and I'm an alcoholic.* Which was not funny. Too many uncles and aunts in my family had walked that path, were on that path, and my grandpa Sean died four years ago from multiple organ failure—at least that was the party line. The organ that gave up the ghost was his liver, his final years spent in a nursing home, where he pled with family to sneak pints of Jameson's. Which we did. I needed to watch my booze intake… and watch it I did, one drink after the next.

Shannon's accusations, spoken and implied, played in a loop. Father Calvin piped in with my litany of sins. He was right; I had born false witness. Maybe I wasn't 100 percent aware of it, but do ignorance and stupidity count?

Waitress Patty kept the drinks coming; she knew I wasn't going to drive. "We're up to last call," she said. It was just me and a few other couples and solo drinkers, all COVID banned from the inside bar and spaced at tables in this tent like satellites in orbit around the good planet alcohol.

"Sure," I slurred. "What's one more?"

"You want a coffee with that?"

"Hell no." Last call in Massachusetts is 1:30 a.m., which left half an hour before they had to shut the doors and kick me out. "You know what, Patty?"

"What, Trevor?" she asked with the amused tone one takes with three-year-olds and drunks.

"Let's skip the drink and get me a check."

"You got it." And she punched a few buttons on her tablet, told me the damage, took my card, inserted it, and asked, "You want the paper receipt or emailed?"

"Emailed. I'll leave the tip in cash."

"Thanks. Hope the rest of your night goes better."

"Me too, and tomorrow is a workday, and I'm fucked."

"It's Sunday."

"Yeah, but not for me." I got up and launched out of orbit and in the general direction of the front door. My feet kind of followed a straight line, but once outside, *I got to pee*.... I looked back at the front door of Carlito's, but the thought of going back in, having someone check my temperature... too much hassle.

I relieved myself in a hedge off the parking lot and aimed for home. The tune from "It's a Small

World" cued up. Most Saturday nights would end with Shannon at my side, either headed left toward her third-story walkup in a building owned by her aunt, or right and back to my place… in the basement of my parents' house.

"What the fuck have I done?"

My toe caught on a break in the sidewalk and I fell hard. I landed on the palm of my hand. "Shit." I scanned for injuries. *You didn't hit your head… did you?* I felt dazed on top of drunk. I rotated my hand in both directions and wiggled all five fingers. The wrist hurt, and my abraded palm started to bleed. Embedded bits of gravel and sand sparkled under the streetlights. *Nothing's broken. Of course, if Godfrey were here, he would have caught me.* My heart pounded.

"Fuck!" I said aloud. *Get your drunk ass home.*

I did. I went around the back of the house. A light was on in my parents' second-story window. One or both were up, their noses in books. Not waiting for me, as half the time I'd spend the night with Shannon, but always eager to chat, though not so much since COVID and my sort-of quarantine in the basement.

Fortunately, I could sneak in through the steel bulkhead doors. *Un*fortunately, and why I rarely used this strategy, the hinges wailed like a banshee, which no amount of WD-40 rectified.

I inserted my key, turned, and pulled up and back.

The sound of rust and steel split the night.

Birds roused, a squirrel jumped from a tree, and I heard someone's feet upstairs hit the floor. A curtain drew back, and the window opened.

Mom looked down, her expression puzzled. "We thought you'd gone to Shannon's."

"Not tonight." I struggled to keep my syllables in tight formation.

"Did you have a fight?"

"Yeah, and I don't want to talk about it. Not now, okay?"

I didn't wait to hear her reply but disappeared down the flight of rough wooden steps and pulled the screaming steel door shut behind. Spiderwebs caught against my cheek, and I coughed as something shot up my nostril… possibly a spider.

The basement was dark and cold; my cheek brushed against a stainless pull chain that hung from a utility light. I heard the scurry of cats, and Aldo, a long-haired rescue, brushed against my ankles. I held still and grabbed for one of the Lally columns that ran the length of the space. I listened to see if Mom's curiosity would pull her down. I did not want to talk, and I did not want her to see me like this. Sloppy drunk… and dumped.

My head spun, or the room did, or some combination of the two. Aldo butted his hard head against my ankle. "Not now." I aimed for the bathroom.

Inside, the LEDs were too bright, and what stared back from the mirror was a crime scene. Matted blood in my hair above a two-inch gash over my right temple. The palm of my hand throbbed. *You hit your head.* I turned on the water, pumped the liquid soap, and cleaned and disinfected. The booze kept me anesthetized. *Nothing's broken.* This awful night would not end with me waiting in an emergency room, having to interact with the same nurses and doctors I'd see on the day job.

There'd be pain in the morning, and not just from the bruises. "You fucked up," I told the bloodied guy in the mirror. That didn't begin to cover it. I wanted to blame someone for all of this—for Shannon, for my drunken fall, for two failed attempts to get into medical school, for blowing off studying, for my freak of a partner. I pointed at the man in the mirror. "He's a drug addict," I said, "and a church decorator... no, desecrator. And you," I said in a stern and what I thought was prosecutorial voice, "need to make amends."

A knock came from the top of the basement stairs.

Mom's voice, "Trevor, are you all right?"

"I'm fine, Mom. Drank too much," I admitted... and wished I hadn't.

There was a weighted silence. I held my breath, my finger still raised in accusation at the drunk in the mirror.

"Drink some water," she said, her tone rich with a mother's disapproval. "We can talk tomorrow."

Goodie. I closed my eyes and steadied against the cool porcelain sink. Aldo forced his way into the bathroom and made furious passes against my ankle.

Drops of blood popped on my palm. I washed it a second and third time, did the same with the gash above my temple, which could have used a stitch, or two, or three and bled... a lot, as scalp wounds do. "Pull it together." And I did, albeit more literally than figuratively. I grabbed a couple butterfly bandages and closed the head gash—*it's going to leave a scar*. Then I ripped open three packs of gauze and wrapped and taped them hard against my palm.

I stuck my mouth under the faucet and drank, brushed my teeth, stripped to my shorts, and fell into bed.

Booze be praised, I passed out. And booze be dammed, I fell into a dream.

I was back in college… *no*, I realized as I looked around. *This is medical school. I made it into medical school.* I stopped and looked around to make certain it wasn't on some Caribbean island, but no… I saw both the John Hancock and Prudential Towers. *Boston. I'm still in Boston.* That left a number of choices, all of them good, and based on the location of the two towers, I was on the other side of the river, which meant Cambridge, which meant. *Harvard.*

I couldn't figure out how it happened, but it didn't matter. I was here. Around me students had their faces buried in laptops and notebooks. "What's going on?" I asked a woman seated next to a pile of books. *How come no one is wearing masks?*

She looked up at me. "Are you kidding me?"

"No, what's happening?"

"Don't be a moron, Trevor; it's the Latin final."

"Latin? But this is medical school."

"Duh," her expression incredulous. "You need two years of Latin for medical school."

She was right. How did I forget? I felt like a moron. I'd finally gotten in and I'd screwed it up.

I hadn't gone to a single Latin class. And now there was a test, which I'd fail.

A door opened, and the students filed in. The girl who told me about the exam gave a pitying look and followed the others.

"You can do this," I told myself. "You took Latin in high school… and hated it." I shuddered at the memory of Sister Robert Agnes's cruel didactics. "In with the ablative," she'd shriek and rap a ruler hard against the nearest desk as she patrolled the rows, examining each homework assignment, none of them ever good enough.

I could not remember a single word of Latin, but I went in. It was a massive auditorium. I took a seat toward the back. *I have to try.* A proctor dropped a test booklet onto my desk. At the podium stood Sister Robert Agnes.

"So nice of you to join us, Mr. Sullivan." She looked at me. "But you don't belong here."

"Don't listen to her," a familiar voice came from across the aisle.

"Godfrey." And then I remembered. "You shouldn't have waited for me. I screwed up."

"Everyone does," he said.

"Why are you dressed like that?" I whispered, trying to understand his choice of outfit, more like a costume, with tight breeches, a purple overcoat, and a green-and-gold vest, his hair tied back with a black ribbon.

"It's comfy."

"You look like the cover of a romance novel."

"Glad you noticed." He opened his test booklet and wrote at a furious pace… with a black feather plucked from his sleeve.

I stared from him to the test packet on my desk. I turned to the first page. "It's in Hebrew."

He looked up at me. "Of course."

"I don't speak Hebrew. Or read it… or…."

He put down his quill and looked at me dead-on. "That's because you've skipped classes, Trevor. I got you in here; the least you could do is make an effort."

"I'm sorry," I said, and I was, unable to pull my gaze from his beautiful eyes. "For all of it."

"Do you even know what you want?" he asked.

The auditorium and Sister Robert Agnes vanished, and we were in a park. "I thought I did." I stared at him. "You're the hero in all those books," I said. "Or the villain. Which is it, Godfrey?"

He smiled. "Both. At some point you have to choose."

"What does that mean?" I wanted to hit him, or kiss him, or maybe one and then the other.

But he was gone. A church bell rang. It grew louder and louder, and then it wasn't a church bell but the alarm on my cell. It pulled me from the dream into Sunday morning and into lots of pain—from the lump and gash on my temple, to a diffuse burn on my palm, to a throb, throb, throb like someone had stuck my head in a vise.

Aldo crawled onto my chest. I went to pet his head as nausea flooded my mouth with salty saliva. I clamped my jaw and dashed for the toilet.

I puked, and it wasn't just remains of calamari, beer, and bourbon that came up and out, but all that I'd done the night before—the look in Shannon's eyes, her anger, confusion, hurt, and betrayal. *I am so sorry. What did I do?*

I vomited and tried to ride out the waves of pain with a minimum of movement. It was six thirty in the morning and my shift began at eight. I should call out… and isn't that one of the road markers on the path to alcoholism? *No… you need to hurt. You need to do penance. You must make this right.*

Chapter Twenty
Godfrey Sunday

ARMED WITH a bag of bagels, cream cheese, and lox from Kupel's and a thermos of their excellent coffee, I came prepared... for Trevor. I should have sent him home.

"Rough night?" I asked as he extricated himself from his AARP-ready Subaru.

"Please don't."

The full effect was stunning. From the dark shades to the butterfly strips across what must have been a gusher over his right temple, to his right hand, swaddled in gauze and tape. Even from twenty paces and after his morning shower, I caught bourbon under Irish Spring and a floral shampoo Shannon had left in his basement shower. "Coffee?"

"Yes, please."

I poured a generous mug, and if it weren't the start of our shift, would have dosed it. Instead I sloshed in cream. "Bagel?"

"No."

"Do I need you to blow into a tube?"

"I don't think so."

"Right. I'm driving… at least till whatever is in your system is out."

"Thanks." He wouldn't meet my gaze.

"You want to talk about it?"

"Absolutely not."

"Rough night with Shannon?" I couldn't help myself.

"Please don't."

"Fine. I'll sign out the truck." Which was usually Trevor's job, like driving, but now he needed to pull his hungover ass into shape. Bad as I knew he felt, he had to go through this. Life is short—at least his and Shannon's were. And seven years of stringing that poor woman along…. Though I do not believe he meant to.

I opened the bay for Eight, grabbed the clipboard, and ran through the checklist. Sundays at Cavalry, which jumbles in my head with Calvary—especially on the sabbath—have a timeless quality—no on-site supervisor, dispatch comes through the city's 911 operator, no dialysis runs or routine medical-cab trips if the EMT trucks are overwhelmed. It's the shift that time forgot.

I popped the hood, checked the oil, transmission fluid, and tire pressure, and ran through the inventory in the back.

I pulled out of the garage and into a crisp October morning, topped off the gas, and watched Trevor through the window, shades on, hands clamped to his coffee in pain and contemplation.

Catholic guilt. I never suffered that affliction, but I had issues of my own right then. Not the least was Trevor's dream question—*which are you, hero or villain?* If yesterday's activities were the gauge, which included ending Rod's miserable existence, my hat was more black than white.

A door clanged shut, and Trevor headed toward me. "We need to talk," he said.

"I'm listening."

He stopped at a distance and grimaced.

He was in pain, lots of it. "What's on your mind, Trevor?"

He stood rooted. "I owe you an apology, and I don't know where to start."

"Spit it out."

He stared at the ground, then up at me. He took off his glasses and revealed a fresh shiner just starting to turn purple and red around his eye.

"Sweet. Have you gotten that looked at?" I asked.

"Nothing's broken," he said. "Let me do this."

But I'd already closed the distance. "You reek of booze," I said as, uninvited, I put a hand to the side of his head.

"I'm fine." He didn't move, though I sensed part of him wanted to and another part didn't.

"Stay still," I instructed as I felt through the pads of my cello-callused fingers for signs of fractures. His unmasked breath brushed my neck and cheek as I let my fingers wander from around his eye to the butterfly strips around the gash to his skull. I felt my hunger and I salivated. It would have been so easy to have a taste, just a little. "You'll live," I said and forced

myself to take three steps back. *What am I doing?*
And Trevor's dream returned to me—hero or villain?

"Would you please shut up," he said, "and let
me talk."

"Go ahead."

"I broke into your place," he spat out.

"I know."

"What?"

"I wasn't a thousand percent certain it was you,"
I lied—of course it was him. "But I don't leave the
door unlocked, and you did."

"It could have been that kid."

And here we go…. "Ricky?"

"Your drug dealer. I saw it, Godfrey. You bought
the same shit that killed James Grant. What in God's
name possessed you? Is that your deal? Is it drugs?"

He was on a roll. "Is that what you think?"

"I don't know what to think."

"Trevor, for an apology, this feels like an inquisition. I wondered what you'd do when I showed you
that letter."

"What are you talking about?"

"My acceptance letter. The golden ticket. You
memorized my address off it, which, had you asked,
I'd have been more than happy to give you. Invite
you over. Like normal people… like friends."

"You live in a church."

"I do." His head of steam started to cool.

"But the drugs… what were you thinking? Are
you an addict?"

"No, at least not to heroin or fentanyl or any-thing poppy related."

"Then what…."

I took one step forward and lowered my voice. "Aren't you curious, Trevor? Every day we save someone from an overdose, maybe multiple some-ones… or we show up too late. If anything, it's ac-celerated since COVID."

He shook his head and winced. "So… you're playing detective? You're not a cop."

Another baby step. "True. But I like to know how things work. So I made a phone call."

"To a dealer?"

"Yes." I watched as he swam through the pain and receding booze to make sense of it.

"Those were the same drugs we saw at the Grants'."

"Yes…."

"But how did you…."

"On that first run, when we resuscitated James, I asked him for his dealer's number." Which was true.

"I saw you lean in and ask him something. That's what it was?"

"Yes, James passed me the digits."

The moment broke with the simultaneous ring of our two company cell phones and the one on board Number Eight. I held his gaze and answered the call. "Cavalry Ambulance." I nodded and told them we were good for the run—a fender bender a few blocks away. "I'm driving," I reminded Trevor, who had started to get behind the wheel out of habit.

"Right." He changed directions, plunked into my usual spot, and synced the address from the dispatcher to the dashboard GPS.

"That was your apology?" I said as I put my elbow out the window, turned on the flashers—no sirens, because what kind of sadist does that on a Sunday morning with no traffic?—and drank in the cool morning air and sips of excellent black coffee to which I'd added a scoop of cocoa.

"I'm sorry," he offered.

"That's better. So, what did you learn?" I asked. "Other than thinking I was on drugs."

"That kid was young."

"Ricky. Yes, he is." And I spotted a police flasher and a burgundy Highlander that had gone off the road. No skid marks, no other vehicle, early morning. "Somebody fell asleep at the wheel," I commented.

"Guy with the cop," Trevor said.

"He's conscious." I pulled onto the curb, hopped down, and headed toward the day's first victim. "Morning." I visually assessed the older man seated on a log—smiling, embarrassed as blood dripped from a cut on the left side of his head, in animated conversation with a young officer who crouched in front of him.

"I must have passed out," the man said without guile as I approached. He appeared shaken.

"It happens," I offered. "Anyone else in the vehicle, Officer?"

"No." And the black-masked cop looked back at me, smiled, and made solid eye contact. "Just Mr. Jordan. On his way to pick up donuts and... then this." He held my gaze, his left eyebrow raised. I caught a tingle of his interest and glanced at his name plate—R. Carmichael.

"Let's take a look at you." I pulled out my flashlight as Trevor joined me with the red kit box. "So, Mr. Jordan."

"Call me Bryan."

"Okay, Bryan, are you on any medications?" I checked his pupils, got a good look at the small gash, probably from hitting the dash, and looked for any asymmetries or facial droops as I worked my way down.

He rattled off a short list that included two pills for blood pressure that he really didn't think he needed and a salt tablet that he swore by that was not prescribed. "But what do these doctors know. I like to sweat, and you have to replace the salt."

"So true. Anything else…?"

Next came a list of nutritional supplements and fresh turmeric, which he added to the daily yogurt smoothie that had done miracles for his colitis.

"Anything that might have made you drowsy?" I asked as Trevor pushed up his sleeve to get a blood pressure.

"My PCP added something for my nerves."

And we have a winner. "You remember the name?"

"It's a little white pill. I don't like to take them, but…."

"Out with it, Bryan," I said.

"It's been a rough morning," he admitted. "Klono… something."

"Got it. Klonopin, a likely cause."

"Yes…." He sighed, and his smile vanished.

My first assessment of Bryan Jordan had been midsixties, but as we chatted, I realized he was an incredibly fit octogenarian. Once I checked his driver's license, that got upped to ninety-three. "Any headache or nausea?" I asked as Trevor retrieved the stretcher from the back of Eight.

"No… but…."

"Out with it."

"My chest feels tight."

"Not to worry." And we helped him up and onto the stretcher. "Describe how it feels." I snaked a plastic tube around his neck and popped in the nasal canula prongs for a wee bit of oxygen.

"Achy," he said.

"Any history of heart problems?" I asked.

"They said I had a heart attack, maybe ten years ago. I'm not convinced. What about my car?" he asked and tried to sit up.

"Don't worry, sir," young Officer Carmichael said. "We'll get a tow. You get yourself taken care of."

"I need to call my wife." He seemed disoriented. "My cell."

"It was on the floor of your vehicle." The officer handed me his Samsung and a World War II veteran's cap. He looked at the cap. "Thank you for your service, sir."

Bryan nodded and tears popped, and while he still did not look his age, whatever emotional burden he carried was heavy.

"It's going to be okay," I said as the three of us wheeled him to the back of Eight.

"I'm not so sure," he said, and he wasn't talking about his accident. With a "One, two, three," we had him up, in, and locked to the side rail. I felt a hand on my shoulder as I started to climb in. It was Trevor.

"Remember, you drive."

"Right." I bit back a surge of annoyance, because I like to be in back. Lights and sirens are well and good, but Bryan, with his WWII cap and donut-run mishap, had a story to tell. I wanted to hear it.

I stepped away, Trevor got in, and I closed the doors. The officer followed. "I'm Raphael," he said.

"Godfrey."

"Maybe I'm off base," he said.

I opened my door. "You're not," I said, knowing where he was headed and admiring both his initiative and… the uniform thing, and how good he looked in it.

"Okay, then. Can I give you my number?"

"Love to have it." I got behind the wheel, rolled down the window, and accepted his hastily written number.

"Call me," he said.

"Will do. Gotta run." I turned back and caught Trevor's gaze. "Bryan," I said, "we're in striking distance to either the Roxbury VA or St. E's. You got a preference?"

"VA. That's where I go for everything."

"You got it."

Officer Raphael stepped back from the door and made the universal call-me sign.

"I will." And with lights, no siren, but an occasional toot of the horn, we rolled.

Chapter Twenty-One
Trevor Diagnoses Godfrey

I FELT like crap and cracked the small side window to let in air as we took our first run of the day, ninety-three-year-old Bryan Jordan, to the VA.

"You okay?" he asked.

Not good. "I think I'm the one who's supposed to ask the questions here."

"Quite the shiner you got." He smiled. "What's her name? And was she worth it?"

"Yeah. Shannon." It felt like someone stomped on my chest as I remembered the look on her face as she got up and left me. "She is… was."

"Sorry about that," he said.

"So, you're a retired psychiatrist."

"No, a mechanical engineer, but I raised four boys and two girls, and I know a broken heart."

"Yeah…." I tried to shake it off. *Focus on him… on work, and did Godfrey just get that cop's number? What the fuck is his deal? And why do I care?*

"So, what happened back there?" I grabbed the tablet from its nook.

"Don't really know." His voice drifted. "Must have fallen asleep. Must have been that new pill."

"The one for your nerves?"

"Yeah."

"Trouble at home?" I asked.

"My granddaughter." And this man who looked so much younger than his age turned ashen. His eyes welled.

"Are you in pain?"

"No."

And taking a note from Godfrey, I abandoned the boxes to be ticked. "What's her name?"

"Melody… a pretty girl is like a melody… and she is pretty and, and smart, and sweet and… throwing it all away. Throwing her daughter away too."

"You're worried about her."

"I don't know what to do. She's on drugs. She can't stay with my son and daughter-in-law because Jilly and Aaron are in high school, and now they have custody of Penelope—that's Melody's little girl, my great-granddaughter. We call her Sweet Pea. But protective services said Melody can't be in the house, so we said she could stay with us…."

"Did something happen with her this morning?"

"Last night," he said. "I don't know what to do. Neither of us do."

I looked to see how close we were to the VA and caught Godfrey's eyes in the mirror. He was listening. He was so much better at this, and I felt a pang of guilt for not being fit to drive. "What happened?"

"It's a boy, but not like in my day when boy-friend-girlfriend stuff didn't wind up with someone almost dead. Sure—" He attempted a smile. "—you might wind up with a black eye and a gash on your head, but that would be it." A look of alarm and he tried to sit up. "I never called my wife."

"Bryan… Mr. Jordan, we'll do that when we get to the hospital."

"She'll be so worried. I really messed up."

"You're going to be okay, and that's the main thing, right?"

"Yeah, it is. We've been lucky, Jan and I." He settled back.

"Jan's your wife?"

"Yup, married seventy-three years. Met her the week after I got out of the Army. She was a fix-up."

"What's that?"

He chuckled. "It's where your busybody aunts invite you to dinner, and there happens to be the most beautiful girl you've ever seen who just happens to be there." Tears rolled down his cheeks.

"Are you in pain?"

"Not physical." His tear-filled eyes stared up at me.

"You're thinking about your granddaughter."

"Yeah. She got out of a program yesterday… a drug program, and she looked great, like her old self. But then she went out to buy cigarettes… and didn't come home till after three in the morning. High as a kite." He grimaced.

"Something happened," I said.

"Yeah. You got some water or something?"

"Sure." I twisted open a small bottle, put in a straw, and let him get a couple careful sips.

"Thanks." He leaned back on the pillow. "Neither one of us could sleep. We just lay there. Our bedroom is right under hers, and around six we heard a crash from the upstairs bathroom. She was passed out on the floor, needle in her arm. Last time that happened I took the lock off the door. We gave her the Narcan… two doses."

"Did you call 911?"

"No." He looked away.

"Why not?"

"She won't go with them when they come. Just gets mad at us. Screams, tells us to mind our own business. She's twenty-seven, and I don't think she's going to make it. And I don't know how to help her."

"I'm so sorry, Bryan."

"Me too. She's a beautiful girl when she's not on drugs." He sighed. "I need to phone my wife."

"I've got his cell," Godfrey called back. "We'll do it as soon as we get you checked in to triage." He turned into the ED entrance, did a tidy J-turn, and backed into an ambulance bay.

"Okay," Bryan said. "People say all sorts of bad stuff about the VA, but they've been nothing but good to me."

"Good to hear." I opened the back doors and un-hooked the stretcher as Godfrey grabbed the foot end.

As we wheeled through the electronic doors, Godfrey fished the WWII veteran's cap with his battalion number embroidered over the bill and propped it onto Bryan's head.

"Thanks," Bryan said, and we got whisked through triage in under two minutes. Before we even had time to get him off our stretcher and onto one of theirs, he'd been assigned a private room in the trauma suite.

"My cell?" he asked as a masked and gowned orderly led us back.

"Right here," Godfrey said, but before he could hand it over, a thin woman with a three-pronged cane, palm-tree patterned mask, and determined expression barreled toward us with a nurse at her elbow.

"Oh-oh," Bryan said. "Here comes trouble."

"Bryan!" She stopped us and steadied herself on the edge of his stretcher. "What did you do?" She put a hand on the side of his face, pulled down her mask, and with an effort, bent down to kiss him. "What did you do?"

"It was that pill," he said.

She exhaled and ran her fingers up and down the side of his face, stopping at the hastily applied pressure dressing I'd put on his temple. She looked up from him to the orderly, to me, and then fixed on Godfrey. "Is he okay?" she asked.

"He is," Godfrey said without hesitation. "He'll have a big bruise on his chest where he hit the steering column, and the cut on his head looks worse than it is. They'll give him a couple stitches and he'll be good to go."

"Thank you, God," she said, her fingers entwined with her husband's.

"I'm fine," Bryan repeated, his gaze fixed on his wife. "How did you know I was here?" he asked.

"I got a call from a police officer."

"He was nice. Local boy. Where's Melody?"

"In the waiting room," she said and lowered to a whisper. "I didn't dare leave her at home."

He nodded and squeezed her hand.

Between the two of us, the orderly, and the nurse, we got him settled into his cubicle, off our portable oxygen, and hooked to an assortment of monitors.

As we prepared to leave, Bryan grabbed for my hand. "Thank you. You're a good listener. And I hope your girl trouble settles out. But maybe she's not the one." He looked at his wife. "You'll know when it's right."

"You take care of yourself, and I hope things work out with Melody."

"Yeah, me too."

As I pulled the stretcher, Godfrey was not on the other end. "What the…?" And there he was, headed at full steam down the corridor, toward the lobby and not the ambulance bays.

"Crap." I parked the stretcher and gave chase. After a year with Godfrey, I almost don't question this stuff. But my head throbbed, I'd barely cracked the surface of the paperwork on Bryan, and what I most wanted was to get back to the station house and crawl into bed.

I pushed through the double doors that led into the ED waiting area and saw Godfrey standing over a painfully thin young woman with skunk root hair and a mask that had slipped off and hung around her neck. Her eyes were hooded as she looked up at Godfrey and then down. As I approached, I heard him try to talk to her.

"Melody, what did you take?"

"Nothing," she slurred and slumped down into the molded plastic chair.

"What did you take?" he persisted.

"I'm fine… just a little something."

He grabbed her drawstring bag—an embroidered Indian sack with a paisley print and fringe—and started to go through it.

She looked up at him. "That's mine." But she didn't seem able to stop him.

He found her syringe and a stack of baggies. I looked in and was not surprised to see the same rubber stamp of the skeleton on his knees, hands clasped in prayer.

"Melody." He sank into the chair next to hers. "How many bags did you just take?"

I connected the dots. In the few minutes that she'd been left alone in the VA waiting room, she had gone into the ladies' room and shot up.

She nodded and barely responded. "Two... three." Her voice trailed and ended with a deep snore.

He looked up at me.

"Should I get the Narcan?" I asked.

He shook his head. "Not yet."

Her eyes shut, and she slumped against his shoulder. Her breath became a series of loud snores and then gasps. Her body stiffened, and she stopped breathing entirely.

Godfrey's expression was unreadable, distant, almost spacey as he looked from Melody, whose lips had turned a purplish blue, toward the window of clerks, one of whom was taking information from a patient. He put a hand on Melody's abdomen and raised his voice. "Code Red. Code Red."

"I could get the Narcan," I whispered.

He shook his head no, his gaze fixed on the ceiling. "Code Red! Code Red!"

The sleepy ED sprang into action.

"Code Red!"

I helped him lower her to the floor and tried to see what he was looking at... something above the row of molded chairs bolted to the floor.

"Code Red!" he shouted.

As the lobby flooded with the code team, I couldn't take my eyes off him. He was fixated on something I could not see, and while his mouth was concealed by the dark mask with the Cavalry logo, his lips moved. It was trancelike, and not the first time I'd seen this. *It's got to be drugs*. I felt bad because he'd said he wasn't on them, but I'd seen him buy them, seen them in his kitchen…. And then I stopped myself as the ED doc took a quick look at Melody and instructed the nurse to draw up a vial of Narcan. *This isn't drugs.* I stepped back and stared at my partner, who knelt beside Melody, one hand on her abdomen, his eyes raised to a blank spot on the wall. His lips moved beneath his mask. He was in conversation with something or someone that I could not see. And suddenly my hypothesis that he was on drugs seemed wrong. People who see and talk to things that aren't there? If it's not drugs, it's insanity.

Chapter Twenty-Two
A Pretty Girl is Like a Melody

"CODE RED!" I shouted as Melody Rinaldi's spirit rose from her body. I think of this universal bit of death like the way you separate yolks from whites when you bake. How and why I can see and chat with these disembodied folk as they shuffle off the mortal coil and head to the great mystery is… a mystery.

Melody hovered, tethered to her body. She saw me looking at her.

"Let me go," she said.

"You want to die," I said.

"It's better that way. For all of them. I tried… I really did."

"There's no limit on tries," I offered, and I spotted a second disembodied wisp.

"They'll be better off without me. Penelope will be better off with my parents. I'll just screw things up."

"And your son?" I asked.

Her expression widened.

I looked from my hand on her still-flat abdomen back to her. "Yup. You didn't know you were pregnant?"

"No… maybe. I haven't had my period, but I just thought that was the dope. It does that."

"Yeah."

"Shit…."

"Can I give you some advice?"

She seemed perplexed. "How is it that you're the only one who sees me?"

"Wish I knew," I said. "Now about that advice…."

"Yes, please."

"As long as you're still breathing, there's hope. And in my considerable experience, your daughter will be much better for having you around. But here comes the rub-a-dub-dub—before you give up the ghost, ask yourself if that's what you really want…. Do it now."

She nodded and gave a wry smile. "I don't want to go, not really. But I can't seem to beat this."

"Do you want to?"

"Of course. What person chooses this? I don't want to be a junkie. I don't want this to be what my daughter remembers about me, or my parents. Or… is my grandpa going to be okay?"

"He is."

She was torn. "That's my fault. I swore I was done with the drugs. I was off everything. Twenty-eight days without a hit of anything. And the day I get out, I overdose." She shook her head. "Twice."

"And this one is different," I said.

"Yeah."

"This is you trying to end it."

"I don't think I want to die."

"Are you sure?" I asked.

"I am. But I don't know if I'll be able to get off drugs."

"That's not the question you need to answer right now. You want to come back into your body?"

"I do."

"Okay, then. You see that little wispy string that comes out of your belly?"

"I see two of them."

"Yeah, but only one is yours. Just walk back down it. It's easy. But before you do, can you answer a couple quick questions for me?"

"I'll try."

"Who gave you the drugs?"

Her tone sank. "My boyfriend."

"What's his name?"

"Dylan."

I nodded. "Is he Penelope's father?"

"He is… and I guess he knocked me up again. What am I going to do about that?" Her gaze was riveted to the strands of yellow-white energy that pulsed from her belly.

"Again," I said, "not a question you need to answer now. You ready to give it another shot?"

"I am."

And as the ED nurse injected a second amp of the overdose medication, Melody and her barely there rider slipped back into her body.

I turned to look at her and caught Trevor's intense hazel-almost-green eyes staring at me. *Damn.* And just like Melody had decisions to make, I needed to figure out what warped game I was in with Trevor. *You're in love with him, you moron. Yeah, but that doesn't mean you have to ruin his life.*

We helped them hoist Melody into a hospital bed. It was the usual Sunday morning suspects in a VA—aides, nurses, docs muscling out on-call shifts. And hanging on the periphery was the strawberry blond from last night's dreams. My gaze flew to her, but no, she was just a beautiful woman doing some kind of weekend pharma work in a high-end suit. But so like the one in those dreams.

"We can't admit her here," a nurse said as they rolled her back into the ED.

I searched for the blond, but she'd vanished. *Like the one from the dreams… different person.*

"We should go," Trevor whispered.

"Not yet." And with a hand on Melody's stretcher, I followed them into an observation cubicle as she opened her eyes.

"Where am I?" she shivered. Gooseflesh popped along the skin of her bare arms.

"Emergency room at the VA," I told her.

The ED doc looked at me and then Trevor from behind her plastic shield. "You brought her in?" she asked. "She a veteran?"

"No. She's a family member of a WWII vet we brought in. Bryan Jordan. He's in a trauma suite right now."

"Great," she said. "So what happened?"

"She OD'd in the bathroom," I said. "And apparently OD'd last night and just got out of rehab yesterday."

"Awesome," the young doctor replied. "You know we can't keep her here. We'll get her some numbers to call, and once she's stable, she'll have to go."

"She's pregnant," I added.

The doctor's wide brown eyes stared back at me. "She told you that?"

"She did, but it's easy to check. My guess, end of her first trimester."

"Crap!"

The room grew silent except for the dings of monitors.

Melody's shivers grew worse. "I'm going to puke," she said.

A nurse helped her sit up and offered her a pink plastic emesis basin.

The ED doc, whose name tag read Rana Chandran, MD/Resident Physician, looked from Melody back to me.

"Do you mind if I make a couple suggestions?" I asked.

"Why not?"

"Get her on some medication to stop the withdrawal." I recommended the drug and the dose. "You don't want to have her miscarry from withdrawal contractions. And then I'd get her admitted to either medicine or gyn, just until you can get her into a program for pregnant women on opioids."

"Those things exist?" the resident asked.

"They do, but it will take a few days to get one to agree to take her, and they're going to want to know that she's medically stable, all of which you guys can handle. Your social worker should know who to call."

"She's not a veteran," the nurse said. "We can't admit her here."

I felt her disdain for Melody. Her contempt was palpable. I swallowed my anger, as it would only bring things to a dead stop. I colored my words. "She's the granddaughter of a veteran and a mother of a three-year-old, and she's got a bad drug problem and a boyfriend named Dylan who's making things worse. Here's the deal…." And I knew that I had the attention of the six socially not distant, masked, gloved, and shielded professionals in that cubicle. "You can save her life today. It's not rocket science. Get her started on meds, get her into a bed, do not let her Dylan visit, and be kind. Because all of the mean things you might think about her… she tells herself far worse. She did not want this for herself. No one does."

Melody curled up on the cot, her knees clutched in her arms. The pink basin had been replaced by a fresh one. Her eyes and nose ran, and with each passing moment, her sickness grew. Plucked from death, she was now in hell, and it would be only another minute or two before she demanded to leave and search out Dylan and drugs. They had a window to help her, but it was about to slam shut.

The resident nodded and ordered the medication I'd suggested. Careful to not further undermine her authority, I scribbled the dose and how often it should be given onto a gauze pad package and slipped it to her.

She read it, nodded, and smiled through her plastic shield. "You get a lot of these?" she asked.

"Every day."

"If she were a vet, we have programs."

"But you know what, Dr. Chandran?"

"It's Rana."

"Rana, you have power here, and when you lose the resident from your name tag, you'll have even more. If doing the right thing means breaking a rule or two…." I shrugged and turned back into the room. "So, Melody." I leaned in to her. "If these people get you on meds, do you think you could give another program a shot? One that's just for women?"

"I don't know…."

"Let them get you feeling better first. Your grandparents are here."

Her expression darkened, and while I could not hear her thoughts, it didn't take a genius to guess. "You've got people who love you." I clutched at straws. "Just get through this moment and the next."

"I'm pregnant," she said and shook her head. "How did I let this happen?"

The nurse returned with the medication. "You need to hold this under your tongue until it's all gone," she instructed. "Don't speak and don't swallow."

She opened her mouth, and the nurse placed a chalky peach oval under tongue.

"We should go," Trevor said.

"Yeah." I stepped back from the bed. No clue if even a portion of what might save this woman's life would happen. Or would she be another James, saved in the morning and dead at night? Plagues inside of plagues.

Rana followed us into the hall. "Those programs that take pregnant women," she said. "do you have any more information?"

I pulled out my cell and did a quick search for Massachusetts residential drug treatment centers for women who were either pregnant and/or had young children. I passed it to her, and she took a picture of the screen with her cell.

"And when she wants to leave AMA?" she asked.

"If you keep her comfortable… and give her some hope, maybe let her family visit… if they don't upset her too much. Just don't let the boyfriend in."

"We have a volunteer we can call," she offered. "You know, someone who used to use drugs but doesn't anymore."

"It might help," I said, and did my best to hide my fear born of experience. *She might not make it.*

"I will try," the resident said.

"I know you will."

"It may not be enough," she said.

"Truer words." We said our goodbyes, retrieved our stretcher, and got back into Eight.

I turned on the engine and backed out.

"You don't think she's going to make it, do you?" Trevor asked.

"I don't know," I admitted, and braced for the inquisition.

"How did you know she was pregnant?"

"She told me."

"She did not," he shot back. "I was there the whole time, and she said nothing close to that."

"You weren't listening."

"Bullshit… wait a minute, she didn't know she was pregnant."

"She did… and she didn't."

He looked out his window, and I pictured the cogs in his still hungover brain creak and churn. "In that waiting room," he began, "you told me not to get the Narcan. Why?"

"Because we needed her to be *their* patient and not ours."

"But what if she'd died because we waited?"

"She wasn't going to." I glanced at him. His mirrored sunglasses no longer hid his blossoming shiner, and the gash on his forehead had oozed through the gauze. "When we get back to the station, you need to let me look at that."

"It's fine, and don't change the subject…." He put a hand to the bandage. "Crap, it must have opened again."

"Like I said."

"Fine… and the boyfriend thing." He was like a dog with a bone. "How did you know his name?"

And before I could answer, he added, "And do not tell me she told you, because again, I was there... for everything. Please, just tell me the truth, Godfrey."

I thought to deflect and suggest a breakfast detour, but there was a bag of bagels and fixings waiting for us at the station. And the thick blood that oozed from his scalp wound made me salivate. Left to my baser instincts, I would have pulled off the road and licked it clean. "Do you really want the truth, Trevor?"

"Yes."

"What if it makes things worse?"

"Just tell me. You saw her, didn't you?"

"Okay. Tell me what you saw, and if you're close I'll fill in the pieces." I stared at the road.

"In the waiting room when she OD'd you were looking up at the wall. Not at her. It was weird, but I've seen you do it before, like with James, like with a lot of them. Like there's someone else in the room."

I turned onto the side road for the station and clicked the remote for the garage bay. "Yes and no." And I cracked open a can of worms.

"Yes and no, what?" he asked.

I drove in, turned off the engine, and stared ahead at shelves of neatly stacked boxes of supplies. *Be careful.* "There was no one else in that room, but...." I turned to look at Trevor, my reflection mirrored in his glasses. "I had a conversation with Melody."

"She was unconscious."

"She was almost dead," I corrected him.

"She was." His jaw hung loose. "You talked with a dead woman."

"An almost-dead woman," I clarified.

Neither one of us moved, and I sat and watched him watch me. I knew that he believed what I'd just told him. But as I'd warned, the truth, my truth, even a whiff, made things worse.

Chapter Twenty-Three
Trevor is Not a Popsicle

"COME ON," Godfrey said. "Let's see what you did to yourself." Without breaking gaze, he opened his door.

I stared into amber rings, the ones that entered my dreams and burrowed into my brain. Questions queued. *He lies. He's playing with you.* I reran the events in the VA. I never left his side. I hunted for his magician's trick, the trapdoor, the distraction, the moment when he asked an unconscious woman for intimate details of her life.

"If you don't like my answers, Trevor, don't ask." He got out of the truck.

"Shit," I muttered. I pictured him staring up at that wall and not at her as he called for a code. It was no one-off. Lots of the OD's, some of the heart attacks, all the bad ones where you don't know if the person in the back will make it. *Is such a thing possible?* Like a plot from an episode of Shannon's favorite shows—*Supernatural*, *Buffy*, and *Lucifer*.

He came around and opened my door. "Don't think about it, Trevor."

"Have you always been able to talk to the almost dead?"

"Pretty much." He stepped back, and I got out.

"You see them too?"

"I do."

"All of them?"

"Yes."

"And you can talk to them?"

"Yes."

"Do they know they're dead… or almost dead?"

"Some. Some aren't sure, some refuse to see it. Let me look at your head, Trevor. The patients are going to think you're the one in need of an ambulance."

"It's not that bad." But I followed him to the kitchen and sat at the table as he assembled gauze, steri-strips, tape, and alcohol. I held still as he undid my drunken pressure bandage. I stared at his throat, his neck like sculpted marble. He swallowed, and I felt his strong fingers tease caked blood from my hair.

"You need stitches," he said.

"I don't care about the scar." I didn't. I deserved punishment for what I'd done. A scar would remind me never to do what I'd done to Shannon.

"Shut up and stay put." He gathered the blood-ied gauze and headed back to the station's business and dispatch office.

I felt numb as I stared at the mirror over the kitchen sink. It was a mistake. I saw him put that disgusting wad of gauze into his mouth. At first I thought it was my imagination, but no, he sucked on it like… like something delicious from an ice-cream truck. Like a popsicle.

I felt the side of my head. I felt warm… fevered. That's what this was. I shouldn't have come to work today. Should have stayed home.

"Here we go." Godfrey pulled up a chair to where our knees touched.

"What are you doing?" I tried to slide my chair back, but the legs caught on the rubberized floor. I started to fall.

"Steady, Trevor."

And faster than I could see, he stopped me… again. I stared at his mouth, full lips, cleft chin…. *No blood. Just my imagination.* My heart pounded in my ears. I struggled to catch my breath.

"You're okay." He righted the chair with a single hand and pulled down my mask. "Just breathe." He cracked a smile. "It's a lot to process. I get that."

I felt heavy in my body. Even if I'd wanted to get away, I couldn't. But I didn't want to get away. His knees pressed against mine. He pulled his chair in.

He ripped open gauze packets and soaked them in alcohol. "This will hurt," he said as he sterilized and cleaned the wound.

I glanced at the table, and among the tape and gauze was a sewing kit used to pop back the occasional button. I pointed. "You're kidding, right?"

"You need stitches," he said. "I'm not going to let your Catholic guilt leave your beautiful face with a Harry Potter scar."

"But that's not sterile. It's….." *And you think my face is beautiful. And when did I turn into a twelve-year-old girl?* "Do you know what you're doing?" But as I watched his long fingers thread the tiniest needle in the pack and run it back and forth through an alcohol-soaked cotton ball, I made another realization. "You've done this before."

"Yes."

The fingers of his left hand landed on my temple and applied gentle pressure to the edges of the wound. I braced for the needle's bite, but it never came. As he cleaned and stitched my wound, I stared at his perfectly symmetrical face, long black lashes around movie star eyes. Another mistake. Because I wasn't the one who was beautiful, who random cops, nurses, and countless others slipped their numbers. He glowed like a stained-glass angel, his hair, like a raven's wing… he stopped and caught me in mid ogle.

"It's okay." He turned back to his needlework.

I felt exposed, ashamed, and worse… aroused.

His arm brushed mine as he retrieved a tiny pair of scissors from the sewing kit. He snipped the threads. "All done."

"I didn't feel it," I said.

He put his hands on my shoulders and looked me dead-on. It gave me a strange sensation in my gut. I stared back at him, and my vision darkened, like a scene that goes to black in a movie. I must have passed out. But I could swear he leaned in and kissed my forehead, but… more like my cat. I think he licked me. I opened my eyes. "What just happened?"

"You fainted."

"Right." His hands hadn't budged, and our un-masked faces were inches apart. A part of me wanted to pull away and to break from his gaze. But another part…. "Did you just kiss my forehead?"

"I did."

Okay. I did not imagine that… or this was a dream. "Did you just lick me?"

"Yes."

"Why?" I tried to swallow, but my mouth was bone-dry.

"You'll heal faster."

"That's not true. Human saliva is filled with bacteria. It's more likely to get infected."

"No," he said without pause. "It will help you heal."

"I'm not a popsicle." I leaned in and slid my hands up the sides of his face, the feel of stubble against my palms. *What the fuck am I doing? Stop. Don't!* I kissed him. I had to know. The instant my lips landed on his, I did. *Not good.* He kissed back. *So good. This is not happening.* My tongue sought his. This was not me. A hunger unlike anything I'd known welled, and I was out of my chair and on top of him. My lips pressed against his; my fingers clawed at the back of his head and ripped that stupid ribbon from his hair. I wanted to devour him. Bells rang, and I could not stop. *I'm going to hell. I don't care.*

His hands pressed against my shoulders, and he pushed me back.

I grabbed for him. *No! More. I want more.*

"Trevor." He sounded distant, sad. "We have a call."

"I'm sorry." I clutched for the back of my chair and made doubly certain it—and I—were steady. "I'm so sorry." *What did I just do?*

"Not your fault. You did nothing wrong." He reached for his cell, which lay among the garbage from his kitchen surgery. "Cavalry Ambulance. What's your emergency?" He wedged the phone under his ear, retrieved the black ribbon from the floor, tied his curls back, and tucked them beneath his collar.

What have I done? I couldn't catch my breath.

"We'll be there in fifteen." He looked at me. "Come on, Trevor, it's not the end of the world."

"You can read my thoughts too?"

"No. Your face. Your beautiful, beat up, mortified face."

I felt my temple. He hadn't replaced the bandage, and I ran my forefinger over his tiny cotton stitches. I stood, grabbed the back of the chair till the dizziness passed, and caught a look in the mirror. With all the strange revelations, what I saw gave me great pause. My wound from last night, which by rights should have brought me to an emergency room, was perfectly dry. The edges were sealed tight around five identical stitches, each topped with a complex knot unlike any I'd seen. "How… how do you know how to do that?"

"Practice." He headed back toward the garage. "It makes perfect."

Chapter Twenty-Four
The Mad Woman of Copley Square

NONE OF this is good... then again... so good. I'd done the thing I'd promised myself not to. I'd tasted Trevor's blood. Behind the wheel of Eight, I savored... him. And then he'd kissed me. It was unexpected, wicked hot, a bit sloppy, and now... he headed toward me, the dark glasses on, cheeks flushed, and his Cavalry mask beneath his chin.

He opened the passenger door, climbed in, and stared ahead, his expression unreadable.

"You okay?" I asked.

"Just drive."

"Okay. But for the record, you kissed me."

"Shut up, Godfrey."

Telling me to shut up is like waving a red cape in front of a bull. I tried... I did, really. But here's the thing. As I drove out into what had turned into a glorious fall day, the sugar maples and sumacs ablaze with reds and oranges, the air cool and dry, and my chest about to burst with an emotion I haven't felt in a long time, I did not want to shut up. I wanted to sing. I lowered my window and hummed an old tune, Spanish. I tried to remember the words and where I'd first heard it… a synagogue… but not in Spain, in Istanbul. The words came back, a prayer in a minor key, the notes slurred outside the diatonic scale, like a baseball player set to steal a base.

I felt Trevor's attention, though he wouldn't look at me. So I sang in full voice and caught glimpses of him as he pulled down the lighted mirror on the back of the sun visor—and yes, ambulances have those—and examined his stitches. When he thought I wasn't looking, he snapped a picture of his forehead on his phone and enlarged it with his fingers.

"I do good work," I said.

"You're freaking me out, Godfrey." His humorless tone matched his words.

"I know. I'm sorry." And I took the Stuart Street exit off the Pike and headed toward Copley Plaza.

"I wish you'd stop."

"Is that what you want?" I dreaded his answer. Because if he wanted me out of his life and he meant it, I would leave. *I am not a rapist. I am not a monster. Yeah, you kind of are.*

"I don't know." He stared at his phone.

I turned onto Clarendon and spotted two patrol cars and a small cluster of pedestrians and uniformed officers in the plaza across from the public library.

I drove toward them and up onto the sidewalk, between a cement planter and a glass-cased map of downtown.

Trevor got out without another word. I followed him.

He approached one of the officers as I spotted our next patient, a homeless woman with a face like a dried apple, her wrinkles both etched and fleshy. A cut bled over her left eye, and she clutched her right arm in pain. She wore layers of skirts, sweaters, and shirts, all in reds and purples. Her feet, covered in high rubber galoshes, pressed hard into the ground as she braced against a toppled shopping cart. "Stay away," she shouted. "Stay away. God sees all. You will be punished."

I broke through the onlookers. "Good morning, ma'am. I'm Godfrey. I can see that you're hurt."

"Devil," she shrieked and pointed at me. "Get thee behind me, Satan."

I smiled and tried for eye contact. From the angle of her arm, even buried in all that fabric, I could tell the shoulder was dislocated. The cut on her head—like Trevor's—gushed and splattered. She ranted and tried to protect her upended cart and its contents. "Ma'am, what's your name?" I crouched down and felt the distance between us. Tears flowed, and the ground was a Jackson Pollock of her blood.

"That's Bonnie." A young dark-haired woman in jeans, flannel shirt, and black Doc Martens boots came up behind me. "She's a regular at our shelter."

"What happened?"

"I don't know," she said, "I was on a coffee run, and she was lying on the ground. I tried to help her up, but she's really hurt. I called 911. Wait a minute.... Bonnie, where's your pocketbook?"

"Devils!" she shrieked and pressed back against her cart.

"It's okay, Bonnie," I offered and held out my hands. "We're here to help."

She shrieked at me. "You are the devil! You want to tear my flesh. You want to devour me."

"Bonnie." The woman from the shelter inched closer. "What happened?"

The woman wailed, "They stole from me! They stole my babies!" She threw her head back and stared toward Trinity church. "Why, God? Why? I want my children. My babies!"

Trevor reappeared with the stretcher and wheeled it up to Bonnie. Without hesitation, he dropped cross-legged to the ground next to her. "Bonnie, I'm Trevor." He held out his gloved hand.

She looked at him wide-eyed, and at his hand, and shook her head no. "It hurts," she whimpered.

"I can see that," he said. "I'm so sorry. Did someone hurt you?"

She sobbed and winced. "They stole my babies. Why? Why?"

"People can be cruel." He looked at me and jerked his head, which I took to mean "Get the stretcher prepped."

The woman from the shelter followed as I undid the straps, freed the backboard, and locked the wheels.

"Bonnie," Trevor said, "we have to get you to a hospital."

"No." She shook her head and blood flew. Then she tried to reach back, but the pain from her wounded arm stopped her. She gasped and hyperventilated.

The shelter worker stepped in. "Bonnie," she said. "It's me, Cheryl. I'll take your stuff back. I'll keep it safe. No one will touch it, I promise."

"Why? They took my babies. Why?" Bonnie sobbed, her voice softer.

"I don't know," Trevor said softly. "It's going to be okay. I promise. My partner, Godfrey, and I will put you on a backboard so things don't hurt so much when we move you. We can give you a shot of something for the pain, if you'd like."

"No." She stiffened. "No shots. I won't let you rape me." She stared at me. Her teeth chattered. "He's a devil!"

"Yeah, he can be," Trevor said. "But he's mostly okay."

"Don't leave me alone with him."

"I won't, not for a second."

"Promise."

"I do. And Cheryl will keep your stuff safe, but we have to get you to a hospital and get you fixed up."

"I don't like hospitals. They're filled with snakes." Her eyes stayed fixed on me. "And devils—devils in white coats and pretty blue shirts. They don't think I can see them, but I do. With their pointy teeth and horns. That one has horns."

"Yes, he does," Trevor agreed as he reached for the backboard that lay on top of the stretcher.

I helped him get it to the ground as he coaxed Bonnie to inch away from her toppled cart and onto the wooden board. An officer stepped in to help Cheryl from the shelter upend Bonnie's cart and retrieve several plastic doll heads and limbs that had fallen out, along with a frayed teddy bear and a stuffed three-legged elephant.

Trevor gentled his hand onto Bonnie's good shoulder. He looked across at me and shook his head.

"She's got bad arthritis," I said, reading his concern and that she'd be in agony if we forced her back onto the board.

"Bonnie," he said. "I need you to sit on the board and hold perfectly still while we lift you onto the stretcher."

"Don't drop me." With her good hand, she tried to steady her injured shoulder.

"We won't," he said. "But you have to keep still."

He helped her inch onto the board, but she looked back at her cart. "Keep them safe," she cautioned Cheryl.

"We will, Bonnie. They'll be waiting for you when you come out."

"You need help?" one of the officers asked.

"Yes, please," Trevor said. "Just grab one of the handholds."

And with a minimum of fuss, Bonnie, seated atop the board, made it onto the stretcher. We strapped it down, and the crowd of masked onlookers parted as we wheeled her toward Number Eight.

"Devil," she muttered.

"True words," Trevor said as we collapsed the legs and got her into the truck. "How can you tell?" he asked.

"Don't be a smartass," I said, but I was relieved that he didn't seem so... off center, freaked out.

"He bears the mark," Bonnie growled. "Pretty on the outside, rotten to the core. Get thee behind me."

"He does have to drive us," Trevor said as he settled her into the back, clicked the stretcher in, and took his seat on the bench.

"That should be okay," she said. "Just because he's a devil doesn't mean he can't be useful."

"Bonnie," Trevor said, "I need to examine you, but if it hurts too much, let me know and I'll stop." He lightly touched her injured but sweater-cushioned shoulder.

She screamed, and he pulled his hand back. "You know what," he said, "let's just get you to the hospital."

I closed the rear doors, got behind the wheel, and called the dispatcher for instructions on where to take her.

As I pulled out, I spotted the social worker from the shelter in conversation with a pair of cops, her hand on Bonnie's toy-filled cart. There was a fair amount of traffic for early Sunday afternoon, but I opted to forego the siren. Instead I cranked the speaker so I could hear what was happening in back.

"About that mark of the devil," Trevor asked. "What's it look like?"

Bastard. He knows I'm listening. I looked in the mirror. They faced one another—an impromptu pair of conspirators.

"A serpent with three heads," she answered.

"How come I can't see it?" he asked.

"You don't have the sight," she said. "I do."

"What is that?"

"I'm the seventh daughter of the seventh daughter, born with the caul. The queer child."

"You see things that others can't?"

"Yes, always have, always will."

"And you think Godfrey is a devil."

She paused. "Not exactly. He *is* handsome. He *is* pretty. He plays a merry tune, but he reeks of blood and dust…." Her voice trailed.

That's not so bad, I mused. But she kept going.

"He is unclean and not of God." She snorted. "Even his name—Godfrey…. God Free…. That can't be good. Especially on a Sunday. My babies." She looked panicked. "They took my babies."

"They're safe," Trevor reassured her. "They'll wait for you."

"No," she wept. "They stole my babies. They need me. Children need their mother."

"They do."

Something in his expression pulled at me. There was no irony, no ridicule of this crazy woman with her shopping cart filled with broken dolls and torn plushies. He tended to her head wound, not so different from his own.

"You live at the shelter," he said as he wrapped a length of gauze around her head to hold the bandage taut.

"It's no place for children," she sighed.

"You said you're from a big family. Can you live with one of them?"

"They're worse than your Godfrey."

"How so?"

"They call me names and tell lies. They say I'm psychophrenic. And the doctors, the ones you bring me to, you have to watch them. Rapists, all rapists."

"I don't think so," he said.

"You don't know. Pretty words and lies, and you have schizophrenia and a jab to the shoulder, or they yank down your pants and jab you in the ass and steal your children and tie you to a bed. If that's not a rapist…."

"Point taken," he said. "You've had a hard road."

She winced as I hit a pothole. "I don't want to go to the hospital. They'll call me names. They'll lock me on a psych ward. I'm no psycho. I don't want their drugs."

"Bonnie." He touched a hand to the side of the stretcher. "Then don't give them the power to do that. Here's what you should do. Tell them you were mugged and that you live at the shelter and have a bed you can go back to. Say nothing about your babies. Cheryl has them and they're safe."

"But they stole."

"I know, but if you want to get treated and released…."

She nodded. "I was mugged and live at the shelter."

"That should work," he said, and he tucked and taped the gauze, his movements tender, his tone kind.

I replayed his kiss, almost violent in how he'd lunged for me and held me. *He should not have done that... but he did.* And the truth was not just that I'd fallen in love with him, but something more I couldn't fathom. It had to do with crazy Bonnie, who experience had taught me might not be so crazy—more like a radio tuned to a station that others can't get.

I backed into a bay at the massive New England Medical Center off Tremont and Washington in the middle of Chinatown and what used to be the red-light district. I got out and opened the back.

"You two got thick as thieves," I offered as I clicked the stretcher release.

She looked at Trevor and shook her head. "I suppose he's your devil." She sighed, and we lifted her down.

"God free. God free." Her voice swelled.

"Bonnie, pull it back," Trevor said as the plate glass doors swished open and we rolled toward triage.

"He's drenched in blood," she hissed. "Bathed in blood. Birthed in blood. God free. God free."

I watched Trevor try to navigate Bonnie through her ED experience. At the triage window, he explained, "She was mugged, her right shoulder is dislocated, probably from trying to hang on to her purse."

The nurse, a woman in her fifties who looked like she'd sat at that desk for decades, grunted. "Any loss of consciousness?"

"Not certain. But she has a laceration over her right temple. She went down hard. She'll need stitches."

And they won't be as neat as mine, I thought, and I remembered the Polish battlefield surgeon who'd taught me how to make them... over a hundred years ago. "Sew in the valley of the wrinkle," he'd instructed me. "Or where the wrinkle will be one day if they don't die here. That way the scar will be invisible."

"Cardiac history?" the nurse asked as she stuck to her script and didn't look at Trevor.

Just doing her job... but what is he doing? Me. And I stopped myself before my head got too big. *Yes, he's trying to imitate me... but for our patient.* My chest ached. It was why I was falling, had fallen, in love with him—his kindness, his belief in right and wrong, even his faith, which I'd once shared. But here he was trying to make this nurse care for poor Bonnie.

"Do you have her insurance card?" the nurse asked.

"No." He leaned in, and I sensed the smile beneath his mask. "They stole her pocketbook." His voice lowered to something sexy, almost a growl.

Well done, Trevor. If she wasn't interested, I was.

She looked up. "People can be awful," she said. "Do you have her last name?"

He turned back to our patient, who moaned and cradled her damaged shoulder. "Bonnie, what's your last name?"

"Why?" Her gaze narrowed.

"So the nurse can get you taken care of."

She shook her head. "I'm not giving it. They'll use it against me in a court of law. I know my rights.

I have a right to remain silent, and you're not going to use it against me. I want my babies."

The nurse looked through her plexi window at Bonnie, took in the layered sweaters and shirts that Trevor had opted to not cut away, a decision I agreed with. "Doe it is," she said, and then in a voice that she thought only Trevor could hear, "It's Canfield, Bonnie Canfield. She's a frequent flyer to psych."

"She's in a lot of pain," Trevor said.

"Yeah. We'll take care of her. Bring her back to Trauma Three." And she smiled at Trevor, her earlier officiousness replaced by warmth. "You did good."

"Thank you," he said.

"She's right," I told him as we found the cubicle and an orderly helped us transfer Bonnie from our backboard and stretcher to their bed.

"I didn't want them to send her back to psych," he said. "She's really hurt, and I feel bad that I couldn't do a better exam on her."

"I would have done the same," I said.

"Right." His gaze narrowed. "Because you don't follow rules."

I said nothing and helped settle Bonnie.

"Unclean thing," she hissed. "I want my babies."

"Okay, then." I stepped back as Trevor, two orderlies, and an ED nurse set to work. "Take your time," I said. "I'll do the paperwork."

"Yeah, right."

"Promise." And I retrieved our stretcher and blood-spattered board, closed the screen to Bonnie's cubicle, and headed back through the ED and out to the ambulance bays.

The sun shone high, and a trio of spindly maple seedlings with flame-red leaves rustled in the breeze. I grabbed the spray bottle of disinfectant from the back and set to wiping down surfaces. I wadded the soiled linen and grabbed fresh from the plastic-fronted cabinets.

Bonnie's accusations echoed. She'd struck a nerve, several if I were honest. And it didn't help that this was the absolute low point of my day. I was famished, and while I can go for long stretches without blood, I prefer not to. The longer I wait, the more it clouds my thoughts, and the more I just want… to nap.

I looked at the bank of glass doors, clicked the lock on Eight, and went back in. The ED was relatively quiet, other than Bonnie's loud protests as they tried to get her out of those sweaters. Had Trevor even attempted to cut them off in the ambulance, we'd be stopped on the road, need multiple backups, and have to sedate and restrain her. It still smarted, those names she'd hurled at me.

"Truth hurts," I whispered into my mask, and I left the ED in search of my lunch.

HALFWAY THROUGH a delicious third-year medical student, my cell buzzed. "Where are you?" Trevor asked.

"Cafeteria," I lied from the cozy dark of a third-floor supply closet.

"That's where I am," he said. "I don't see you."

Oops. "On my way to the cafeteria." And I pressed a finger to the lips of the ecstatic young woman, soon to be pediatrician, as she moaned and shivered the length of her body against mine.

"Are you with someone?"

"I'm on my way." I hung up.

"You good?" I asked the young woman, whose name tag was obscured by the collar of her short white jacket.

"So good."

"I've got to go."

"No…. Don't."

"Sorry."

"Can I give you my number?"

"Of course." And into the patch pocket of my pants it went.

Sated and more awake, I went to find Trevor.

He was easy to spot—the back of his light blue Cavalry shirt and his thick auburn hair that sparked red and gold in the light that spilled through the high cafeteria windows, almost like a halo.

He sensed my approach and turned. "Where have you been?"

"I turned over the ambulance."

"Yes, I saw… thank you. Where have you been?" he repeated.

I sank into the chair across from him. "You okay?"

"Godfrey, please stop the lies. Just tell me where you've been. It's not a difficult question."

"I was on the wards." I hoped he'd let it drop.

"Why?"

A list of plausible lies flew to mind. *I was bored. I wanted to get my steps in. I have an aunt in a COVID ward.* But the truth—*I was hungry, and there was a luscious dark-haired medical student who was all too happy to give me a quick bite*—would have gone over about as well as trying to cut off Bonnie's hard-won clothes in the back of Eight. I met his suspicious gaze and said nothing.

"You're not talking."

"I'll take the fifth."

"Right. How much of what she said was true?"

"You know she's crazy."

His jaw tensed. "What are you doing with me?"

It was a horrible question. I saw he was in pain, and not from his injuries or the hangover that had finally abated. Words would not come.

"I'm sort of dying here," he said. "What were you doing on the wards… or should I say who were you doing up on the wards?" He looked down at a half-drunk coffee clutched in his hands and then back at me. "Say something. Please."

"I can't," I admitted.

"You won't," he corrected, "because you know it's not what I want to hear."

I startled. "True. I don't want to hurt you, Trevor."

"Too late." He pushed back from the table and stood. "We have a call." He looked at the screen on his cell. "And when we finish this shift, Godfrey, I'm going to ask for a new partner. I can't do this."

Chapter Twenty-Five
Love and COVID

GODFREY DROVE toward our next call—a Peter Hardwick in Cambridge—in silence. There was nothing to say, and I wanted to hit him. To demand answers. Why was he doing this to me? His weirdness, his games, his crazy stories about seeing… and talking to people, as they hovered between life and death. I stared out the window as we left Chinatown and drove past the Commons and the Gardens, past the Taj Hotel that used to be the Ritz, then down the mostly shuttered shops of Newbury Street. Some had reopened since COVID. Some had closed forever.

Bonnie called him a devil, and wasn't that the truth? Prince of lies, one heaped onto the next. *And I kissed him… after he licked me.* "Is everything a game with you?"

"It's not a game." He took the right onto Mass Ave across the Charles River to Cambridge.

"Yeah, it is, Godfrey." And all the jumbled thoughts, the twisted emotions, the Catholic guilt, and who I thought I was, erupted. "I'm a toy to you. Let's seduce the straight boy and get him to break up with his girlfriend. Get him to break her heart. Won't that be fun? Well, it's not."

"It's not a game." He turned down a side road and parked in front of a weathered brick 1920s apartment building. "You're not a toy. And you're right, we should not work together anymore."

Shit. And why does he sound so sad... so sincere? I wanted to say something, to take back everything I'd said... but it was true. So why did I feel worse? Like something in my chest was set to break.

"Come on." He opened his door. "Let's just get through this shift. You feel up to driving now? 'Cause it's not my favorite."

"Yeah." My hangover had dimmed to a dull ache, no longer the steel torture device around my head.

He tossed me the keys and fob. "Good."

I pulled on a new mask and followed him out as a woman in her fifties or sixties appeared through the building's outer security door. She held it open as Godfrey approached. He asked her a few brief questions and gestured to me to get the stretcher.

I climbed into Eight and piled on the kit box and portable oxygen, my thoughts a jumble. *I shouldn't have said anything.... He licked my forehead, that's not normal.* He appeared at the back and unclipped the stretcher from the retaining bar. With a practiced "One, two, three," we dropped the wheels and rolled.

"He didn't want me to call," the masked woman said as we walked up the half flight and entered the lobby.

She pressed the button for the elevator, and Godfrey asked, "How long has your husband been ill?"

"Two weeks—fever, chills, all of it—but it's his breathing… it's gone too far. For such a brilliant man, he can be an absolute moron."

"Has he seen a doctor?" Godfrey asked as we got in.

"He won't go. He never does. I tried." She pressed the third-floor button.

"He hasn't been tested for COVID?" I asked.

"No. But several of his colleagues at the college had it… what else could it be?"

With Godfrey at the front and me at the back of the stretcher, we followed her to an apartment, the door left ajar.

"He'll be furious that I called," she said.

"You did right," Godfrey said as we wheeled over dark parquet floors and past tightly packed floor-to-ceiling bookshelves.

She led us down the corridor to an airy bedroom, where light spilled through sheers that billowed on a soft fall breeze. Godfrey went to the bed and sat on the edge.

I took in the thin white-haired man propped on pillows. I could see his skull through his taut flesh and wondered if we were too late.

"Peter," Godfrey said in a soft voice. "Dr. Hardwick."

I wondered how he knew to add the doctor—maybe something in the conversation he'd had with his wife, or he just figured it out from the books, or….

The man's eyes cracked open, and he struggled to draw breath through parched lips. He looked from Godfrey to his wife and then to me. He coughed, and his body shook as he hacked uncontrollably and violently.

"Dr. Hardwick, my name is Godfrey. That's my partner, Trevor. We need to take you to the hospital."

The man shook his head no, and a wave of coughs overtook him. He doubled over, his face reddened, and he grimaced.

Godfrey placed a gloved hand on the man's forehead and a stethoscope to his chest, but even from ten feet away, I heard the COVID gurgle in his lungs.

"It's going to be okay," Godfrey said.

I slid the stretcher in tight next to the bed, and we gentled the frail man from the comfort of his four-poster to our stretcher.

"No hospital," he wheezed.

His skin was hot to the touch.

"Peter," his wife interjected. "Don't be a twit. You're going to the hospital. If you die on me…."

"I'm not dying." And again, explosive coughs as he tried to clear fluid-filled lungs.

I saw him want to argue, but there was no fight left, almost no life at all as he struggled to breathe, like a drowning man. I ripped open the package on a plastic rebreather mask and passed it to Godfrey.

He strapped it onto Dr. Hardwick and handed me the tube. I cranked the oxygen.

"Eight liters," Godfrey said as we followed the now-routine COVID protocol that hadn't existed before March.

"What should I bring?" the woman asked as she closed the bedroom windows.

"His insurance cards," Godfrey said. "You can ride in back with me."

"Thank you." And with no further argument, we were out the door and en route.

I pulled out with lights, but as traffic was sparse, no siren. I called the dispatcher with a five-minute ETA and focused on the road ahead... sort of. I flipped the screen from the GPS to the cabin camera that gave me a bird's eye to the action in back. I swallowed my frustration with Godfrey's refusal to do paperwork in transport and focused on what he did so well—take awful situations and make them better. I drove and I listened.

"Try not to talk, Dr. Hardwick," he said. "They'll give you some steroids when we get to the emergency room. It will make your breathing much easier."

The man nodded, and his gaze flitted from Godfrey to his wife.

She gripped his hand. "I should have called sooner," she fretted.

"You tried to," Godfrey said.

"Yes... for days. He hates hospitals."

"They're not good places," Godfrey said. "But in this case, necessary."

"You've seen a lot of COVID?" the woman asked.

"Yes. He'll be okay."

She nodded. "You're just saying that."

"No. I'm not. He'll stay for about a week. We caught him soon enough to where they won't have to put him on a ventilator, but just. They'll want to make sure of that before they let you take him home."

"How can you know?" she asked.

"Lots of little things," Godfrey said. "His color is still good, so he's moving enough air, he's a non-smoker, generally in good health... runner?"

"Yes, we both are. But how...?"

"It shows, though he's going to need some major nutrition when this is done. How long have the two of you been married?"

"Almost thirty-five years."

"And you're both professors?"

"Yes... we met in graduate school."

And through the tiny screen, I saw something pass between her and her husband—a squeeze of the hand, a hint of a smile through his oxygen mask.

"From your library," Godfrey said, "I'd guess one of you is medieval studies and the other is...." He paused. "Genetics?"

"That's spot-on," she said. "You're a very astute paramedic"—she stared at his name tag—"Godfrey Hesse."

"Observant."

"And young," she said. "Is this your career path?"

"For now. Then medical school."

"Good," she said. "And your partner... Trevor?"

"The same."

She turned from him back to her husband, who had closed his eyes and took small careful breaths of oxygen-enriched air.

"May I make an observation?" she asked.

"Of course, Dr. Hardwick."

"Please, it's Elizabeth. I'm Dr. Hardwick during office hours."

"And on the cover of a couple dozen books," he added. "*Death and Rebirth of the Italian City States*, *Love and Commerce Amid the Great Pestilence*, and one that I thought was excellent—*Giovanni Bocaccio, Witness to History*."

"You read that?" she sounded incredulous.

"It won a heap of awards, and the reviews did *not* do it justice. So good. Almost like you were there. And the chapters that summarized the latest medical theories on the pestilence… I think they're damn close. It wasn't a single pathogen—not possible—but at least three, probably two viral and then yersinia pestis, the bacteria that everyone focuses on," he said.

"Now you're showing off. But I can do that too, Godfrey Hesse. Your Trevor…."

The way she said it made my breath quicken. *I'm not his Trevor.*

"Yes," Godfrey answered.

"You have feelings for him," she stated.

"I do."

"Does he know that?"

"Yes… sort of. It's a problem. And if you can pardon my language, it sucks… for me."

"Why is that?" she asked. "Oh." She glanced my way. "He doesn't feel the same."

"Worse," Godfrey said. "He doesn't want to."

"I'm sorry," she said.

I tried to read his expression, but between the mask, the plastic shield, and the camera angle, it was hard, but I heard.

"Heartache is not all bad," he said. "It reminds you that you're alive."

Distracted by their conversation, I missed the ED ramp for the accepting hospital. I hit the siren, checked for oncoming traffic, made an awkward U-turn across four lanes, corrected my error, and shot into an open ambulance bay.

We finished the run at the hospital and took our leave of the Doctors Hardwick. But all that Godfrey had predicted came to pass. They gave him a shot of steroids in the ED, hooked him to an intravenous, kept the oxygen flowing, and decided not to intubate but to send him to a medical floor for observation.

"I need to make a call," Godfrey said, and he ducked into a staff lounge.

I stood in the hall and tried to process what I'd heard. The piece that ran like a mouse in a wheel, around and around? He has feelings for me. *And I have feelings for him, fucked-up and twisted feelings that I should not have… but I do.* And from there I was back at that kiss, that wonderful, life-fucking-up kiss. He was right. I did not want whatever this was. If I could have taken a knife and hacked it out, I would have. *But....*

I peered through the open door of the lounge. He had his phone under his ear and a yellow stick-um I'd seen earlier that morning in his fingers. "Fuck him," I said aloud... too loud, as it got me a curious glance from a pair of nurses as they walked past. *He has feelings for me, all right.* Final straw. I needed to get far away from Godfrey's bullshit. I knew what was on that paper, probably one of dozens that swirled in the patch pocket of his pants like a fish-bowl lottery. And the lucky winner of a strings-free hookup with Godfrey is... that fucking cop from this morning's run. Disgusted, I went out to Eight and wrote an email to our boss to request an immediate change in partner. I read it, reread it, and hit Send.

Chapter Twenty-Six
Pus Under Pressure

I FISHED into the Velcro-closured pocket on my right thigh. My finger caught on the goo of a stick-um, and I pulled it out. *That's the one.* Not into this, but if I only followed my emotions, I'd stay in bed under the covers, eating chocolates with the curtains drawn.

I looked at the name and number and dialed.

"Officer Carmichael."

"Raphael?"

"Who is this?"

"Godfrey, the medic from this morning."

"Hello, Godfrey. That old guy do okay?"

"Bit of family drama." I paused. "Truth is, the best thing that could have happened to him was driving off that road."

"How's that?" Raphael asked.

"Like a boil," I said.

"That's weird."

"It's something surgeons say," I explained. "Pus under pressure must be lanced. If you don't get the infection out, there's no chance to heal. It festers and worsens." The first time I'd heard that truism was from Gaius, who might well have coined it. Only then it wasn't a pimple, ingrown hair, or boil, but massive pus-filled buboes that he'd slit with a Damascus-steel knife in the neck, under the arms, or the groin. And the smell when they burst.... Sometimes it worked and healing would take hold, but often it was too little too late.

"Gross. But makes sense." Brief pause. "And can I see you?"

And here's where I felt like a bit of a shit, but... "Raphael, can I ask a favor?"

"Maybe. Is it contingent on my getting to see you?"

"No. Two separate things."

"Okay, then. What's the favor?"

There was no way to massage this. "If I gave you a license plate number, could you run it?"

Silence. "Why would you want that?" All flirtation gone. He sounded wary.

I went with a modicum of truth. "We've had a slew of ODs recently. All with the same batch of fentanyl."

"Yeah. It's gotten worse since COVID."

"Right... I think this plate belongs to someone midway in the supply chain of a particularly deadly batch."

"You trying to do my job, Godfrey?"

"Do I get to carry a stick?"

"Would you like to carry my stick?" he asked.

"That was cheesy." *And we're back on track... sort of.*

He laughed. "It was… and I'm usually not. It just slipped out. And I don't give my number to random hot guys. After I did, I was like… Raphael, what the fuck did you just do? You have to believe me, Godfrey. I don't do this kind of thing. And now I'm rambling, so I'll shut up."

"Don't sweat it." And I pushed everything I had over the airwaves. But the phone is not as good as in-person for my skills.

"If I got you the information, what would you do with it?" he asked.

"Work my way back," I said.

"That's how people get killed. I'm sorry, God-frey, but there's no way in hell I'll do this. But it could be good information. I won't waste it." There was another silence. "You still there?"

"Yeah."

"I'm thinking you're no longer interested in meeting up…."

"Like I said, two separate things."

"Glad to hear that. When does your shift end?"

"Not till 8:00 a.m."

"Could I take you to breakfast?"

"You could."

"And now I've got your number."

"Yes, you do," I said, but in truth, he had no clue.

"Breakfast at eight?"

I resisted the urge to rhyme—*sounds great, don't be late, that's my sister Kate*. But couldn't stop myself. "It's a date."

"Cool. I'll pick the place?"

"Excellent."

As Raphael hung up, I glanced up and saw Trevor pass through the ED's electronic doors. Things had taken a nosedive, and I couldn't see a way to pull out of the inevitable crash. I'd let him glimpse behind the curtain, and what he saw was unacceptable. *I* was unacceptable. *And why are you surprised? What did you expect? You are what you are.*

"Buck up, little camper," I told myself as the company cell buzzed from its holster. It was our next call—a five-year-old with a backyard mishap—followed by a message ding from Trevor telling me to move it.

There was a hollow buzz between my ears, a pit in my gut, and pure ick as I climbed into the passenger side of Eight. Trevor would not look at me.

"Let's go," he said.

It was obvious I'd done something else to piss him off. Not certain what, but at this point, did it matter? I glanced at the clock on the GPS screen. It was 5:00 p.m., and we weren't even halfway through the shift, which would be followed by a date with Officer Raphael. Although what Raphael hoped to get and what I intended to learn were different. I looked out my window and studied Trevor's reflection. He hadn't put his mask back on, and his jaw ground in anger.

Right. Pus under pressure must be lanced. "So, Trevor. Out of curiosity, and seeing as you want a new partner, why did you kiss me?"

Chapter Twenty-Seven
Mount St. Trevor

"SERIOUSLY?" I asked. 'Cause wasn't this pure Godfrey? Take a bad situation and... I put the truck into gear. If I focused on work, and hopefully we'd stay busy, then I could get home, switch partners, and never have to deal with his bullshit again.

"Absolutely."

"Why do you care?" I glanced at the GPS and picked the most direct route. "Is it so important to have me as another notch on your bed? Am I supposed to be flattered? I kissed you because I was still drunk, hungover as hell, and.... Just fuck off. I did it."

"And enjoyed it."

I clamped my jaw shut. I had enjoyed it... a lot.

"While we're at it," he said, "when you broke into my home... because you thought I was doing drugs, which to repeat, I am not... at least not those, did you go up to my bedroom, take a look around, peek inside the drawers?"

"I said I'm sorry." And I pictured his bed, framed by organ pipes, the room flooded with rainbow light that spilled through the stained glass.

"Yeah, you did…. We both know that doesn't count."

I put on the siren to get through a weirdly empty Harvard Square, with no street performers or throngs of Sunday shoppers, and caught his stare. Mistake. Framed in the window, I got the full effect—his amber-rimmed eyes and raven's-wing hair, and something about his face that was hard to pin down. At times he looked younger than me, almost like a teenager, but then a shift in his mood or the light and he seemed older, much.

A Prius honked as I nearly clipped it.

"Eyes on the road, Trevor," Godfrey said.

I course corrected and shot over the bridge. The image of his face hung in my mind's eye—no lines or wrinkles, skin like marble, and I remembered the feel of him, his hair, his flesh, how he tasted. My throat went dry. "What do you want from me?" I croaked.

"I'd rather not say." He sounded sad.

"Why?" I risked a quick look at him.

His brow knit, troubled. "Because you're going to break my heart."

That's not what I expected. The tips of my fingers tingled on the wheel. *Stop this. Stop this!* It was hard to focus, and then I pictured that yellow stick-um. And knew I was being played. Just lies, lies on top of lies. "You called that cop from this morning."

"I did…. And you're still spying on me. Didn't Father Calvin tell you to stop that?"

"Don't turn this back on me." *Why am I so mad?* "You got his number, called him, and then tell me that *I'm* going to break your heart. You are so full of shit, Godfrey, it oozes out of you."

"That was descriptive. But you're wrong, Trevor. You've jumped to a wrong conclusion."

"Okay. So, you telling me you're not hooking up with that cop?"

"That's what I'm telling you."

"Bullshit. Does he know that?"

"No."

"And?"

"And what? What is it you want from me?" he lobbed the question I'd asked back to me.

I hit the gas and focused on the traffic. "Why won't you just answer my questions?" I drove across the Charles and headed toward the Fenway. "Tell me why you called that cop if it's not to get your rocks off." *Why do I care?*

"I want him to run a plate for me."

"What?"

"A license plate, you know, those metal things on the fronts and backs of cars."

"Dick. Why? Whose plate?"

"A woman two rungs up from that kid who sold the drugs that killed James and nearly killed Melody."

Again, unexpected, but things now clicked. His meeting with that kid, the drug purchase…. "What are you doing, Godfrey? You're not a cop."

"No, but I am wicked curious. Aren't you?"

"About those drugs?"

"Yes. They fascinate me."

"Why?"

"It's a plague," he said. "Like COVID, like Ebola, like… the great pestilence that killed half the world seven hundred years ago. But what's unique about this one is that it's completely man-made—no virus or bacteria or worm. Humans. Every step in the process… it fascinates me."

"And that cop is going to run a plate for you? Seriously? Seems like a lot of rules to break. Why would he do that? What's in it for him?"

He said nothing.

"Right…. Jesus, Godfrey." And then, three minutes from our destination, I lost it. "So you lied to him." My voice way louder than intended.

Not a peep.

"He thinks he's going to get seven minutes in heaven with God's-gift Godfrey, and you're going to use him. And if it's ever discovered… what? He'll lose his job. I'm sure there are rules about tracing license plates for random hookups. You don't give a shit for anyone but yourself… and your fascination. It's all lies and games with you." I missed the side street I was supposed to take, but this part of Brookline was a grid, so I shot for the next right. "And it's the same with me, and you don't care."

"Not true."

"Yeah, it is. But here's the thing—how do I know what's true and what's not true? You lie. All the time." All the weirdness of this year with him bore down on me. "I'm not going to get into Harvard… so we can go together. I have no clue why you deferred, but that's not it. You take the things I most want, what I care about, and you use them. Like Shannon."

"That was not me."

He had a point, but I was in no mood to hear it. "It's all you—what you want and your little games. I feel bad for that cop. You're going to screw him over, and he won't see it coming. But I'm done."

"Message received."

He sounded awful. But that was all part of God-frey's package. I needed to get away from him and put his weirdness behind me. Maybe I'd go to medical school and maybe I wouldn't. And maybe if I begged Shannon, I could undo the damage done. "Good." I spotted our destination and pulled up in front of a Tudor mansion on Woodland. "Shit. These people have money."

"Yeah." He got out. "But it's the root of all evil, Trevor… I'm not."

Great. Let him have the last word. We were nearly halfway done with this miserable twenty-four, and then I'd be free of him.

A tall thin balding man in khakis, a pressed red polo, and loafers appeared at a side gate. "Took you long enough."

Awesome.

Godfrey took the lead. "Where is he?"

"This way," the man said and retreated through the gate.

"You bring the stretcher. I'll see what we've got," he said.

Glad for the distance, I retrieved our gear, trailed after them, and checked out the house. These turn-of-the-century monsters started in the millions—a quick hop to the city with lush gardens, towering evergreen hedges, and sweeping drives. I turned the corner and greeted a Norman Rockwell vignette. A freckled kid sobbed on the ground by a high-end swing set and playhouse. His concerned mother with the face of a Madonna, her dark brown hair tied back, knelt at his side as his worried dad tried to manage the morning's mishap.

"It's not that bad," the man told his son. "Don't be a baby. You need to be a big boy, Kyle. And big boys don't cry."

"Kyle fell," the woman said in a tentative voice as we approached.

Godfrey went down on one knee. "Hi, Kyle. I'm Godfrey, and that's Trevor. We're paramedics, and we're going to get you fixed up and go for a ride in an ambulance. That sound okay to you?"

"Okay. It hurts." The five-year-old whimpered and cradled his wrist.

"I can tell. So what happened?"

"It hurts."

Godfrey laid a gentle hand on the boy's shoulder. "Looks like it might be broken."

"That's obvious," his father said.

Godfrey ignored him. "Kyle, look at me."

The boy turned his tear-streaked face upward. "It hurts a lot."

"I know. What happened?"

The boy looked down. "I fell."

"Okay, then." Godfrey traced his fingers over Kyle's shoulders and down both arms. "Anything else hurt?"

"I don't think so." But he winced as Godfrey touched a point over his upper arm.

"Trevor, get me the shears."

"What are you doing?" the man asked.

"My job." Godfrey snipped off Kyle's right sleeve.

What I should have done with Bonnie but had not.

His mother gasped, and his father made a guttural sound in his throat.

Not only did this kid have a fractured wrist….

"It's a dislocation," Godfrey said. His brow knit. "Kyle, that must have been quite the fall. You're a very brave boy." He ran a finger down the kid's upper arm, careful to not move it. He stopped at a reddened band midway down his humerus.

"It hurts a lot."

"I bet it does. Now here's what we need to do."

The kid was great, and I almost rethought my decision to get another partner. Godfrey moved fast and with a confidence that astounded me. *How did he get this good?* He wrapped and stabilized Kyle's wrist on a board and then gentled the arm into a sling.

"Can I ride with him?" his mother asked.

"Of course," Godfrey said.

"I'll come too," the father said.

Without a beat Godfrey answered, "No. It's better if you bring a car. You don't want to get stuck at the hospital."

"Fine." The man glared but did not argue.

I held my tongue because he could have ridden up front with me. But something was off. I sensed it, and Godfrey was all over it.

We wheeled Kyle out the back gate to Eight, his mother at his side. "My purse," she said.

"Ask your husband to bring it," Godfrey said.

"No. I'll be two seconds." And she ran into the house.

Godfrey shot me a look from the head of the stretcher. He gave an almost imperceptible shake of his head and then spoke. "Kyle, we're going to lift you into the back, and then your mommy will sit next to me, and we'll all go to the hospital."

"Okay." The kid's gaze was fixed on me at the foot of the stretcher. I smiled, which was pointless because of the mask.

"You're going to be fine," I offered. And then I remembered the one thing I could bring to this party that a five-year-old might like. "You want me to use the siren?"

"Yes, please."

"You got it. We'll go lights and sirens all the way."

"Oh boy." And he smiled through his pain, and damn if that didn't make me feel like this whole crap day was worth it. Godfrey stared back at me over his mask. *Fuck him and that yellow stick-um. And why do I care?*

His mother raced through the front door, her hair now disheveled, her cheeks flushed. "My mask!" She stared at her pocketbook and then back toward the front door. She hesitated.

"Don't worry," Godfrey said from the ambulance back doors. "We've got tons."

"You're sure? I could…."

"Come on, and I never got your name."

"It's Marti."

He helped her in, to where she sat at the head of her son's stretcher, and he followed, showed her the seat belt, and shut the doors behind. "Let's roll," he said.

"On it." And to Kyle in the back, "Lights and sirens all the way."

And then before I turned them on, I heard Godfrey ask her, "What happened to your face?"

I stared in the mirror and saw it as she shook her head.

"It's nothing," she whispered and took the paper mask.

All traces of that Norman Rockwell fantasy vanished. She'd been hit—an openhanded slap across the cheek. I looked at the boy and then caught Godfrey's gaze in the mirror. He knew… and once again I realized I was twelve steps behind. That's why he'd lied to Kyle Senior and said he couldn't ride along. It all made sense—the dislocation and the band of bruises around the boy's arm. He hadn't fallen… at least not on his own. He'd been yanked off that swing with enough force to pull his shoulder from its socket. *Why? What could make someone do that to a child?*

And I flipped on the siren and pulled away from the mansion.

Chapter Twenty-Eight
I Can Name that Tune

AT TIMES the ambulance reminds me of game shows from early TV. They tumble disconnected through my memories, some from this life, others the one before. *What's My Line*, *The Newlyweds*, and right then, *Name that Tune*.

Because of that, and this too-familiar melody in the key of domestic violence, I trod softly. I pulled the tablet from its niche and booted up the call sheet. If Trevor weren't so pissed at me, he'd be thrilled. I usually left those for him, not because I'm computer illiterate, it's just… they're dull, lots of tick-off boxes when the time in the ambulance is so short, intense, and precious… at least to me. "Okay, Marti, let's get all the information so when we land at Children's Hospital, we can get you taken care of right away."

"Thank you," she said.

"No problem. We've got young Kyle Griffin with what I guess to be a combined radial-ulnar fracture on the right and a pretty nasty shoulder dislocation."

I winked at the boy, impressed at his efforts to not scream in what had to be horrific pain. "You're doing great, kiddo."

He stared wide-eyed at his mother, and tears trickled down. "It hurts bad."

"I know," I said. "The best thing is to close your eyes and listen to the whirr of the siren. Can you do that?"

"I'll try."

He shut his eyes, and I saw him focus on the muted sounds of the sirens through the ambulance's insulated shell. I switched the tablet to my left and touched the fingers of my right hand to his forehead and soothed gentle circles that lulled him into a nod. Without stopping, I pivoted on the orange bench toward his mother.

"Not the kind of thing a child should have to go through."

She stiffened.

"It's okay." I balanced the tablet on my knee and pulled down my mask. I looked at her. The flush on her right cheek had blossomed into the shape of her husband's fingers. I imagined the scene when she'd gone back inside for her purse. "He must have been pretty mad," I said in a voice too low for the boy to hear.

She shook her head. "No."

"I get it." Other than my fingers, that drew gentle circles on Kyle's forehead, I held rock still, my gaze on hers.

"It's not like that."

I watched as she weighed her words and lies within.

"It is," I whispered. "He did this to Kyle."

"I don't know."

"You didn't see," I clarified. "But you know."

"I was in the kitchen."

"Did you hear?" I asked.

"Yes. Kyle… his father, was shouting for him to stop swinging so high, to not make so much noise. He was trying to get work done. It's not easy for him."

"And then?"

"I don't know. There was a crash, and Kyle screamed, and I came out, and…."

Her expression was painful to behold—the palmprint on her cheek, the fear in her dark eyes.

"I should have been there. I should have gone out the first time he yelled at Kyle. This is my fault. I was trying to get supper ready. I should have gone out."

"It's gotten worse since COVID," I said.

"Yes. He doesn't go into the office, has to work from home, and Kyle makes too much noise."

"Do you have family you can go to, Marti?"

"My mom, my sister. But I always come back. He promises… and I believe him. He tries. He really does. He gets so angry."

"But this is too far. You know that."

"He was so angry."

"I can see that."

"I don't know what I'm supposed to do. He's so angry. He didn't want me to call the ambulance."

"You had no choice. He really hurt Kyle."

"I know… and it's my fault…. Will he be okay?"

"His injuries, the physical ones, will heal. That's not the issue. You know what you have to do." I kept my voice soft.

"It's not that simple," she said. "He controls everything. I have no money, no friends. I can't just leave. And…."

"And what?"

"I don't think he'd let me, not for good."

"You're right," I said. "He won't, not without a fight. But it's going to get worse. Is this the first time he's hurt Kyle?"

She tried to look away. "Never this bad."

"Marti." I pulled her back. "Do you have your cell?"

"Yes, but he monitors my calls, my messages, my internet history."

"Of course he does." I pulled out mine. "Who has the safer house? Your mother or your sister?"

"My sister Joe… Joan. She's like a bulldog. They hate each other. She told me not to marry him. Said he had a mean streak."

I handed her the phone. "Call her. Have her meet you at Children's Hospital." And I pulled out the yellow pad from my pocket and wrote on a stick-um. "Give her my number and keep the phone as long as you need it. And hurry," I added as we neared Brookline Ave and Hospital Row with an ETA of two minutes.

I looked back at Kyle, who'd fallen into REM sleep. The lids of his eyes twitched, but at least he lay still. I listened to Marti.

"Joe," her voice tentative. "Can we stay with you?"

"What happened?" her sister's alto audible and concerned.

"Kyle had an accident."

"Don't lie to me, Marti. What did that bastard do?"

"I'm in an ambulance. We're on the way to Children's in Boston. Can you meet us there?"

"Yes. How bad is it?"

"Broken bones, a dislocated shoulder."

"Goddamn him!" Joe spat back.

"What am I going to do?" Marti asked.

"Breathe," her sister advised. "I'll get there as fast as I can."

As I stared at the sleeping boy and listened to his mother and his aunt, I thought about Gaius's pus under pressure. Like many aphorisms, Benjamin Franklin truisms, and twelve-step adages, it sounded pithy and carried some truth. But, but, but, this was a great example of what could happen when things festered. This boil was about to burst. What I did not know now, as Gaius did not know then, was whether the cure would come in time or just hasten death.

"We're here," I said as Trevor eased into a bay. "It's going to get ugly," I said. "Give me the phone for a sec."

She passed it to me. I flicked to the camera app. "Turn your head to the side," I instructed and captured the palmprint on her cheek. "And roll up your sleeve." I had noted her rub her wrist several times during the ride. Without comment I snapped shots of angry bruises, some fresh and some yellowed with age, around her wrist and forearm. "Okay if I take some pictures of your son?" I asked.

"Do it."

Careful not to wake him, I framed crisp images of his bandaged wounds. "When we get inside, my partner and I have to report this to protective services. We have to."

"He'll be furious. He's a lawyer."

"He *will* be furious. But it's the law, and it needs to happen."

"He'll make it my fault, and it was. I should have stopped it. Should have brought Kyle into the kitchen with me, kept him quiet." Her anxiety spiraled and panic set in.

"This was not your fault," I said. "But moving forward will take courage."

"You don't know what he'll do," she repeated.

"I do. But he can't stop himself, and you must protect yourself and your child."

Trevor opened the back doors.

"How did you get him to sleep?" he asked.

"I have skills." I strapped on my mask. "We have to file a 51A."

Trevor nodded. "I figured." He looked at Marti. "You doing okay?"

"No. But this has to happen, doesn't it? This is too much?"

"It is," I said, and I waited for Trevor to release the stretcher. "At least this is the right place for it." As we pulled out the stretcher, I managed a last Godfrey swirl of my fingers across little Kyle's forehead and temples to help him stay asleep. I told Marti some of what to expect. "There's a Department of Children and Families hotline I'll call once we get through triage. That gets followed by a written form."

"He's going to hate this. It's going to make things worse. You don't know him. Do you have to do this?"

"Yes."

As we passed through triage, the pediatric nurse behind a plexiglass wall—a Nordic blond with ice-blue eyes—took a quick assessment of Kyle's injuries and drew the obvious conclusion. "Will you file or will we?" he asked as I gave report.

"We both should," I told him. "And I'd alert security that the husband should not be allowed back."

"Yes," the nurse remarked as he made a copy of Marti's insurance card. "Kyle Senior is already making a fuss in the waiting room. So what did you give the boy?"

"Nothing. Sang him a lullaby."

"You must have a good set of pipes."

"I can carry a tune." And in different circumstances, I might have pursued the spark of interest in this attractive man.

Marti, who held little Kyle's good hand, looked up.

"Is she hurt as well?" The nurse had spotted the red mark on her cheek.

"Marti," I said, "have them look at your injuries."

"They're not that bad. Just a slap and some bruises. Nothing's broken."

"Wow. Just a slap and some bruises," the nurse managed. "Mrs. Griffin, can I offer you some advice here?"

"Sure."

"Have them examine you."

"I won't leave Kyle."

I held my tongue, aware that at some point in the coming hours, Kyle would be removed and interviewed. Neither parent would be present for that.

"You won't have to," the nurse said. "But it's in your interest to document everything."

"Right," she managed. "I called my sister. Can she come back?"

"What's her name?"

"Joan Burrows." She shook her head. "I can't believe this is happening." She gripped Kyle's hand. "How did I let this happen?"

An intercom announced, "Code gray waiting room. Code gray waiting room."

Two uniformed security officers who'd been in the break room outside the ED doors ran out, as did several orderlies, a nurse, and finally an ED doc.

A man's shouts rang out. "I demand to see my child. I'm a lawyer and I will sue each and every one of you for everything you have! I demand to see my child. You have no right to keep me from my son."

The triage nurse gave a wry smile from behind his plexi shield as a masked and gowned aide rolled a portable blood pressure cuff toward us. "And so it begins."

Marti looked from her son to me, her expression one of pure and paralytic terror.

"It's going to be okay," I lied. "Everything is going to be okay."

Chapter Twenty-Nine
Tears

I LISTENED as Godfrey tried to calm Marti. She looked like a trapped antelope about to be shredded by a lion on the Discovery Channel.

Her husband's furious shouts rang out from the waiting room—"How dare you! Get your hands off! That's assault. I will sue. Get away from me!"

Godfrey headed toward the melee.

"What are you doing?" I asked.

"Don't follow, Trevor."

But I did.

The scene in the waiting room was tense—a standoff between five uniformed hospital security officers and Kyle Griffin Senior, dressed for a day of golf, unmasked and enraged. "You cannot keep me from my son."

"Sir," the head officer spoke. "We have orders to not let you go back."

"I demand to see my wife and son."

"The ones you assaulted," Godfrey said, his voice clear as a bell. It filled the room. "The son whose arm you just broke and ripped out of its socket?"

What the hell is he doing?

"You!" he screamed at Godfrey. "This is your fault!" And with that, the ex–high school and college linesman charged toward us and the ED doors.

Godfrey pushed me aside as the guards gave up their attempts at de-escalation and tried to tackle Mr. Griffin. A pair of uniformed police officers ran in through the patient entry and the now-out-of-control lawyer went berserk. His elbows and fists flew, and his knee connected with a guard's groin.

Godfrey pressed back against the wall and watched. "That's called resisting arrest," he said. An officer cursed as Kyle Senior's fist caught him on the side of his face. "And that's assaulting an officer in the line of duty. That's a felony."

"You did that on purpose," I said.

"Of course."

My heart pounded as seven men and two women subdued the furious Mr. Griffin, handcuffed him, and tried to remove him from the waiting area. He swore and threatened lawsuits, and when a woman with close-cropped dark hair entered, he spat out, "And here comes the dyke sister! You keep your filthy hands off my son!"

She glared at him, took in the handcuffs, his red face and torn polo shirt, and walked past.

"That must be sister Joe," Godfrey said.

My cell buzzed. It was the dispatcher with a new call. "We're kind of hung up," I said. "How long do you think we'll be here?" I asked Godfrey.

"Couple hours at least."

"Really?"

"Yup. We have work to do." He headed toward sister Joe.

I stood and watched as they dragged the indignant Mr. Griffin out the doors and perp-walked him to a parked cruiser. I tried to imagine what could make someone so angry and out of control that they'd hurt their own child. I hated these calls, and as pissed as I was at Godfrey, I was awed by his calm and how he seemed to know exactly what to say and do.

I followed him as he walked up to Marti's sister.

"Joan Burrows?" he asked.

"Yes."

"Hi, I'm Godfrey Hesse," he said to her. "My partner, Trevor, and I took the 911 call and brought in your nephew and sister."

"Can I see them?" she asked.

"Of course." And like he worked there, he walked her back through the double doors.

Joe spotted her sister and little Kyle, who'd been transferred from our stretcher to a hospital one.

She rushed over. "Marti? What did he do?"

Marti Griffin shook her head and sobbed. "What am I going to do?"

"Oh Jesus, Marti." And Joe hugged her tightly as she took in her still-sleeping nephew.

"I don't know what to do. He won't stop." She stared wide-eyed at her sister.

"I know," Joe said.

My gut ached. I felt Marti's desperation, her panic.

"Breathe, Trevor," Godfrey whispered. "Let's get some coffee. This is just something to get through." And then to the sisters, "Joe, Marti, we're going to get coffee. Either of you want something?"

Marti looked back at him. "You gave me your phone." She sounded confused.

"Yes."

"Why? Why would you do that? You don't know me."

"You needed it," he stated. "And now you don't."

"But you don't know me," she persisted. And she handed him his iPhone—the newest one that I coveted and could not afford.

"I do know you," he said. And while his mouth was covered, I pictured his quirked smile. "Remember, we talked in the ambulance. I know you, Marti."

And before she could wrap her head around his obtuse utterance, he turned to her sister. "Joe, I've got a bunch of pictures on here. You'll need them." And he airdropped them to her. "And even though I'm sure they'll do it, when they take off Kyle's bandages, take lots of pictures and back them up."

"I will," Joe said. "Anything else I should know or do?"

He rocked back on the heels of his rubber-soled shoes. "Keep them safe."

"Easier said," she replied. "He's a bastard."

Marti stiffened and glanced at her unconscious son. "Please don't, Joe. Not in front of Kyle."

Joe shook her head. "I'll do what I can."

"Is that a yes to coffee?" Godfrey asked.

"That would be great," Joe said. "And thank you. Both of you."

"Our pleasure."

"YOU KNEW he did that from the beginning," I said as we followed the overhead signs to the cafeteria.

"Pretty much. Let's duck in here." He detoured into a family conference room and pulled out his company cell. Then he sighed and dialed the number for the DCF Child-at-Risk hotline. He looked across at me as he gave the verbal report, the 51A.

I sat mesmerized and realized that some of this bizarre attraction was because I wanted to *be* him—calm, effective, on top of things—and there were those amber-ringed eyes, thick black lashes. I swallowed hard and listened as he gave the facts and just the facts.

"Arrived at 17:15 and found five-year-old Kyle Griffin on the ground with a probable compound fracture of his right wrist, dislocated right shoulder, and significant bruising around his middle upper arm." He did not editorialize and gave no vocal inflection to imply anything more than what we'd observed. But it was nuanced and clear. "Mother, Marti Griffin, went into the house to get her pocketbook, returned with significant redness and erythema over her right cheek in the shape of a palmprint. Photographs were taken.

In the ambulance, Mrs. Griffin described a pattern of escalating domestic violence and that this was not the first time her husband has struck their son."

The person on the other end asked a question.

Godfrey responded, "She told me that she and her son can stay with her sister, Joan Burrows, and that it's a safe environment. Ms. Burrows is currently with her in the ED."

He paused and listened.

"Yes, my partner and I both met Ms. Burrows, and in my professional opinion, she represents a viable option for both physical safety and emotional support."

Another pause.

"The husband has just been arrested in the emergency room. There will likely be multiple charges, including a felony assault against an officer. Although that's speculative at this point."

Pause.

"Yes, I directly witnessed Mr. Griffin assault an officer. Both my partner and I did."

Mind you, he neglected to mention how he'd fanned that fire. *Which was brilliant.*

"My recommendation," he continued, "is that you send an investigator to the ED now…. Yes, I'm aware it's Sunday. The father is an attorney, and regardless of the charges, will likely post bail. The child's injuries are significant, and in discussion with the mother, I believe the threats she is under are credible and could easily escalate."

Another pause.

"Yes, we've informed our dispatcher, and we will be available."

He completed the report, and his hand trembled as he ended the call.

"What's wrong?" I asked.

He was crying.

"Seriously?"

A tear glistened on his left cheek. Fascinated, I watched it absorb into the band of his mask. I don't know why, but I said, "I'm sorry." I fought back an impulse to hug him, to tell him whatever had him so upset would be okay.

"I know you are, Trevor." He batted back his tears, sniffed, and got up. "This shit happens. It shouldn't and it does. Coffee."

I trailed after him, uncertain as to what had just happened. We've had DV calls before, and yes, this one was scary, and I hate that children go through this. But something had struck a nerve with Godfrey.

I watched as he loaded a plastic cafeteria tray with muffins, four lidded coffees, and a pile of creamers and sugar packets. He slotted his credit card into the machine and without a word headed toward the ED.

"When I was young, I believed in a loving God," he said as we got buzzed back through the electric doors.

"What changed?" I asked.

"Life." He sounded distant.

"Your life?"

"Yeah." He headed toward the cubicle where they'd brought little Kyle. It was empty, our stretcher parked outside.

"They must have taken him to X-ray," I said, curious as to what was up with Godfrey. "So what about your life got you to give up on a loving God?"

He placed the tray down on a stainless Mayo table by the bed, uncapped a coffee, and loaded in sugar. "The babies." He pulled down his mask and took a sip. "Great, and now we're on to the nature of an indifferent, if not downright cruel, God."

"You're talking about Kyle."

He shrugged and cracked his neck. "I mean all of them." His eyes welled.

What the fuck. And the weirdest part, it was contagious. I wanted to bawl and no clue why. "God is love," I said, and I hated how canned that sounded, like a choir boy reciting his catechism.

"No, he/she/it is not." He stared at me over his dark gray Cavalry mask. "We can choose to be loving, but God is not. Or we can be total bastards. Doesn't make a difference."

He sounded haunted, distant. I remembered how we'd fought and all the weirdness of the last forty-eight hours. I broke into his house… church… the church of Godfrey. He'd bought drugs from a Mexican teenager and was apparently investigating a fentanyl ring. He'd performed minor surgery on my forehead, licked the wound… *right, and I kissed him.* And kind of, sort of, really wanted to do it again. Like now. "Why do you have to be so fucking weird?"

"I'm just me, Trevor."

I grabbed the curtain and pulled it shut. "What is up with you?"

"I'm sad. It happens."

"Because of this case?"

Steam rose from his coffee. "Yes, and because of you. We just have to get through this shift, you and me. Isn't that right? Then you're done with me and my weirdness."

"Why do you care?"

"Because I love you, Trevor. Am in love with you and have been... almost since we met."

I pulled down my mask. I couldn't breathe. *Was that a joke? Why would he say that? Why does he look so sad?* I couldn't stop myself. I lunged for him and pressed him back against the wall. His coffee sloshed and spilled down the front of our uniforms. I felt the heat and the burn as I pressed my lips to his. Only this time, he did not kiss me back. Confused, frustrated, I raked my fingers through his hair and felt a pressure against my chest. He pushed me back. *No!* His palm like a rock against my chest.

"Company is coming," he whispered.

Before I could pull away, the curtain flew open and Joe, Marti, little Kyle—who was now awake, albeit sedated—a nurse, and an aide got a full view of the two of us, masks around our necks, both covered with dark sticky coffee, his hand pressed against my chest.

"Are we interrupting?" Joe asked.

"Trevor spilled my coffee," Godfrey replied. "He can be a klutz."

What have I done? I stepped back to the far side of the room as they wheeled Kyle into the cubicle.

"What did the X-rays show?" Godfrey asked as the nurse flushed the boy's IV with heparin.

"Fresh fractures of both the radius and ulna, dislocated shoulder, and a healed greenstick fracture of the humerus."

An ED pediatrician appeared and looked at Joe and Marti. "Who's the mother?" she asked, her tone brusque.

"I am," Marti answered.

"Would you please come with me."

Joe spoke. "I'm her sister and Kyle's aunt. Would you like me as well?"

"Not yet," the pediatrician said, and her expression softened. "We're going to need to do a more thorough evaluation of your son," she said to Marti. "I would like your permission to obtain additional images."

"I understand."

The doctor looked at Godfrey and me. "DCF has an investigator en route. Did you already give the verbal?"

"Yes," Godfrey said.

"Good. We'll do our best to get you out of here, but you know how these things go," she said. "I'm pretty sure the police will also want statements."

"Not a problem." Godfrey grabbed a wad of paper towels from a dispenser and passed a clump to me.

The touch of his fingers against mine sent a shiver, or maybe it was the cold coffee that had soaked through my uniform and T-shirt. The room felt close—too many people, no social distance—but I wasn't worried about COVID. I stared at him. He said he loved me, was *in* love with me. I hadn't expected that. *He lies. Can't be trusted. And literally catches me when I fall.*

He'd pulled his mask back up, and I did the same. It was impossible to read his expression. *Why did he say those things? Why didn't he kiss me back? He lies. Yeah, he does.* I was in freefall. A couple hours ago, I'd convinced myself that I never wanted to see him again. Which was *my* lie. And then he said he loved me, was in love with me. And maybe that was true, and maybe it wasn't. But the big question, the one I did not want to ask, screamed inside my head.

Are you in love with Godfrey?

Chapter Thirty
I Digress and Throw a Pity Party

(YOU CAN skip this chapter)

Throughout this book I've been mindful to show and not tell. To not ruin things for you, my beloved reader. But in this moment, in this sad emergency room, with a broken child, his panicked mother, and his berserker attorney of a father, who it is not my intention to paint the villain, I am lost. In truth, if we spent more time with Kyle Senior, we'd see he is more victim than perpetrator. That is my experience with men ruled by rage and violence. It's no excuse for their behavior; it just makes it understandable. Perhaps I'll visit him in his jail cell, or more likely, back in the comfort of his king-sized bed as he plots vengeance against his wife, which he will do. But I digress because I am in pain.

I have no one to talk to. So, tag, you're It.

And yes, this is selfish, and maybe I'll trim this chapter and leave it on the metaphorical cutting-room floor. Though in this case, it's just Shift,

Highlight, and Delete. Trevor will break, is breaking, my heart—not the first time for me and probably not the last. I need to let it happen. I know this. I have to let him go.

Heartache dogs me. This is not a call for pity, but… but what? Something about the little boy, about my own brothers and sisters. We were a nest of fragile chicks with round cheeks and bright eyes that got hollowed and snuffed out by disease. I've walked through hell.

In that emergency room I caught echoes of Gaius, the doctor in his bird mask and black robes who cared for those beyond hope. He came into my father's house as each of my brothers and sisters died. On his final visit, he held my father's hand as he breathed his last. His beak pointed toward the ceiling, and he whispered, "Find the light, Bo."

I was fourteen—the youngest and the last of nine. By rights I should have died with my siblings. But the pestilence did not want me.

As I touched my father's dead-but-still-hot forehead, Gaius pulled off his beaked mask. To say he was beautiful is to compare Michelangelo's *Pieta* to… well, anything. He glowed. His long waves of silver hair sparked in the candlelight, his deep-set brown eyes were ringed with gold, and his face was pure symmetry, without a wrinkle, though his age was immeasurable. "Giovanni, you come with me if you'd like."

I struggled to remember. *Did I take anything?* No. Not even my father's precious masonry tools that were mine by rights. Just walked away.

But follow Gaius I did, through that awful world, from Florence to Venice, dressed in black—the doctor's apprentice. Our stiff leather masks were shaped like a crow's head—two birds that wandered west with the pestilence, across Europe, through France, the boat to Dover, the wake of devastation. Vibrant towns and great cities, deserted, desperate caravans as people escaped one charnel house only to die by the side of the road. Husbands fled fevered wives; mothers abandoned stricken babes. Those with wealth locked themselves and their families behind steel-banded doors in country villas. Arks to weather the storm, and some floated, but most did not.

I did not know what Gaius was. And as you've probably gathered, I still have some confusion on his, and now my, taxonomy. He was my first true love. Though it was not carnal on his end, and I tried… repeatedly. "No." He'd kiss me and push me away, and I'd marvel at his strength and shiver from his touch. "Find someone your own age, Gio. I am old beyond measure."

"But it's you I want."

"You are wrong in that."

I wasn't. I loved him with my whole heart, and I listened to him and learned. I watched as he tried to help, to isolate and quarantine the ill, to comfort the bereaved, to treat those with any hope of survival. I'd hold the basin as he slit open the purulent buboes and try not to retch at the stench of bodies rotted from the inside.

And when the spirits departed the flesh, he'd nudge the confused off this plane and toward whatever comes next. "You see their spirits," I said.

"I do."

"Where do they go?" I asked.

"I can't see that part," he admitted.

"Heaven?"

"That would be nice."

"But you don't think so."

"I do not."

"Why?

"Too convenient. A nice story, but an unlikely one."

His reply, like much he said and did, puzzled and at times infuriated my younger self. But I would give anything to have him here, to have him back as my true companion as I was companion to him for ten years. A decade that wiped away great cities. A flood of a different sort, like a Reset button on a video game. Everyone dies, but you can start again. In hindsight, while the plague had no taste for my flesh, it took Gaius. A different sort of infection, and I now wondered if that is what has happened to me. His sadness and his pain grew as we traveled. Each dead child, desperate mother, and grief-racked orphan weighed on him.

Now, in this ED with Trevor at the opposite end of a long counter set up with computers and printers and bottles of hand sanitizer, I felt the fabric of my pain… Gaius's pain. It was a tapestry woven over centuries, with themes and cadenced patterns. And he dies and she dies. And he suffers and she suffers. Around and around.

You need to snap out of this. I stared at Trevor, his gaze on me. And then he looked down at his tablet. *And now he's up and headed toward me.*

He settled on the chair next to mine. His smell, his heat, his Catholic guilt, and his knee brushed against me.

"I don't know what to do here," he said. His face was inches from mine, his mask improperly fixed under his nose.

"Neither do I," I admitted.

The corners of his mouth peaked up beneath the edge of his mask.

At least he's smiling. And I remembered how I'd thrown myself at Gaius, and he pushed me away. And how jealous I got as he'd disappear with comely young women and men... but not me. And that's what I needed to do here.

"I wish you weren't such a freak, Godfrey."

"Me too," I agreed, and I wondered how he'd react if I dropped another veil or two. It was obvious. *Not well.* My decade with Gaius taught me much, and when he ended his life and I bathed in his blood, I glimpsed his true nature. *Let him go.*

He dropped his voice to a bare whisper. "Why did you say that you loved me?"

"Because I'm an asshole," I answered.

He pulled back.

And I ripped off the Band-Aid. "I've been messing with you, Trevor. I'm a bastard, and I'm sorry. Go back to Shannon. Do it before it's too late."

And I promise, dear reader, that this pity party is now over. And the story may continue.

Chapter Thirty-One
Screw Godfrey and the Turtle He Rode In On

IT WAS after 7:00 p.m. when we left the ED. A cop took our statements, little Kyle had been scanned top to bottom, and a team of child-protection investigators had grilled us for details. We'd even gotten a call from Cavalry's big boss, Margorie Carlucci, who'd gotten wind of this shitstorm when Kyle Senior lawyered up, posted bond, and threatened Margorie with financial ruin.

"Document carefully," she advised. "This shitstorm is going to court."

I drove in silence, furious, hurt, and confused. *He played me.* Nothing like a sucker punch from someone you consider a friend, who quite possibly saved you from severe bodily harm—possibly death—who stitched my booboo and who I threw myself at… twice. Who said he loved me, and then said it was a lie. *How fucked-up does someone have to be to do that?* And then random scenes from earlier today—how he'd assessed the scene with the Kyles, separated the dad, attended to the child. He always knew how to say and do the right thing in any situation… but not here. *Not with me.*

I parked back at the station.

"I'm going to order a grinder," he said. "You want one?"

"No." Though I was hungry. "I'm going to bed."

"Suit yourself."

I wanted to scream at him. How could he blow my life up and then say, oh, it was just a joke? And the question I'd dodged from Father Calvin and Shannon but mostly from myself had now been answered. This kind of pain, this hole in my gut that felt like it would swallow me, was not caused by a spat with a friend, a bro, a bud. I shut the dorm room door and caught my reflection in a cracked mirror tile. My eyes looked wide and confused. *How is it possible to hurt so much and not have any physical signs of pain?* Something should be broken.

Your heart, moron. And that's what this was. I was in love with Godfrey, and this is what every love song gone bad was about… *please make this stop.*

I sat on the edge of the bottom bunk and caught my breath. I pressed my hands against my head, and the fingers of my right brushed against Godfrey's stitches. I remembered his kiss on my forehead… *and then he licked it.* Which while gross on the one hand, sent a shiver and made it all hurt worse. I tried to sort things but couldn't. Too sad… muddled. I looked at the carefully made bed, the cotton blanket

and sheet—the same ones we use on the stretch-
ers—and couldn't bring myself to lie there. Instead
I climbed to the top bunk, the one he always took.
If, when, he'd come to bed—if we weren't called—I
couldn't stand the thought of him looking at me. *He
played me. Why?*

At least I sent that email asking for a new partner,
though just a few hours earlier I would have gladly
rescinded it. I lay on the thin pillow, my heart pound-
ing in my ears. I pictured the blood as it pumped
through my body and tried to calm myself. Then I
ran through study mnemonics, all pornographic, like
the one that described the Krebs Cycle and the break-
down of carbohydrates. It would get me through a
good ten questions when I retook the entrance exam.
"Come Charlie, It's Only Kinky Stuff So Fuck Me
Over." *Shit!* That was Godfrey's. They all were, and
they'd never leave my brain. He'd joked as he taught
them to me. "Swear to God," he said, "it will now be
impossible for you to ever forget the twelve cranial
nerves. Here goes… "Oh Oh Oh To Touch And Feel
Vagina Gives Vinnie A Hard-on"—Olfactory, Optic,
Oculomotor, Trochlear, Trigeminal, Abducens, Facial, Vestibulocochlear, Glossopharyngeal, Vagus,
Accessory, Hypoglossal."

How could he do this? Why?

The gross plastic cover under the pillowcase
crinkled. I stared at the dark ceiling. *What am I going to do?*

I closed my eyes, and not knowing what else
to do, I prayed. The words were a balm over my

troubled thoughts—words my mother taught me, the Lord's Prayer, my own mantra, over and over. *Our Father, who art in heaven, hallowed be thy name.* And I'd see Godfrey and push him away. *Thy kingdom come, thy will be done.* But he's the one who pushed me away. *On earth as it is in heaven.* And that acceptance letter… he got into fucking Harvard. *Give us this day our daily bread, and forgive us our trespasses, as we forgive those who trespass against us. And lead us not into temptation, but deliver us from evil. Amen.* Why did he do this to me? And I prayed, over and over, and let the words do what they often did, lull me to sleep. And sadly, into a dream.

"Get over it," Godfrey said. I was pissed at him. He wasn't wearing a mask or much of anything. just a ridiculous pair of red silk boxers and bunny slippers.

"You can't go to class like that."

"Of course I can. It's anatomy, what am I supposed to wear?"

He had a point, and I caught my reflection in the mirror. I'd also forgotten to put on pants and couldn't help but compare and contrast my gray Kirkland boxer briefs to his flashy red paisley undies. Worse was the amount of his ripped anatomy on display. *How much does he work out?*

"Someone's getting a stiffie." He smirked and pointed.

"Don't be a dick."

"That's right, you're not gay. You're Bulgarian."

"What are you talking about. I'm Irish, mostly."

"Get over yourself, Trevor. You're Bulgarian as the day I was born. Did you do the homework?"

"Sure." But I hadn't.

And then we were outside the lecture hall at UMass Boston, where I'd taken my EMT and then paramedic training. Only it wasn't UMass. "This is Harvard," I said.

"Duh." And nearly naked Godfrey pushed through the double doors.

I looked down at the front of my boxers. They tented out; it was obscene. I looked around and grabbed a basking turtle from a stack of them on a log by the window. I hoped it wasn't a snapper, pressed it in front of my crotch, prayed no one would notice, and went inside. *Just keep the turtle firmly in place, don't look down, don't draw any attention.*

I found myself in a large room with covered bodies on stainless steel tables. Godfrey was nowhere in sight. I went up to the first table and pulled back the white plastic sheet. It was the young woman, Rachel, her chest cavity open and empty, her eyes gone. "We took your heart," I said.

"That's okay," she said. "I was done with it."

"Are you my cadaver?" I asked, relieved that she had no eyes and wouldn't be able to see my turtle-covered erection.

"No, you've got James."

"Okay, then." I covered her and went in search of my body.

I went from one table to the next, had quick conversations with the dead, none of whom seemed to know what had happened to mine. A couple of times I was sure that I'd find dead James under the sheet, but no, my uncle Harry, Grandma Rose—"Grandma, it's so good to see you." She looked awesome.

"You too, sweetheart. Are you going to Mass?"

"I am."

"Good boy. And confession?"

"Yes, Grandma."

"Wonderful. And you know that I love you, Trevor."

"I do."

"And I'm always here."

"I haven't been here before." But as I said that, I wasn't certain, because it did feel familiar.

"Sure you have." And she took the sheet from my fingers and pulled it over her head.

And then I spotted Godfrey at the far end of the room, hard at work on a body... our body. "Is that James?" I shouted.

"Who else would it be?"

And I was by his side, and somehow he'd found scrubs and a lab coat while I was still in my underwear. "I lost my turtle."

"No one cares, Trevor," he said. "Get an IV started."

"But he's dead." I looked hard at James's lifeless face on the table... his eyes flat, blue, and wide open.

"So? How do you ever expect to bring him back to life? Get the fucking IV."

"Right. How do you know all this stuff?"

"Because I listen. You should try it."

"I do listen." And I hated how smug he sounded, but he had a point.

"You don't. Not really."

"Fine, what am I supposed to hear?"

"This." A buzz filled the room. It grew and pulsed and pulled me from the dream. Adrenaline surged as I opened my eyes onto the darkened room. My cell rang, and I heard Godfrey's in the bunk beneath me. My breath caught as I heard him answer.

"Right," he said. "We'll be there in twenty... you up, Trevor?"

"Yeah." I looked at my cell. It was 3:40 a.m. "What is it?"

"Probable cardiac at a nursing home."

In the dim light, I felt and heard him get out of bed. He was dressed, no red silk boxers. I smiled at the thought and climbed down. Fragments of the dream clung to me as I pressed the remote for the garage bay and went out into the chill October air. I had a sad thought. *This could be my last run with Godfrey.* I'd asked for a new partner. He'd made it clear that whatever weird game he was playing was just that, a game. But the image that lingered and that I could not pull from my thoughts was James's face on that table, his blue eyes both alert and dead, waiting to be cut apart by a pair of medical students.

I glanced at the GPS and drove out with lights and no siren. I felt the dream fall away.

Grandma Rose was there. But something else. It felt important, and the harder I tried to remember, the further off it seemed.

For his part, Godfrey was silent.

We arrived at Marion Manner—a two-hundred-bed skilled nursing facility—and were met by a nurse in blue scrubs and a heart-print lab coat.

"What happened?" Godfrey asked.

She rattled off the details. "Ninety-two-year-old man with Alzheimer's found next to his bed, screaming."

With him at the front of the stretcher and me at the rear, we followed her inside and heard our patient from the elevator as it opened onto his floor.

"Jeanette! Jeanette!"

"His wife," the nurse explained. "Poor thing, she died eight months ago. Did everything she could to keep him at home. Don't know how she managed."

"Who's his decision maker?" Godfrey asked.

"Daughter Marie in Vermont."

"She been called yet?"

And we parked the stretcher outside his room and found the frail nonagenarian on the floor, his bird-thin legs tangled in sheets, wearing nothing but an adult diaper.

Godfrey looked down at him. "His left hip is fractured," he said.

How the fuck does he know that? And the thing that had eluded me, like the misplaced word on the tip of your tongue, came back. The punchline from the dream—*"You don't listen."* I watched as he knelt beside our patient and soothed a hand across the man's back and shoulders. *So what am I supposed to hear?*

"It's going to be okay, Mr. Collins."

"Jeanette. Jeanette." His screams softened to whimpers.

"Yes, Jeanette will be there."

"Jeanette."

Godfrey looked back at me and shook his head. He spoke to the nurse. "What's his code status?"

"Full. He's not hospice," she said. "Should be but isn't. Daughter insists we do everything to keep him alive."

"Got it. He have anything ordered for pain?"

"Just Tylenol."

"Right." He pulled out his cell, called the receiving hospital, ran the case by the ED doc, and got an order for morphine.

In the early morning, under the harsh fluorescent lights, in a room that smelled of urine and pine-scented disinfectant, I watched and I listened.

"Jeanette. Jeanette."

"Yes," Godfrey said as he drew up and injected Mr. Collins with two milligrams of morphine. "Jeanette will be there."

And if he's a full code, shouldn't we start an IV? Which of course Godfrey would know to do… and wasn't doing.

"Jeanette. Jeanette."

"Let's get him on the stretcher, Trevor."

"Backboard?" I asked, knowing that was protocol but that with a fractured hip the amount of pain Mr. Collins would have to endure would be excruciating.

"No," Godfrey said without hesitation. He gentled a hand around Mr. Collins's back and under his arms. He looked to the nurse. "If you could steady his legs, and Trevor, get his middle. Let's try to move him as a unit."

Right. Listen.

"Jeanette. Jeanette."

"Yes," Godfrey repeated as we got his contracted frame onto the stretcher. "She's waiting for you. Jeanette will be there."

Chapter Thirty-Two
And We Kissed

I DO believe in God. Beyond that, I search for answers as to his/her/its nature, and my own. But as we secured Layton Collins, with his fractured hip, advanced dementia, and wasted body, into Number Eight, I knew what needed to happen.

"Jeanette. Jeanette."

"It's a beautiful name." I turned off the cabin lights. I did not want Trevor to see this, to see me, the real me.

"Jeanette. Jeanette."

"Yes." I gentled my hand onto his shoulder. "Look at me, Layton."

"Jeanette? Jeanette?"

"That's right." Such an odd sensation, to feel a live body when the mind has departed. Dead but not.

I had no hesitation. This is who and what I am. In that pure chill night, surrounded by darkness, this is when I am most myself. I glanced toward Trevor, his eyes on the road, his auburn hair mussed. The dashboard screen, as I expected, not on the GPS but on me and Mr. Collins. *Fine.* I angled my back toward the camera and leaned in.

"Jeanette. Jeanette?" he called into the dark.

"Yes, my love." I pressed my lips to his and drank the remains of his life. His tortured and broken body relaxed as he surrendered his final breath into me. I sampled treasured images of his wonderful Jeanette, his children and grandchildren, an office and a retirement party, a fiftieth anniversary cake, cruise ships, a golden retriever, cocktail parties, hikes, kayak trips, a lawn with stripes, Jeanette on her knees with a bag of crocus bulbs, their first night as newlyweds. "Goodbye, Mr. Collins."

I pulled back, the taste of his blood in my mouth as the fullness of his life surged through me.

His spirit separated from the flesh and appeared as a robust man in his midforties. Not at all like the withered husk on the stretcher. *"Wow,"* he said.

"Yeah."

He looked at his body and then at me. *"That was rough. Thank you."*

"You're welcome."

And without a prompt or nudge, he dove into the light.

I watched and hoped it wasn't a lie, that Jeanette was waiting. He seemed to think so. *Let it be.* And I wept.

I handled the paperwork at the hospital. The ED doc pronounced him dead on arrival. And while not prone to clock-watching, I needed this shift to end.

The proximity with Trevor and the realization that whatever I felt for him needed to be ripped out and buried, hurt… a lot. It was times like this I understood what Gaius must have felt when he transferred whatever this is into me. I was furious. Everyone I ever loved was gone.

"Coffee?" Trevor asked as we headed back to Eight.

"Sure." It was almost six thirty, and in ninety minutes, we'd part. I had picked wrong, not that I have much choice in who I fall in love with. I don't have a type, at least not physically, or even gender. I stared out the window as we drove through dark and quiet streets.

"Did you see him leave his body?" Trevor asked.

Right, that veil I dropped. "Yes."

"And?"

"He was relieved."

"Was he different?" Trevor asked.

"Yes. A much younger version of himself."

"And was his wife there?"

"I don't know. I hope so, but I don't know that, Trevor."

He pulled off the road onto a stretch of dirt and gravel.

"Why did you stop?" I asked.

He turned off the engine and the lights. *Not good.*

"Did you kill him?" he asked.

"And if I did?"

He faced me in the darkened cabin. "What are you, Godfrey?"

His question shot volleys in my head—different companions and lovers, different centuries, but always this moment. *What are you, Giovanni? George? Geoffrey? Godfrey?* Like Beethoven variations, with one melody embedded in myriad frames. I did not want to look at him, but I did. His crazy hair and hazel eyes, the stitches on his forehead, his full lips and strong jaw.

"What are you?"

"Just me." I wanted this to end… but not really.

"You are so full of shit," he said.

"I'm aware of that."

He bit his lower lip and would not look away. "And you hurt people."

"I'm sorry."

"Not good enough."

"What would you have of me?" I asked, and I winced at my regency turn of phrase.

He shook his head and threw it back. "Why, I would have the truth of you, Sir Godfrey."

"I can't do that."

"Yes," he said, "you can."

"Then I choose not to."

"Why?"

"Jesus, Trevor, you're a dog with a bone. Let's get coffee, finish out this shift, and then you can be done with me."

"I don't want to be done with you," he spat back.

"I'm sorry, Trevor."

He grabbed my hand, and before I could stop him, he was out of his chair and over the molded beverage holder and console that separated us. And in that cramped and awkward space, he mashed his lips to mine.

I resisted for a moment, as all the reasons this was a bad idea sprang to mind. But no, he wanted me, I needed him, and we kissed. He raked his hands through my hair as I felt the weight of him on top of me. He was hot, feverish, and it felt as if he wanted to devour me.

I fought the urge to draw blood from him, but my biology would not oblige. Our lips mashed, and our tongues entwined. *Don't.* I could not stop. *Just a taste*, like James with his beloved heroin and fentanyl, *just a taste. I can stop anytime I want.* I couldn't. And then I felt his hand leave mine, and he pressed back against my chest and broke the kiss.

Suspended over me, his lips parted, blood-tinged spittle at the corner of his mouth and on the tip of his tongue, he shook his head slowly.

"What?" I asked.

"You taste like death, Godfrey."

"And?"

"Everything tells me I should run from you."

"You should," I said.

"Fuck you. We're not done." And doing a one-handed push-up against my chest, he lowered down, and we kissed.

Chapter Thirty-Three
Three Strikes You're Out

"YOU'RE COMING with me," I said. This was not me, but to have the shift end with no clue as to what the fuck was going on with me and Godfrey seemed awful.

"And where is that?" he asked.

I stared down at him and realized I must have cut myself or him. I tasted salt and blood in my mouth. "The back."

"Okay," Godfrey said, and I didn't move till I heard the click of his door. "Worried I'll try to run?"

"Yes."

"I won't, unless you want me to."

"No… I'll meet you in the back." I swallowed. *Who the fuck said that?* My hand pressed against his rock-hard body.

"Then you need to get off me."

"I don't want to." I lowered back to his beautiful full lips. My body, my brain, sizzled as we connected, like I'd stuck a finger into a live socket. His hands moved up to my shoulders, and I marveled at his strength as he pushed me back. *No!* Frantic thoughts intruded. Once again I'd thrown myself onto him. This would make number three, and three strikes you're out. He bench-pressed me back, and I gasped as our lips broke contact. "No."

"I'll meet you out back," he said. "But I have to warn you."

"Of what?"

"You'll see."

"Okay." I tried to breathe, to steady myself as he watched me.

"Are you okay?" His expression unreadable.

"Sure." I felt for the door handle and stepped out onto loose gravel, my legs like rubber. I was on fire. Twenty-four years of Catholicism, confession, Mass. All of it was clear—hate the sin and not the sinner. *Though didn't Pope Francis say civil unions were okay?* I shook my head. *No.* If any of that was right, I would burn, and I didn't care. My left hand on the cool flank of Eight as I walked around back. My thoughts on Godfrey. The taste of him on my lips, the feel of his hard body beneath me. *You don't know what you're doing.* I rounded the back. He wasn't there. I coughed. My heart sank. *He's not here.*

And then he was, bathed in moonlight, his ponytail dislodged from the rumpled collar of his Cavalry shirt. He was glorious and… bathed in silver. "You glow."

"So do you." He closed the space between us.

"But you're…." I gripped his upper arms and shoulders, all hard muscle and sinew. My breath caught as my fingers vanished in the silver glow that surrounded him.

"Trick of the moon," he whispered, his breath cool and sweet against my face.

"I don't care," I said, because it was no trick. "You glow."

"Have it your way."

Awash in a dying moon and the first rays of dawn, we kissed. It felt like falling, weightless. I reached back for the door handle. My throat constricted, and I had no saliva to speak. "Get in."

His eyes narrowed. Then his hands came up to the sides of my head and one of them brushed against my forehead.

He pulled away.

"What?"

"You're burning up, Trevor."

Cheesy lines popped to mind, but his expression and the chilled sweat that rose up my back and across my chest stopped me.

"Get in," he said. "You're on fire, Trevor."

"I'm fine." But I climbed up, the moment gone. I sat on the edge of the bench and didn't want to feel the hard scratch in my throat. It hurt to swallow.

"You've got a fever." He pulled out the electronic thermometer and stuck the probe in my ear. His fingers lingered on my skin, and shivers ran as beads of sweat popped on my forehead. "102.8." He pulled out a stethoscope and unbuttoned my shirt.

"We going to play doctor?" I asked.

"Yes."

"Well okay, then." I knew that I was sick. It was probably COVID, and in that moment, in the back of Eight with Godfrey, I didn't care. His fingers on my bare flesh, his eyes, his warmth.

"Take a deep breath."

I did.

"Another." He snaked the stethoscope around my back. "You're soaked," he said.

My teeth chattered.

He pulled out the scope and buttoned my shirt, but his hand strayed on my chest, and I grabbed for his wrist.

"This is fucked-up," I croaked.

"It's not." He rested his forehead against mine, his breath against my lips.

"I'm so sorry."

"You're sick, Trevor. Don't apologize."

"It's probably COVID." It hurt to speak.

"Yeah, lie down, we'll get you tested."

"I've probably infected you."

"You probably have." And he eased me off the bench and onto the stretcher. I shivered and couldn't stop my teeth chattering.

He pulled sheets from the cabinet, heaped them onto me, and cranked the cabin heater. Then he pulled out his cell. "At least our shift's almost over."

I was soaked and sweating, hot and cold at the same time, the pores of my skin out of control. "I don't want to go to a hospital." I pulled the thin sheets around me and tried to get warm. My teeth chattered so hard I had to clamp my jaw. "I don't want to go to a hospital." This was awful. And the worst part was I'd probably infected him, and if this was COVID, that meant Shannon, my parents, Father Calvin, every single person I'd interacted with for the past two weeks would have to quarantine.

"It's okay, Trevor."

"What are you doing?" I tried to ask, the words staccato through my clanging teeth.

"It's okay." And he lay next to me on the stretcher, his body hard and warm. "It's okay." His lips against my sweat-soaked scalp.

The shivers eased and my teeth stopped chattering.

"It's okay."

And while none of it was okay, I closed my eyes.

"It's okay." He kissed the side of my head. "It's okay."

It is. And I fell into a deep and fevered sleep.

Chapter Thirty-Four
Quaranta Giorni

"CRAP!" KATE summed it up. "You're sure?"

"Yes." And I was as I drove Eight down the gravel path to my carriage house. But hope springs eternal, and I threw her a bone. "They did the quick read at the hospital. Those have a ten percent false-positive rate."

"But not with symptomatic people. Crap, crap, crap. I hate Mondays."

"Don't shoot the messenger."

She caught herself. "Is Trevor okay? Are they keeping him?"

The ED I'd brought him to wanted to admit him, but he refused. I could have, possibly should have, insisted and persuaded, but I did not. "No."

"This means everyone has to be tested, starting with you."

"It does. And my quick read was negative." Which was true. I imagined her nimble mind at work on the action plan. By day's end, every Cavalry employee would have had their nostrils swabbed, and she'd have called in reinforcements for two weeks of contact tracing. It would run into the hundreds, maybe a thousand or more.

"So where's Eight?"

My cell buzzed, and I checked the ID. *Right, Raphael the cop.* "I'm in it, and I've got another call. Let me get right back to you."

"No. Wait, Godfrey!"

I hung up.

"Godfrey."

"Hi, Raphael, bit of a snag."

"You bailing?"

"My partner got sick this morning."

"Partner as in boyfriend?"

Not yet… maybe. "As in the guy who sits next to me on the ambulance. You met him this morning. It's COVID, and guess what?"

"Fuck no."

"Yup. Congratulations, you're the first on our people-to-contact list."

There was a pause on the line. "You going through the health department?"

"I'm sure we are." If there was a protocol, Kate would follow it in an obsessive state of bliss, after she'd memorized it, bulleted the key points in an all-staff email, and bullied everyone into obeying her three-step action plan.

"So…," he said. "I'm looking at up to two weeks of full-pay self-quarantine?"

"Could be. At the very least until you get your test results back. So maybe just a couple days."

"I'll take it. And a raincheck with you?"

"Also correct."

"Happy birthday to me," he said. "Got to love a Monday."

"Yes you do… did you run that plate?"

"Jesus, you don't let up." His tone was still upbeat.

"I don't. So did you?"

"I did."

"And?" I pushed. 'Cause if you don't ask for what you want, you'll never get it.

He lowered his voice. "I passed it to the narcotics bureau and the high-intensity drug unit. They wanted to know where I got the information."

"And?"

"Said I couldn't reveal my source but that it was someone a notch higher than they've found."

"Do you think they followed it?" I asked, hoping that this well had not already been poisoned.

"They will. So *how* did you get it?"

"A dead patient told me"—and I caught myself—"before he died, of course." *Although I guess pedophile Rod wasn't really a patient, but James did lead me to Ricky, who led me to Jeff, who worked with Rod, who chased the dog that bit the cat that killed the mouse that ate the cheese….*

"Of course."

"And the tag belongs to?" I pressed.

"This can never come back to me."

"It won't."

"It's not registered to a who but a what. It's a company tag."

"Which company?"

"That's the weird thing. It's a pharmacy... a large one."

"Maybe not so weird. Which one?" I asked.

"A Bainbridge. The branch in Cleveland Circle, and you did not hear this from me."

"Hear what?"

"Right, and you're not going to bail again."

"No."

"Okay, then, hope your partner feels better."

"Yeah." And I looked at the on-screen video of Trevor passed out in the back. "Me too. And Raphael...."

"Yes."

"Happy Monday. Enjoy your quarantine."

"You too, Godfrey."

I hung up, ignored a call from Kate, and went around back. I knew that COVID was nothing like other plagues and pandemics. It was bad, and it killed, but not a healthy twenty-four-year-old like Trevor Sullivan. I knew that, but it didn't register as I opened the rear doors of Eight and looked at him passed out, drenched in sweat, his hair plastered over his forehead, his breath labored. *I should have let them admit him. I could have made him say yes.* But he'd been adamant. "Don't leave me here." His voice desperate. It was unexpected, especially from someone determined to become a doctor.

"I won't leave you," I said, but as I stared in at him—on fire, shivering—I weighed my options. Bring him back, take him to his parents. I climbed in and felt his forehead. I didn't need a thermometer to tell me it was over 103, maybe 104.

"It's COVID," I reminded myself. "It's not the pestilence."

Trevor's eyes cracked, and he smiled. "You're the pestilence. Yersinia pestilence. Yersinia Godfrey."

"And you're my Rattus rattus."

"Where are we?" he rasped.

"My place." I waited for his response.

He swallowed and winced with pain. "Okay. I'm sorry."

"Don't be." I lowered the stretcher bar and helped him swing his legs onto the ambulance floor. I reached behind and got him to sit. The fabric of his polyblend shirt clung to his back and was damp to the touch.

"I feel like shit." His teeth chattered.

"Don't talk. Lean on me." And I got him up and out the back.

He blinked in the sun and looked from the fall-blooming roses to the squat tower of my church. "Saint Godfrey," he muttered.

"Just a minute ago I was a disease."

"Range," he croaked. "I'm so dizzy."

I scanned for possible onlookers, but the back of the property was surrounded with hedges and, except for a couple windows of the next-door apartment complex, was not overlooked.

I scooped his 185 pounds into my arms.

"Did we get married?"

"Stop talking." I carried him up the side stairs.

His head nestled against my chest. He felt so hot. *Is this a mistake?* But there was nothing the hospital could do for him that I could not or would not.

My iPhone and company cell buzzed in unison as I shifted Trevor to an awkward one-handed carry and pulled out my keys.

"Godfrey," he whispered, half-asleep.

"I'm here."

"Do you love me? For real. No bullshit."

"Yes."

He shivered and pressed into me. "Good." His head lolled back, his jaw dropped, and he snored.

I closed the door with my hip. His weight and his heat were like an anchor. The phones stopped and started—Kate and God knows who else. I pictured Bela Lugosi, or maybe it was Frank Langella, in one of the many Dracula movies, or even Rhett with Scarlett, as they carried their objects of desire up the grand staircase. I cradled unconscious and fevered Trevor tightly and headed back through the light-filled sanctuary and up to the organ loft and my bedroom. I felt sick with fear. *He does not have the pestilence. He is young and healthy. He will get better. But what if he doesn't?*

I settled him on my bed beneath the rose window, his mouth open, snoring, the rattle of fluid in his lungs. I pulled off his shoes—the same style of black New Balance leathers that I wore. I peeled off his sweat-caked socks. "I'm going to get you into some dry clothes," I said.

But he was out, and I tried not to be too big a
perv as I stripped him to his sexy boxer briefs and
dressed his lean and fevered body in cotton pajamas.
I retrieved his cells—both with missed calls—from
his pocket and stacked them on the ancient trunk by
the bed. He had fallen into a deep dreamless sleep.
It's the best medicine, Gaius taught me. "The golden
slumber," he called it, "that restores the body and
the mind." Within just the past few years, science
had reached a similar conclusion. This deepest sleep,
when the brain pulsed to the beat of the heart, was
what Trevor needed.

I covered him with quilts and tried to calm my
fears. *This is not the pestilence.* I thought back through
the stupid arguments we had and how I'd pushed him
away. *Be careful what you ask for.* I could not take my
eyes off him, because what if he stopped breathing?
Then you'll breathe for him. Glad to have the ambulance with its onboard and portable oxygen tanks
and a full buffet of masks. I'd get the pharmacy in the
adjacent plaza to fill the prescription for steroids I'd
gotten from the ED doctor. *You've got this.*

My pocket buzzed, and I reached in and pulled
out my phones. I glanced from him to them. As predicted, Kate was on the company line, but the other
on my iPhone was Trevor's home number. I hit the
answer button.

"Hello?"

A woman's Boston twang. "Hi, I'm trying to
reach my son, Trevor Sullivan."

"Mrs. Sullivan, this is Godfrey. Trevor is with me." Strange, how after a year of working with her son, this was the first we'd spoken.

"I got a call from his supervisor at the ambulance company. She said he was sick, that he had COVID. What's going on? Where is he? Is he okay?"

Her anxiety pinged my own. "He's okay. He's sleeping now."

"Are you at a hospital? Which one? We'll be right there."

"I brought him to my place."

"Why? How sick is he? He should either be here or at a hospital."

"I've got the space," I said, "and as he's infected and we've been together in an ambulance for forty-eight of the last seventy-two hours, it seemed like I could isolate with him and take care of him."

"And if you get sick? You should have brought him home."

I don't get sick, but too much information. And she was right... at least from her perspective. But I would not let him out of my sight, not without a fight. "If I have it, I'm asymptomatic, no fever, nothing. I can take care of him here." Which would not fly with her.

"Where are you?" she asked. "We're coming over."

I did not argue and gave her the address.

"I'm Liz, by the way," she said.

"I'll see you in a bit."

Her tone softened. "Should we bring anything?"

"No need. I was going to make a pot of soup. It's probably all he'll be able to handle."

"I'm on it," she said.

We hung up, and I had this powerful urge to tidy. Normally I have a crew come in twice a week to clean the church. I'd have to cancel them and tell them to get tested. *This is not the pestilence.* "Lazzaretto," I said aloud—a term Gaius coined as he went to the leaders of Venice and urged them to isolate the sick. *Quaranta giorni*—forty days. The two islands… Lazzarettos Vecchio and later Nuovo, mass graves, sailors and soldiers, mothers and their babes. Forty days in hell. Most survived a bare fraction of that time, and few ever left.

I stared at Trevor, his forehead and upper lips beaded with sweat. His company cell buzzed, went dead, and then mine vibrated.

I got up from the bed and answered.

"What the fuck is going on, Godfrey?"

"Hi, Kate."

"The GPS has Eight in Brookline. Where are you?"

"It's parked outside my house."

"Why there?"

"Because I live here."

"Don't be a dick. Where's Trevor?"

I stopped myself from saying *in my bed*, as that would have sounded wrong. "Here."

"I just spoke to his mom. She's freaking," Kate said.

"She's on her way."

"How sick is he?"

"Pretty sick. Temp about 104, sweats, chills, kind of what we've been seeing."

"He breathing okay?"

"So far," I said and listened to the faint sounds of fluid in his chest. *Not worse… not better.*

"His mom will take him home."

"I'll convince her to have him stay here."

"Why? Won't he be better off with his folks?"

"No, I don't think so. And I have to isolate anyway."

"True. This is one major clusterfuck. Everyone in the station has to get tested now… I'll send a team out to pick up Eight."

"No rush," I said. "It's going to need a deep clean. It's going to be out of commission anyway, and I want it here… in case…."

"Right… not company policy… crap. So it's okay to stay there?"

"I can stick it in the garage if you'd like."

"Your unit has a garage?"

I pictured her on Google maps, assuming as most did, that I lived in the complex next to the church. "It does."

"Okay, we'll let it sit. What a mess. You guys need anything?"

"No, we should be set."

"Okay, but call me if anything happens or you think of anything you need."

"I will."

We hung up.

"Quaranta giorni." And how the hell did Gaius settle on forty days? *Because he knew.* I stripped down, tossed my uniform into the hamper, and headed for the shower. I kept the bathroom door open so I could keep an eye on Trevor and make sure that his chest moved air. My thoughts split between him and a haze that clouded my years with Gaius. *He knew how long it would take to clear the disease.* For COVID it was two weeks. *Why forty days for the plague? Because he knew.* "It wasn't a single disease."

I toweled off, pulled my hair into a ponytail—bypassed the satin ribbons and went with a Dollar Store red elastic—threw on jeans, a Red Sox tee, and loafers. Then I stopped by the side of the bed. Trevor's slumber had shifted into dream sleep. His eyeballs twitched beneath his lids, and it took a force of will not to lie beside him and enter that intimate theater. "Where are you?"

The iron knocker rapped three times on the church's front door. "Time to meet the parents. Liz and Colin," I reminded myself as I headed down to the seldom-used front door.

I grabbed a fresh black mask from a box I'd left beside the carved-oak donation box, shot back the hand-forged bolt, and opened the massive door on two familiar faces.

"Godfrey?" his mom asked. She held a bouquet of autumn flowers, and behind her, in a navy Boston Fire Department zipper hoodie and jeans stood her silver-haired husband, his arms around two brown shopping bags. Both wore paper masks.

"Yes, come in." While I've seen Trevor's parents many times in his dreams, this would be their first gander at me, and there can be a huge distance between how someone appears in another person's dream and how they are in the waking world. For instance, Liz and Colin Sullivan were a good decade older than the pair that featured in Trevor's dreams. His father was in his early, maybe mid fifties, tall and with a flattop in need of a cut, and his mom was right on the cusp of fifty. Both were fit, Liz in desperate need of a trip to her colorist, or else on the cusp of the decision to let the blond go gray.

"We thought we had the wrong address," his father said with the nasal vowels of a true Bostonian.

"Happens to everyone, Mr. Sullivan."

"It's Liz and Colin," he said. "I've always wondered about these places."

I ushered them in.

"You know, these old churches that have outlived their congregations. Rude to ask, but what did it cost?"

"Not at all. Five fifty."

"That all?" He sounded incredulous. "I would have thought a lot more, especially in this neighborhood. Damn shame."

"White elephants." Glad for the bit of chitchat. "The upkeep and utilities are insane."

"Where's Trevor?" his mother asked, less interested in the purchase, care, and upkeep of nineteenth-century neo-gothic structures.

"He's asleep upstairs, Mrs. Sullivan."

"Please, Liz." And she held out the bouquet. "Do you mind if I go up and look in on him?"

"Of course not." I took the fragrant mix of fall blooms—mums, daisy-faced asters, pink sedum with soil that clung to its shallow roots, sprigs of vivid purple beautyberry, topped with three floppy balls of blue hydrangea. They hadn't come from a store and had been hastily but artistically assembled. "These are beautiful. You're a gardener."

"I try. Who takes care of those roses?" she asked.

"I do the gardens."

"Someone taught you." Her accent was less strong, her curiosity high.

"They're not hard," I said as I led them back through the sanctuary. But yes, she was correct. I had been taught by the master groundskeeper at Balmoral. I repeated his words, minus his dense brogue. "Roses are like people. Feed them, water them, and they thrive."

"Yes." She looked back as we passed beneath the organ and the choir gallery. "He's up there?"

"Yes."

"Do you mind?"

"Go ahead, either staircase gets you there."

She looked around the sanctuary, where I'd removed the pews except for the rows under the side galleries. My cellos stood in their cradles like a row of parishioners before the apse, along with an assortment of amps and a tangle of cables.

Her eyes narrowed, and I sensed her curiosity. "It's beautiful," she said. Her gaze fixed on me. "Really beautiful."

"Thank you." I felt the weight of her scrutiny and was glad I'd ditched the ribbon. Not that she didn't have enough to think about.

She broke gaze and headed up.

I stared after her. *A boy and his mother.* Having never met mine, it was a world I did not know. Though my father did remarry—Margherita. And while I don't often care whether or not someone likes me, I did then.

"Really something, this place," Colin said. "You got a kitchen where I can drop these?"

"This way." And while part of me wanted to follow Trevor's mother up those stairs—*what will she think of her son in my bed?*—I brought Colin back to the industrial kitchen.

"I see your point about the utilities. Must cost a fortune to keep it heated."

"It does." I spotted the stack of drug packets, still on the kitchen table. *Shit!* I waved the bouquet toward the side door. "I put up a slew of solar panels on the back of the carriage house." I grabbed the fentanyl packages and stuffed them into my back pocket.

"Yeah, we saw the ambulance round back and figured this had to be the place. So that building is a part of this?"

"There was a parsonage too, but I sold that to the strip mall. It was a fifties split level and they tore it down for parking."

"Lot of property for someone so young."

And here it comes. Why, Granny, what a big house you have. "Trust fund." Two words that have gotten me through many a meet-the-parents rough spot, though it struck an odd chord. Poor dead James and the trust fund he'd never receive. But it would go to Annie and the baby James would never see.

"That explains it." He sounded skeptical as he put the groceries on the island. "Then why be a paramedic? And Trevor says you plan on medical school. Must give the two of you a lot to talk about. Though I think Trevor may be on his third strike you're out. I hope not. He wants it bad."

"He'll get in," I said.

"And what about you, if you don't mind me asking. How old are you?"

An excellent question. I paused to check my pseudo facts. "Twenty-six."

"Had to think about it," he noted, his expression unreadable through the mask. "So why medicine?"

"It's my passion—science in general, but medicine in particular—how things work, what heals, what hurts. I can't think of anything more fascinating, and it always changes, new discoveries, new theories… new diseases." I hated how pompous it came out and stopped the next sentence from leaving my mouth. It would have been something like *It's what I always do. Feel compelled to do. In fact, I've been a medical professional for seven hundred years.*

"I get that." And he unpacked the groceries. "Mind if I use that?" he pointed toward a stockpot under the stainless island.

"Not at all." Bemused at how the two of them just walked into my home and….

"I used to cook at the fire station all the time. This place reminds me of that." He stopped. "You sure you don't mind? It's sorta weird, us just having met and all, but I figured if you're looking after Trevor, least we can do is make you some soup."

"No explanation needed," I said as he dropped a whole chicken into the sink and unwrapped a stick of butter. "Knives?" he asked, and before I could respond, "There they are." He grabbed a parer and chef's from the block and proceeded to smash garlic with his fist, hard on the side of the blade. Then he peeled and diced ginger on the butcher-block counter.

"You're the cook," I commented, and just as I knew he was sizing up me, I gathered information not found in Trevor's dreams. His dad was at least six three, fit, and with the straight-spined posture of career military. His movements in the kitchen were efficient and practiced.

"I am. I love my wife more than life itself, but everything she learned about cooking came from her Irish mother, God bless her sainted soul."

"Not a good cook?"

"Clean as you go. And she boiled everything." He dropped half a stick of butter into the bottom of the stockpot and turned on the burner. It was followed by a long slug of olive oil from a deep amber bottle. "For a long time. Had to get every bit of taste out."

"Got it."

"Awesome stove, by the way," he said, taking in the restaurant-style twelve burners with an embedded grill that could serve up scrambled and sausage to feed a congregation.

"You a cook?" he asked.

"Not much," I admitted. "More of an eater."

"You don't look it." He focused on a trio of Vidalia onions that he peeled, sliced, and slid into the sizzling mix of butter, garlic, and ginger. "Me, I do both. You like sausage?"

"Sure."

"Good. So, trust fund, twenty-six, lives in a church, going to be a doctor, and has a stack of drugs lying out on the kitchen table... you're an interesting man, Godfrey Hesse." He looked back at me.

"I don't use drugs."

"Good to hear. And I try not to judge, except when it comes to my kids."

"Got it."

"Good. You going to flush those?"

"No. They're evidence. And I did flush the contents."

"Go on."

"I thought you were a retired firefighter?"

"Fire marshal for my last ten, and I pick up some freelance and consultative investigative work to keep me busy."

"Trevor never mentioned that."

"Too hard to explain, and the family wasn't thrilled when I took the job. Carry a gun, get people pissed off, Liz didn't want me to do it. Most people don't understand what marshals do."

"Investigate fires."

"Correct. Now, about those drugs...."

"Fentanyl. It killed one of our recent patients and likely a whole lot more."

"What's the deal? Why do you have them?" He turned briefly to stir the savory mix, then grabbed the sausage and a knife, placed them on the island between us, and sliced with hand-blurring speed.

"I'm giving them to a cop friend, along with some information." Which was mostly true, and I supposed it wouldn't hurt to give Raphael the envelopes with death on his knees.

"Word of advice?"

"Yes, sir."

"It's Colin," he repeated. "Be careful. If someone doesn't care about killing their customers, they won't think twice to get rid of someone who might hurt their business. Does that pot-filler work?"

Chapter Thirty-Five
Twenty Questions with Liz Sullivan

I LAY in bed… Godfrey's bed, and shivered and sweated and shivered. I pulled the quilt tight around my neck, my teeth chattered, and awful as I felt, the image of him in the shower, full front, rear, and side, left no doubt I was into him. And while I've looked at guys in the shower and even had the odd thought about what might it be like to be with one, it never held much interest. I was attracted to women, to Shannon in particular, and all was right with the world. I loved her curves and soft breasts and the feel of her in my arms. We'd marry and have kids. Maybe I'd make it into medical school, maybe I wouldn't, and that would have to be okay. I'm a medic, like my job, could probably work for the city, do like Dad did with the fire department and retire with a good pension… but Godfrey's ripped and naked body in the shower…. If I'd been in any condition to get out of bed and join him, I would have.

I glanced toward the open bathroom door. He was gone. Maybe I'd just dreamed it, and as I lay still, I heard voices from below… familiar ones—Mom, Dad. Colors through the stained glass pooled around the room. I inched back against the pillows and saw clear across the sanctuary to Christ on the Cross, his side pierced with the sword of Longinus, the two Marys, one in white and the Holy Mother in blue, at his feet, angels with trumpets on either side, his head crowned with thorns, his face serene and filled with love, his hair long, dark, and curly like Godfrey's in the shower. His body, taut and—*Stop that.* I tried to swallow. It hurt. *I'm going to hell. Hate the sin, not the sinner. Impure thoughts. His kiss.*

I heard footsteps up the stairs. I looked up, expecting to see Godfrey. "Mom!"

"What have you done?" she said, her mouth covered in a blue paper mask.

"Stay away," I managed, and my throat burned.

"Not on your life." She sat on the edge of the bed. "COVID?"

I moved to the far side. She and Dad had been so careful, and I'd been stupid and somehow managed to catch this thing. "Please. You shouldn't be here."

"What happened to your forehead?"

"I fell." And I remembered Godfrey's stitches, *and he licked me. And I kissed him. And why does Mom look so… worried.* "I'm fine."

"Well, that's a lie. You're certain it's COVID?"

"They did a quick read at the hospital."

Her ungloved hand landed on my suture-free temple. "Well, you sure have a fever. Don't you think you should be in a hospital?" Her blue eyes, lined with fine wrinkles, shone with love and fear.

"No." And I remembered how I'd argued with the ED doctor and nurses to let me leave with Godfrey. I did not want to die in a hospital, alone with strangers. The thought, *I could actually die*, bolstered by this weight in my chest and fatigue unlike anything I've ever known. It was hard to get enough air, like drowning on land. "I'll be fine."

"We'll take you home."

"No." I wanted to list the reasons why that was a bad idea, starting with the risk to her, Dad, and Emma. Or that I felt so weak that the thought of having to get out of this bed… not possible, or that Godfrey would get me oxygen if needed. "No. I'm good here."

"In Godfrey's bed?" Her gaze held fast.

"Yes."

"He's a good friend," she said, more question than statement.

"He is." Like a crash in slow motion, I knew where this was headed.

"Is there more to it, Trevor?" she asked, her tone calm.

"Yes," I said, beyond caring. Hell, if I was about to die, I didn't want to rack up more sins, and bearing false witness toward your mother was a ten-commandment double banger.

"And Shannon?"

"We broke up." I did not look away. If I could have opened my brain for her to rummage around, I would have. It would have been less painful.

Her mask puckered in as she gasped.

"The poor thing. So she knows about Godfrey?"

"Suspects. It's kind of a mess."

"You sound awful." She picked up a glass of water that Godfrey left by the bed. It had a straw in it. "Can you sit up?"

I pushed back against the linens, and my teeth and jaw chattered as the chill air hit my flesh. I sucked on the straw and took a cool sip. It hurt to swallow, and I winced. Mom's hand brushed against my bangs.

"I don't feel good about this," she said and quickly added, "leaving you here. You're absolutely sure about this?"

"It's best. He knows what to do." Though I don't think that's what she meant, not entirely. The water helped lubricate my voice. "He'll throw me in the ambulance if he has to."

She put the water back on the bedside chest. "Do you love him?" she asked.

I sank against the pillows. "I do." And we stayed frozen in each other's gazes, but at least I'd said my truth.

"And what does he feel?" she asked.

"Not sure."

"I'm glad you told me, Trevor. I knew something was up. Didn't know what exactly. And did not see this." She pulled her mask down.

I shook my head and tried to move away.

"I love you," she said. "Don't ever forget that. And don't ever think you can't talk to me… or your father."

"Put your mask on," I groaned. "Where's Dad?"

"With Godfrey."

"Not good." And of all the awkward meet-the-parent scenarios one might imagine, my by-the-book fire-marshal father alone with Godfrey? It would not, could not, go well.

"I'm sure they're fine," Mom said. "It's best to go with the truth, Trevor. Don't you think?"

"Yeah." Though I knew that pearl would be lost on Godfrey.

"Is there anything you need?"

I thought about my highlighted and carefully underlined and notated textbooks. "My books."

"Seriously?"

"Yeah…."

"What's wrong?"

"Godfrey got accepted to Harvard Medical."

Mom's gaze narrowed. "He's quitting the ambulance… but wouldn't the school year have already started?"

"He deferred."

"Why would he do that?"

I reached for the water.

"Let me." And she held the glass as I sipped.

"He said he did it for me." It felt like someone was sitting on my chest, each breath an effort. "He said he wanted us to go together."

"That's quite a thing to say." She put the glass down. "You should try to sleep."

"Yeah." And I eased back down. I'd stopped shivering, as waves of heat made me bat away the covers. "Do me a favor?" I asked.

"Of course, sweetie."

"Rescue Godfrey from Dad."

"I'll think about it."

Under her inscrutable and masked gaze, I sank into Godfrey's bed, and as sleep overtook me, I felt a weird relief. *I just told my mother that I'm in love with Godfrey. I'm not gay... I guess I'm bi... and I just came out to Mom.*

Chapter Thirty-Six
On with the Denouement

MY INQUISITION with Colin Sullivan ended with instructions on the care and management of an aromatic church-sized stockpot of what's best described as "chicken soup meets the slaughterhouse." At some point I'd lost track of how many different animals had slid beneath the bubbling surface. "We're Costco people," he explained. "And with only four of us in the house, all leftovers land in the freezer."

It smelled amazing, and I was impressed by his investigative approach. He'd distract with a frozen lamb shank, run it under hot tap water to loosen it from the zip-lock bag, plunk it into the stew, and ask, "So what made you buy a church?"

"Lots of reasons. Great acoustics, it's beautiful, private, good location."

"A lot to manage… for someone so young." And without pause, he pulled a freezer-burned turkey carcass out, and under it went. He peeled and chopped root vegetables—beets, yams, carrots—and the questions never stopped. But I got it. Who wouldn't?

As he ripped open and poured in a pound bag of pearl barley, I said, "I will take care of Trevor."

And that's when Liz Sullivan rejoined us. "That's all we can ask," she said, and she went next to her husband and ran a hand up his back. "Smells delicious."

"I try," he said, and the two made eye contact.

It's at times like those I wished my skills included mind reading.

"How's he look?" Colin asked.

"Sick. Very sick. Go up and say hello to him. I'll stir the pot," she said. "And Colin…."

"Yes."

"He and Shannon broke up."

Colin handed his wife the long-handled spoon. "I figured."

His answer was unexpected and led me to wonder what else he'd pulled together.

He turned the burner down to simmer. "Don't burn my soup."

"I would never," she protested.

"Yeah, you would and you have. Just stir."

"Yes, sir."

And off he went. I wasn't certain if the good cop or bad cop had left the room.

Liz put the long-handled spoon down on a plate next to the burner. She looked me dead-on as we listened to Colin's footfalls fade through the sanctuary and then up the stairs.

"He said you got into Harvard medical school."

"I did."

"And that you turned it down."

"I deferred."

"Right… why?"

"I think he told you that," I said.

"He did. But I want to hear it from you."

"I wanted the two of us to go together."

"Past tense?"

"It's complicated. I'm not sure what Trevor wants."

"You," she said.

Something stuck in my throat and in my chest. Words, my constant companion and dear friends, would not come. "All right, then," I managed and tried to read her expression.

"What does that mean, Godfrey?"

"I care for Trevor."

"That's obvious, but in what way?"

"In every way."

"All right, then," she mimicked my words. "Anyone tell you, you have Sophia Loren's eyes? And are you wearing eyeliner?"

"A couple times. And no."

"Did not see this one coming," she said.

"He didn't either."

"And you?"

"Since I first met him… or just about."

"It was the same with me and his father. Our first date has lasted twenty-seven years." She sniffed and turned to the pot. "Darn!"

I smelled it too, the faint whiff of something burnt.

"Don't stir it," I warned, knowing that something had stuck to the bottom. I grabbed a fresh stockpot from under the island, grabbed potholders, and transferred thirty pounds of carnage into a fresh pot.

"I should never be left alone in the kitchen."

"We caught it," I said as I deposited the scorched-bottom pot into the sink.

Colin reappeared, assessed the damage, and thanked me for my quick response and salvage of his stew. "She does it on purpose," he remarked.

"That's a terrible thing to say," Liz protested.

"Not if it's true."

My Cavalry cell buzzed. I pulled it out and saw Kate's extension. "I should take this."

"And we should get going," Liz said.

"I'll show you out." And I pressed the button. "Kate, I'm with Trevor's parents. I'll call you right back."

"No prob."

And I took them out the side door. "When you come back," I said, "just park around back."

"Take care of my stew," Colin said.

Liz rolled her eyes. "And our son."

"Yeah, him too," Colin said, and as they walked down the side stairs, he looked back at me. "This place suits you, Godfrey. Shades of *Wuthering Heights*."

"I'm no Heathcliff," I said, aware that his interrogation had not ended.

"True enough. Maybe more Carfax Abbey."

It felt like I'd been punched. "I'm not him either."

"I hope not."

And I watched them head back toward the road, their masks pulled down, deep in conversation.

I sighed and ripped off my mask. *Parents, wanting nothing more than to protect their son.* Colin's parting shot, way too close. I am not Dracula. *And just keep telling yourself that… do you drink blood? Yes. Do you die? No. Do you sneak into people's rooms while they sleep? If the cape fits…. But I can't turn into a bat… unless it fits with someone's dreams. And I'm happy as a clam in the sunlight… but you're stronger at night. But you don't sleep in a coffin*, and my thoughts drifted up to Trevor in the choir loft.

I headed in, pulled out my cell, and called Kate. "What's up?"

"How's Trevor?"

"I'm checking on him now." And there he lay, fast asleep, propped up on three pillows, his mouth open with trumpeted snores loud enough for her to hear.

"He sounds like crap."

"Yeah, but he's moving air on his own. They gave him the first shot of steroids in the ED."

"And you?" she asked.

"Not a sniffle."

"Want to make a little extra money?"

"Not particularly."

"Let me rephrase, want to make amends for causing a global shitstorm?"

"I did not cause COVID."

"So you say. But here's the deal. I told corporate we'd get in front of this and do our own contact tracing."

"And why would you say that?" My gaze fixed on Trevor.

"Let me think… because it's the right thing to do. Because DPH is overwhelmed and won't do as good a job as you will."

"Excuse me?"

"It's not rocket science. You retrace everyone you and Trevor have been in contact with for the past two weeks, call them up, ask them if they have any symptoms, and tell them they should get tested and self-isolate for ten days. Just start with the most recent and work your way back. Please tell me you'll do it."

"I'll do it."

"There are a couple forms," she said.

"I'm sure there are."

"And the good news is you have your work tablet with you."

"Good news, indeed."

"I'll attach forms to an email. Just fill them out as you go and send them back."

I smiled at Kate's enthusiasm—a bureaucrat comforted by ticked boxes and forms.

"On it."

"Thanks, Godfrey, and if you, or Trevor, need anything, don't hesitate."

"We're good." And I added, "His parents just left, and his dad made enough soup to feed a regiment."

"Parents are good that way. Surprised they didn't take him home."

"He's better here."

"Something I should know?"

"Catch you later." And I hung up, but her words lingered. *"Parents are good that way."* My birth father, what I remembered of him, worked hard, tried to provide for his children, who died one by one, and in the end, had a horrible death. And Gaius, my second father and mentor, bathed and birthed me in his own blood. He ultimately gave his life to me... for me. *"Parents are good that way."*

I grabbed a pad of lined paper and settled cross-legged on an oak pew in front of the bed. My gaze fixed on Trevor, I imagined my mind as a kind of recorder and pressed Rewind. I jotted down names I remembered and all those I didn't, like the triage nurses behind plexiglass shields, the myriad doctors and aides, the spouses and onlookers, each of yesterday's calls.

"What are you doing?" Trevor rasped, and his eyes cracked open.

"Contact tracing." I turned the pad to show him the list.

"Shannon."

"Right. What's her number?"

"You can't call her." And he coughed.

It sounded awful, and he couldn't stop. His face turned red, and I heard fluid in his lungs. He needed sleep and more steroids and maybe some oxygen. And just as Kate found comfort in her forms, I turned to medicine. "No." I crossed to the bed and settled on the mattress beside him.

"Mask," he croaked and was racked with explosive coughs.

"I'm fine." I soothed circles across his back and did what I do, what Gaius had taught me. *Sleep. Sleep.*

His hacks lessened.

Sleep. Sleep.

He settled back, his eyes hooded, his expression pained.

Sleep. Sleep.

His mouth dropped open, and he snored.

Shannon.... I scrawled her name at the top of the list, grabbed his cell off the side table, and tapped in his pin. He had not given it to me, but after a year on the ambulance together... okay, after a week, I'd figured out it was the four-digit street number of his parents' house. I found her number and called.

"Trevor?" She picked up.

"No, this is his partner, Godfrey."

"Why are you calling?" She sounded exhausted.

"Trevor has COVID."

"Crap.... Where is he?"

"My house."

"Of course. Well, this is just perfect."

"You should get tested. I can give you places that will get you right in."

"Don't bother. I'm a physical therapist. I'll get it done at work." She sounded pissed.

"Sorry to be the bearer of bad news," I offered, and mission accomplished, I wanted off the line.

"Hold on," she said.

"Yes?"

"What did you do to him?"

"Nothing."

"Bullshit. Before he met you, I don't think he'd ever thought about being with a guy. So what did you do to him?"

"You should get tested," I said.

"I really want to know," she persisted. "Because this is so fucked-up, and you're at the center of it. What did you do to Trevor?"

I heard it—her heartbreak, the betrayal, all of it. "I'm sorry." Because what else could I say?

"Yeah, and now I've probably got COVID on top of this. Fuck you, Godfrey!" And she hung up.

Through the conversation, I hadn't taken my gaze off Trevor. He hadn't roused, and his expression was troubled. She was right to be furious. I had seduced the love of her life. It was cruel and it was unfair. I may not sleep in a coffin or turn into a bat, but this was not the first Shannon who'd wanted me dead. I made a check next to her name, thought about getting my tablet from the truck so I could fill out Kate's forms, but figured it could wait.

I looked down my list. It ran to three pages, single spaced. I called Joan Burrows, whose number was in my work cell.

She picked up.

"Hi, Joan, this is Godfrey Hesse. I'm one of the medics who brought in your nephew and sister."

"Yes? I remember."

"Bad news."

I heard her tense inhale over the line.

"My partner has COVID. You all need to get tested."

"That's it?" She sounded relieved.

"Yeah, if you get a pen, I can give you places that will get you to the front of the line."

"Sure."

"You guys doing okay?" I asked.

"Not really, but this had to happen," she said. "Hold on. I want to go into the other room so Marti can't hear."

I waited.

"It's not good. None of it," she said.

"What happened?"

"We just left the ED a little while ago, spent the whole night. DCF investigators came. They're keeping Kyle at the hospital, and there's a good chance they'll put him into a temporary foster placement. It's killing my sister. And then we've got her asshole of a husband, who's threatening to sue everyone… or worse."

"Worse how?"

"You saw," she said.

"You think he'll hurt her."

"If he gets the chance."

"Did they let him out?"

"Don't know. Like I said, we just made it home. She's a mess. All she wants is her son and a husband who doesn't beat the shit out of her and nearly rip her son's arm off."

"Reasonable things."

"Yeah, but we don't always get what we want." She sighed. "Anything else I need to know?"

"Get tested, do the self-quarantine thing till you have the results, but they'll tell you to do it for the full ten days, regardless. And can you give me Kyle Senior's number?"

"Why?"

"He may be a bastard, but I still have to inform him."

"I suppose." She read me his digits. "Do me a favor, Godfrey."

"If I can."

"If he's out of jail, let me know. We might have to go somewhere safer."

"You got it. And that's a good idea."

We ended the call, and I looked at Kyle Griffin Senior's number. I logged on to the state's Department of Corrections website and entered his name into the inmate locator. He was out. I checked his charges on the Department of Justice page; they'd been downgraded to misdemeanors. *Not good.* One way or another, he'd come for his wife and son. *It won't end well.*

So what you going to do about it?

I circled his number and called Joan back. "He's out," I said.

"Shit!"

"Get somewhere safe that he doesn't know about."

"He'll find us. Marti is so scared, and frankly, so am I."

"With reason. But Joan, things sometimes work out. Get somewhere safe, tell DCF you'll foster your nephew. It will work out."

"You don't know that."

"True." But I did know that. "Trust me on this. Just get through the next few days, one foot in front of the other. It will work out." And we hung up a second time.

My gaze wandered down the names on my list. I drew a line through Mr. Collins. *Dead, and hopefully in a better place. You killed Rod, and no need to call Kyle Senior, as you'll visit him after Trevor improves. And the cause of death will be....*

I felt the wad of drug packets in my back pocket. Perhaps Kyle Senior has a heretofore unknown drug habit. Which, in the COVID fall of 2020, would get written off as just another overdose. I filed that away and stared at Trevor. He'd rolled onto his side, the snores softer. *What am I doing with him?* The list on my lap, with two names crossed out… because I'd killed them, and a third about to go. His father's words. *"More like Carfax Abbey."*

I'm no Dracula.

Yeah, you are.

I pulled the drugs from my pocket. I pictured young Ricky, Jeff, and dead Rod, and the beautiful blond in the white BMW. Little fish, bigger fish, bigger fish still, but nowhere near the top of the food chain. Raphael's information that the BMW was owned by a downtown pharmacy presented new possibilities. It was a tiny cog in a giant chain that, according to *Bloomberg Reports*, which I read religiously, had been purchased by a pharmaceutical company as they strove for greater integration and profit. The most likely scenario was a local distribution of fentanyl…. No, I thought of Ricky and what I'd learned from Jeff, and Rod with his excursions to Mexico to recruit young runners. *It's more organized than that—bigger. But how big? And to what end? Obviously money, but….*

My gaze drifted from Trevor, to the drug packets in hand, to the pad on my lap. I spotted another name in need of a line through it—James's. But pregnant Annie required a call, and for that I'd need the tablet.

I crammed the drug bags into my pocket and went downstairs. My mind ran back through the faces and names from the last couple weeks. I thought how impressed Gaius would be with this technology and wondered what he'd make of our twenty-first-century epidemics, opioids, COVID, malaria, and Ebola. But really, nothing new.

"Hmm." I opened the back of Eight and retrieved the tablet. Then I settled on the bench in the back and pulled up the log sheet from the last of our two calls with James and Annie. He was dead and gone when we arrived. Not much different from the first call, but… no James's spirit hanging about. "She waited before she called," I said aloud. "Why would she do that?"

I called her on the company cell.

She answered on the third ring.

"Annie Grant?"

"Speaking."

"Hi, this is Godfrey Hesse. I was the medic who took you and your husband to the hospital last Friday."

"Yes? What is it?"

"My partner has COVID, and you need to get tested."

"Okay." She sounded numb. "Sure, whatever."

"I'm so sorry about James."

"Me too."

"You doing okay?" I asked.

"No, but life goes on."

As I looked down my list and at the number of dead, I could have poked holes in that truism. Life goes on till it doesn't, like a light switch, Off and On. Like reversing an overdose—dead and then not dead. And discordant bits that had bothered me about the case rose to the surface. "You didn't give James Narcan," I said.

"What are you talking about?" she shot back.

Don't. I told myself, but I did. I reread the call sheet on the tablet. Neither Trevor or I found Narcan at the scene, and I remembered seeing the box in her pocketbook. The ampules I'd injected had been too little too late. "You didn't give him Narcan."

"Please don't."

"Why?" And as the word left my mouth, other questions queued.

"Don't do this. Please."

"How long did you wait, Annie?" I asked.

"No." She started to sob, and I wondered if she'd hang up on me.

"How long?"

Silence.

And I had my answer—long enough to ensure that he was dead... for good. "Why, Annie?"

"I'm going to have a baby." The words choked over the line.

"But you loved him."

"I did."

And I envisioned what her life would be with a baby and a drug-addicted husband. "You couldn't see him as a father."

"Oh God… what have I done?"

Like a dentist with a cavity, or a surgeon inside a cancerous patient's abdomen, I realized there was more rot than just a delayed 911 call and the omission of medication that might have saved his life. I knew this story. "Where did he get those drugs, Annie?" Because I knew from Ricky that James's woman, Annie, had been a customer. I also knew she did not use. So *A* plus *B* equals…. "How did he get those drugs?"

"You don't understand."

"I do. You bought them… or more likely had them saved for this. You did what? Left them out where he could see them? Couldn't resist them?"

"Oh God."

"I don't think it's actually murder… but it kind of is." *And with two I've committed in the past forty-eight hours, who am I to judge? And what was it James told me about a trust fund? His grandparents.* And like the tumblers on a safe, the last bits clicked home. "And now that he's dead, whatever is in his trust fund is yours."

She gasped. "How could you know?"

"He told me."

"He would have spent it all on drugs. He got lump sums when he was twenty-one and twenty-five, and that's what he did. He couldn't stop. He'd go through all of it."

"Probably."

"What kind of life is that for a child? I could not bring a child into that kind of life, wondering when… if, her father would come home. When he'd finally kill himself. I couldn't."

I held the phone and mulled the information. This was murder, this was deliberate, *and who am I to judge?* What she'd done, not far from how I'd dispatched poor pedophilic sadistic Rod.

"What will you do?" Her voice was breathless with fear.

"Nothing." I told her where to go to get COVID tested, and I hung up. *She killed the love of her life.* I tried to process that. I don't think it was about the money, though that factored into the equation. And every time she'd look at her daughter, she'd see traces of blue-eyed James—the man she loved, the man she killed. "What the fuck?"

I patted the names and stared out at the street. I needed steroids and a few other things from the pharmacy. I could have asked his parents to stay. I did not. I thought to lock the church door. I did not.

So many things I could have done. But did not. I was at the mall for less than a minute, maybe longer. Hard to tell. I bought steroids and lemon cough drops and vapor rub. It could not have been more than five minutes… ten tops.

When I got back, Trevor was gone.

Not a little gone. Not like "I've gone for a walk." Gone. I searched the church repeatedly, then I phoned his parents. "Is Trevor there?"

It was not a conversation I wanted. It did not go how I imagined.

"I'll be right there," his father said.

"Thank you." And I meant it. I hung up and methodically searched the church again. *I should hear his breath.* When his dad showed up, he'd figure things out… sort of. But where could he be? My mind was not ready to entertain the unimaginable. No one would *take* him. Why would they?

Clearly, he got up and….

I looked out the window and let my eyes wander as far as they could in either direction, hoping to see his pajama-clad body.

Nothing.

No one.

I stared at the bed and searched for clues. But nothing. No one. Just a tight knot in my stomach.

I've been here before.

The End

Keep reading for an excerpt from
Dark Blood

Chapter 1

Wednesday, July 4, 1998

MILES'S SIX-YEAR-OLD legs churned as he chased Amos, his golden retriever puppy. The boy and the dog flew down the sandy lawn of Grandma Anna's house, its borders hedged by tangles of beach plum and wild rose. Overhead, the sun shone through clouds of spun sugar. Grandma Anna was inside the white clapboard house with Mother and little Maya. Father had to work the holiday in Boston but had promised there'd be a long weekend where they'd drive to Provincetown, go out on a whale watch, and handpick a box of saltwater taffy at Cabot's.

Amos turned, stopped, and dropped the drool-covered red rubber ball. He pawed the ground and nudged the toy with his nose. He barked. It was a game, and Miles knew if he approached too fast, Amos would grab the ball in his mouth and race off.

He inched forward. "I'm not going to take the ball. Nope, not me. Not interested. Who'd want that stinky thing?" He skimmed his red sneakers forward like the ninjas he'd watch on TV with Grandma Anna. His eyes and the dog's locked. The space between them narrowed from ten feet, to nine, to eight. The animal's lustrous red-gold fur sparked in the sun. Muscles in his back twitched as he tracked Miles's stealthy approach.

"I don't want the ball. It's slimy. Who'd want a ball like that?" Ninja sneakers slid forward, seven feet, six feet. Boy and dog focused on each other and the game. Five feet, four feet. "I don't want it." Three feet, two feet. "Uh-uh, not me."

As though each could read the other's thoughts, Miles and Amos lunged for the ball. The pup was closer and faster. He gripped the prize between his teeth and raced down the hill with Miles in pursuit.

Caught in the moment and the ecstasy of flight and pursuit, neither Amos nor Miles saw the heavily laden burgundy Dodge Caravan as it turned off Highway 6A.

Likewise, the driver was distracted by his oldest daughter punching her little brother in the arm. It had been a miserable six-hour drive with no AC, three children, including the new baby, and his largely unresponsive wife, who suffered an emotional meltdown after giving birth three months earlier. He did not see the dog or the boy. What would become seared into his memory was the sequence that started with his daughter's scream—"*Daddy!*"—followed by a dull thud and single surprised yelp as the two-ton vehicle going thirty-five miles an hour made impact with the dog. The animal flew for what seemed an impossible distance.

His pulse jumped as he slammed on the brakes. He saw the dark-haired child racing toward them as he broke through a beach plum hedge, and for a split second he feared there'd be a second impact. Tires squealed as they burned rubber and ground fine white sand into the asphalt. He spotted the red dog in the rearview mirror, not moving save for blood that pulsed from an open wound onto the hot tar. From the angle the dog lay, it was clear his neck was broken.

"Don't look!" he barked to his family, who stared in horror at the unfolding tragedy. "Shit," he muttered.

His wife turned, her lip trembled, her mouth opened into a scream: "No!" He saw condemnation in her eyes.

I didn't see him. This wasn't my fault. One more sin that would be laid at his doorstep. He opened the door, not certain what he was supposed to do. "Kids, stay in the car! Don't look."

His feet touched the pavement, his attention riveted on the dying animal. He wanted to warn the little boy away from his pet. "I'm sorry," he muttered. "I'm so sorry."

Up on the hill, two women emerged onto the porch of the two-story white house, a few hundred feet from the accident. The younger held a toddler's hand while the older, dressed in black, her silver hair in a bun, started to jog toward them. She screamed at the little boy who crouched in the middle of the road, touching the dog's unmoving head, "Miles, no! Don't!"

What happened next the man would never understand and would never forget. As he stood frozen, the little boy lay next to the fatally wounded animal. He knew he should intervene to pull the kid away, but there was something so tender in how he wrapped his little body around the puppy.

The woman's screams grew as she ran on arthritic knees.

"Miles, don't! Stop! No! Please, God, stop it. Now!"

All the man could see was the child, his body fused to the dog's, moving his lips as though singing. His hands fluttered across the dog's fur; they blurred like hummingbird wings. *There's something wrong with this kid. This isn't normal. The boy was drawing designs across the dog's body. He trilled his fingers impossibly fast, first this way and then that.*

And then it happened. The animal convulsed. His hind legs, which at first glance the driver thought were broken, kicked back. They were synchronous and straight. He found purchase on the pavement with his front legs. The boy rolled back on the asphalt. He stopped the freakish movement of his hands, and for a moment the man wondered if he'd been hit as well. The kid's face was flushed and smeared with blood, his striped shirt was drenched in it. His green, green eyes stared, unmoving.

The dog stood up, shook his head, and then his entire body, starting from his tail and ending with

*his fuzzy golden nose. Blood whipped off the animal
in all directions; the droplets sparkled like garnets.*

*The dog turned to the boy. His broad pink tongue
licked the kid's face from chin to forehead.*

*The man held his breath. He stared at the blood
on the boy's chest. Don't be dead. Please God, don't
be dead.*

"Amos." The boy recoiled from the dog's
tongue bath and threw his arms around the animal's
shoulders.

"Miles!" The woman had made it through
the hedge to the road's edge. She looked from the
boy and dog to the man standing ten feet from the
minivan.

Her eyes were a vivid green like a cat's, like
the boy's. She glared at the driver. He felt her rage
and fought back a childhood memory of a fairy-tale
witch. "Get out! Get in your car and get out!"

He wanted to argue, to say he was sorry, to give
her his insurance information, to….

"Leave!"

He looked at the boy and the dog. He saw the
steaming pool of blood on hot asphalt. Too much of
it for the boy and dog to be unhurt, for the dog to be
alive… *but he is.*

"Leave now!"

He could almost feel the words of a curse about
to be hurled in his direction. Of course that was a
ridiculous thought, and he pictured the boy's hummingbird hands. The kid stared wide-eyed at the

woman. Maybe it was a trick of the summer sun, but his eyes glowed as though lit from inside his skull.

"I'm sorry," the man finally said.

"Get out," she said as she walked to the child.

"Okay."

He turned back to his van. The hood had crumpled under the impact; an inch higher and the windshield would have shattered. He got into the vehicle. His family, for the first time since they left Norwood, was silent. His wife's teary gaze was fixed on the ruined hood. He put the Caravan in gear and looked in the rearview mirror. The old woman in black pulled back her right hand and struck the child across the cheek. It looked far harder than any well-deserved spank he or his wife had ever administered.

He thought of getting out, but then he thought of witches and curses and of the two-thousand-dollar-a-week cabin he'd rented to bring some fun to his family. He'd have to get the hood fixed.... *You'll say you hit a deer. You should call the cops... and say what? The dog's okay.* He looked from the mangled hood into the mirror as the old woman, gripping the child's shoulder with her long fingers, disappeared through the hedge, the barking dog trailing behind. *He shouldn't be okay. He wasn't moving. Too much blood. How can he be okay? But he is. Get out of here. And he drove away.*

CALEB JAMES is an author, member of the Yale volunteer faculty, practicing psychiatrist, and clinical trainer. He writes both fiction and nonfiction and has published books in multiple genres and under different names. Writing as Charles Atkins, he has been a Lambda Literary finalist. He lives in Connecticut with his partner and three cats.

Website: charlesatkins.com
Blog:calebjamesblog.wordpress.com
Facebook: www.facebook.com/
Caleb-James-536765356387453

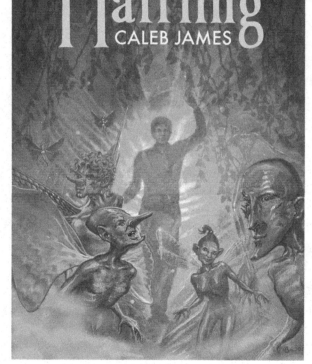

The Haffling: Book One

All sixteen-year-old Alex Nevus wants is to be two years older and become his sister Alice's legal guardian. That, and he'd like his first kiss, preferably with Jerod Haynes, the straight boy with the beautiful girlfriend and the perfect life. Sadly, wanting something and getting it are very different. Strapped with a mentally ill mother, Alex fears for his own sanity. Having a fairy on his shoulder only he can see doesn't help, and his mom's schizophrenia places him and Alice in constant jeopardy of being carted back into foster care.

When Alex's mother goes missing, everything falls apart. Frantic, he tracks her to a remote corner of Manhattan and is transported to another dimension—the land of the Unsee, the realm of the Fey. There he finds his mother held captive by the power-mad Queen May and learns he is half-human and half-fey—a Haffling.

As Alex's human world is being destroyed, the Unsee is being devoured by a ravenous mist. Fey are vanishing, and May needs to cross into the human world. She needs something only Alex can provide, and she will stop at nothing to possess it… to possess him.

www.dsppublications.com

For more
great fiction
from

DSP PUBLICATIONS

visit us online.
WWW.DSPPUBLICATIONS.COM